Readers love The Wheel Mysteries
by SUSAN LAINE

Sparks & Drops

"*Sparks & Drops* contains so many different elements and combines them admirably… It all works here and works exceedingly well."

—Joyfully Jay

"*Sparks & Drops* is both a good mystery and a sweet romance… I really admire the way in which author Susan Laine always strives to write a better story, deeper and more involved characters and humorous and entertaining plot lines."

—Reviews by Jessewave

"*Sparks & Drops* is a beautifully crafted tale, layered with intrigue and secrets, plenty of sexual desire... all wrapped up in a clever tale of mystery."

—The Romance Reviews

Devil's Own

"This is a fantastic installment to this series…"

—multitaskingmommas Book Reviews

"The plot is complex enough to keep you guessing and the characters are likable and engaging."

—Love Bytes

"Susan Laine gives the reader so many wonderful elements to enjoy in this story… I can't wait to see what happens next!"

—Scattered Thoughts and Rogue Words

By SUSAN LAINE

Falling for Rain
Haunted Heart
Sage Advice
Sauna Lover
The Sensualist & the Untouched
Two Tickets to Paradise (Dreamspinner Anthology)
The Witching Hour

ISLESHIRE CHRONICLES
Lofty Dreams of Earthbound Men
Wishing Wings

LIFTING THE VEIL
The Wolfing Way
Genie's Wish
Hunter's Moon
Love of the Wild
Monsters Under the Bed

SECOND CHANCES
Accidental Chemistry
Twice by Chance

SENSES AND SENSATIONS
Love in Plain Sight
A Luminous Touch
Sensible Commitments
Sounds of Love
The Sweetest Scent

THE WHEEL MYSTERIES
Sparks & Drops
Devil's Own
Fireworks & Wild Cards

Published by DREAMSPINNER PRESS
http://www.dreamspinnerpress.com

FIREWORKS & WILD CARDS

SUSAN LAINE

DREAMSPINNER PRESS

Published by
DREAMSPINNER PRESS

5032 Capital Circle SW, Suite 2, PMB# 279, Tallahassee, FL 32305-7886 USA
http://www.dreamspinnerpress.com/

Fireworks & Wild Cards
© 2015 Susan Laine.

Cover Art
© 2015 Brooke Albrecht.
http://brookealbrechtstudio.com
Cover content is for illustrative purposes only and any person depicted on the cover is a model.

ISBN: 978-1-63216-934-1
Digital ISBN: 978-1-63216-935-8
Library of Congress Control Number: 2015904663
First Edition June 2015

Printed in the United States of America
∞
This paper meets the requirements of
ANSI/NISO Z39.48-1992 (Permanence of Paper).

Chapter 1

"I NEED your help, Gus. I think someone's stealing from my coven."

Sitting in the dim, dusty backroom office of his occult shop, The Four Corners, at the end of a long workday, Gus Goodwin was trying his best to work on the books. His balance sheet wasn't quite adding up, though. Was it the Greek salad he'd had for a working lunch last Tuesday or that teenage Goth girl buying the emerald green amulet for luck last Friday that messed everything up? The difference, after all, was a mere $5.99. Certainly nothing to merit an audit. Where the heck had he put that receipt?

A gentle hand tousled his hair. "Hey. Are you listening to me?"

Frowning in disorientation, Gus looked up. Then his cheeks flushed in embarrassment. "Sorry, Jules," he murmured sheepishly. He straightened up, shoved the ledger and the cardboard box full of receipts aside, and nodded firmly. "Please, sit. Tell me again."

Chuckling—probably because she knew his habits so well—Juliette sat down in the rickety chair opposite the desk. Juliette Hayes was a high priestess in the Wiccan faith and the leader of a coven of twelve witches. Today the voluptuous brunette wore a dark green, formfitting velvet dress, the hem reaching her ankles. No one could have easily guessed she was in her forties as her roundness gave her skin a youthful glow, the spark matched by the warmth in her brown eyes.

"I suspect someone is stealing from my coven," Juliette repeated slowly, enunciating for his benefit.

Gus resisted the urge to roll his eyes. He loved his mentor to bits, but he swore that sometimes she thought he was too laid-back for his own good. "Aha. Why do you think that?"

"Because money's missing from the till, so to speak." Juliette sighed, her gaze darting about as though she was trying to get her thoughts in order. "I keep a small box at the Emporium. In it, I store the money for the coven's needs. Everyone pitches in now and then, when they've got spare change or a couple of rumpled bills in their pocket. I've never had cause to doubt anyone's honesty."

Juliette sounded concerned, and Gus could relate. Trusting people wasn't always easy, and if someone you knew betrayed your trust, well, it made it that much harder to trust again. Juliette owned the Blue Goddess Emporium, which catered mainly to the Goddess-oriented Wiccans rather than practitioners of other neopagan faiths, and from the shop she tended to her Moonlight Haven Coven, to which Gus himself had once belonged.

"Is the box kept locked?" Gus asked.

"Yes. I keep the key here." Juliette showed him a simple necklace with a key hanging from it. "There are no other keys. I take it off during the night, though."

Gus cringed inwardly, hiding his eyes behind his bangs. He didn't want to ask his friend if she invited men and/or women for sleepovers. His mentor's sex life wasn't something he felt a burning need to delve into. So he moved on to another line of inquiry. "Do a lot of people know about the key?"

Juliette nodded and shrugged, as though it was a small matter that those she trusted had access to such knowledge. She was a good human being, who focused on the good in other people too. "Those in the coven know. Many have seen me with the key, off and on my neck."

"You think one of them, maybe…?" Gus was reluctant to finish the sentence, out of respect for Juliette's judgment.

Juliette frowned, a stubborn jut to her chin. "I'd like to think not. I sure hope not. I've known most of them for years, a few for decades."

"How much money is usually there on any given day?"

Juliette pondered briefly. "Just what we need for esbat and sabbat supplies and such. Not much. At most, perhaps… fifty dollars?" She snapped her fingers. "Last Yule there was about two hundred, though. But that was a special occasion, as sabbats often are. We had that big party, remember?"

Their chuckles matched. Gus recalled the midwinter sabbat celebration with warmth. He'd gotten drunk off Juliette's mulled wine, as only one of the five jugs of the stuff had been nonalcoholic. Last thing he remembered about that night was dancing in the snow in his underwear with reindeer horns on his head and red, gold, and green glitter all over his body, while singing "Jingle Bell Rock" at the top of his lungs. Consequently, he'd been sick with the flu on New Year's.

"Vaguely," Gus replied with a grin. "So, how much is missing?"

"I keep a record of what people give so I have an accurate sum for any purchases that need to get done." She dug into the old brown leather satchel she carried on her shoulder most of the time when out. Juliette had inherited it from her grandfather, and though it wasn't exactly all that feminine, she cherished it. The old leather gleamed and creaked. "Here."

She handed Gus a thin stack of notepapers on which she had written dates, the amount of money given and by whom, plus the final sum. Meticulous and precise, Gus thought. But then again, Juliette had always been that way.

As he studied the notes, Gus asked, "When did you start noticing a discrepancy?"

"About two, three weeks ago. At first I didn't think much of it. After all, anyone has permission to take money, provided they account for what they took it for."

"I thought you said you kept it locked?"

Juliette blushed, clearing her throat. "It's at the Emporium, right by the cash register. I admit, sometimes I… I forget to lock it during the day. I'm very busy at the shop, you know."

Gus suppressed a sigh. Juliette sounded defensive but only halfheartedly, as if she had an inkling she should have been more careful with the money collected from the coven members. "There's someone at the register at all times, though, right?"

"Yes. Either Joy or myself." Juliette nodded firmly.

Joy Bennett was a friend to both Juliette and Gus. She belonged to Juliette's coven, and Gus had been integral in saving her life from a vicious murderer a couple of months back. She was a good and honest girl, but also young and impressionable. Gus seriously doubted she would, or even could, resort to petty theft.

"I take it you know most of the customers who come to the shop." Gus could attest to that fact since he also knew about 90 percent of the people who came to his shop too—mostly local witches, pagans, and occultists, all harmless and simply wishing to worship their chosen gods and goddesses in peace.

Juliette smiled, and her dimples made a charming appearance. "Of course. Sure, there's the occasional tourist, amateur, or scholar, but mostly local folk. And I doubt any of them would know the lockbox contained anything valuable. I mean, that's what the register is for."

Gus nodded. "Yeah, I get it. So, in total, how much money has gone missing?"

Juliette pointed at the notepapers. "I wrote it down there. All in all, $317.69. And that's just for the past two months. I haven't yet gone back farther. I'll give you my notebooks on all the deposits from this year."

"Jules, does anyone else know that you've noticed this... discrepancy?"

Juliette shook her head. "No. I was going to tell one of my coven members, Hollister Baines, who's an accountant and who used to work for the IRS before going to work at a private firm. But I decided against it."

Gus quirked an eyebrow. He didn't know the gentleman in question. "You think he's involved?"

Juliette pursed her lips in dismay. "I doubt it. He's a former government official. Plus, he's well-off. He doesn't need to steal from petty cash."

"Yeah," Gus said slowly. "And yet you decided not to inform him."

Juliette gave him a patient, mildly scolding glance. "That doesn't mean I suspect him. Just that I wanted to do some checking into this on my own first."

"You mean, on *our* own," Gus clarified with a smirk and got another reproachful glare in return. "It's been ages since I've last attended any of your coven gatherings, esbats or sabbats. Is anyone I know still there?" When Gus became a Wiccan, his first coven had been Juliette's, as she was his mentor into the faith. He'd gotten to know most everyone there. But that had been years ago. He practiced alone these days since he rarely found the time. His occupation consumed most of his work *and* free time.

"Tom and Aeryn are still there, and so are Rodney and Syd. The others are new."

Gus nodded. Thomas Hardy, named after the poet, was a former soldier who lived off disability. Aeryn Newton was a defense attorney for a private firm, notorious and wealthy, unlikely to need to steal pennies. Rodney Easton was a former scholar who had burned out due to the stress of trying to get on the tenure track and sought relief from spirituality. He was poor and down on his luck, so he was a candidate for the crime. Sydney Keen was a renowned journalist, aggressive in matters involving the environment and politics, and was quite affluent, which made her yet another person who didn't need to resort to theft, let alone thrills since she was often the target of smear campaigns and political intrigue.

"How are they?" Gus asked, glad to hear news about friends he hadn't seen in a while.

Juliette smiled, showcasing her dimples again. "Fine. You should come by. We're going to celebrate next esbat together at Jason's place. He's got a huge house in Bellevue, practically a palace. I've been there twice. It's fabulous."

Gus frowned. "Who's Jason?"

"Jason Upton," Juliette replied. "He's a financier or a developer or something. As rich as the gods, for sure. I admit when he gets to talking about piles of money, expensive business trips, and high-end estates, I tune out." Her cheeks flushed cutely as she confessed this, and Gus smiled back, amused. "I don't know how into Wicca he really is," she added. "I doubt he's a true believer."

"Why is he there, then?"

"His boyfriend, Alec Hope, has been a member for quite a while. He came in shortly after you took over the shop full time." Juliette uncapped a bottle of water from her bag and took a sip. "You might remember him from last Yule. The sweet young man dressed like a World War II nurse?"

Gus racked his brain for the elusive memory. Most of his recollections from that night were blurry and distorted. *Damn wine.* Out of the blue, an image of a short, whip-thin young man with a swarm of freckles, long reddish-brown hair, and the cutest dimples ever rose to the forefront of his mind. "Oh, yeah, that guy. A nurse or some such. A cutie." He grinned and winked at Juliette, who rolled her eyes.

"Right, that one. Alec brought Jason to the coven earlier this year."

Gus cocked his head to the side. He'd known Juliette for so many years that he heard the things she left unsaid. "You don't like him." It wasn't a question.

Juliette squirmed, clearly hating being put on the spot. "Jason's nothing if not polite."

"But...?" Gus encouraged.

Juliette harrumphed, irritated, and swept her hands about. "I honestly don't know what it is about that man that vexes me so! But something does."

"It's okay, Jules. Whatever it is that troubles you about this guy, it'll come up when the time is right." Gus consoled his friend with a soft smile.

Juliette sighed and relaxed. "Yes, I suppose you're right. I just... I hate that I get this weird sense of... of discomfort with him. I have no rational basis for feeling that way. That annoys me. I don't like to be led by my emotions all the time."

"Perhaps your instincts simply—"

"No, Gus. I'm not a slave to my instincts. I'm not an animal." Juliette straightened up as if she were discarding the whole topic off her shoulders, like shrugging off a heavy coat. "In any case, in addition to the ones I mentioned, there's Hollister, of course."

"Of course." Though Gus hadn't known Hollister Baines was an ex-tax official, he was aware Baines was in the coven. Gus had never met the man but had heard about him. Hollister was a senior citizen, and he had health issues that often excluded him from attending esbats held under the full moon, or late night sabbats.

"There are two new younger members as well," Juliette went on. "Matty Osborne is in college. He's nineteen, into computers and gaming, and he's very nice. He loves baking, so he's the coven's designated deliverer of goodies." She smirked, and Gus chuckled. They both had a bit of a sweet tooth. "Then there's Pine Seed Tash, also a college student, in the arts program, if I recall." Gus started to speak, but Juliette waved him silent. "Yes, yes. What a name to subject a child to. But she's amiable and apparently at peace with the name. Who knew?"

"Got it." Gus did a simple calculation. "Including you, that's eleven. You still prefer to have the full twelve like you used to?" There was no standard number of coven members. Thirteen was popular, but it wasn't written in stone. Not much in Wicca was. Juliette preferred an even number, so twelve had been her focus. She especially liked gender balance, so she typically chose six women and six men.

"Yes. I admit it's old-fashioned. But still…." Juliette took another gulp of water, and Gus realized he was hungry. He should get something to eat, maybe takeaway or pizza. "The last lady is Kerry Pryor. She's a personal assistant to a congressman or some such. She comes from an ultraconservative religious family, and she has authority issues, spiritual issues, daddy issues, and so on. She's a tough nut to crack. But she seems to have embraced the freedom of worship Wicca provides, so that's positive at least."

Gus nodded and made a small acquiescing sound to show he'd listened. Juliette had been the High Priestess of her coven for over two decades, and in that time, the turnover had been significant. There were no original members of the coven left, as most of them had gone off to form their own covens, continued as solitary practitioners, or simply left the area to pursue other interests. Of the current members, Tom Hardy had been there the longest—more than nine years.

That accounted for everyone in the coven. Gus still had two more questions left. "So… want me to bring Niall into this?" Niall Valentine was Gus's boyfriend and a private investigator. A good one. His most successful recent cases had been celebrated by the papers and had earned him a reputation as a PI who cracked cases, no matter what kind. Gus valued Niall's opinion. He had a nose for suspicious things.

Juliette frowned, seeming pensive. "I did think of that."

"But…?" Gus urged quietly. Juliette liked Niall, but Gus didn't know if she trusted him like he did.

Juliette apparently came to a conclusion. Her gaze took on a focused look. "I'd like someone to come into the coven, to see and hear and learn about these people firsthand."

Gus blinked. "You mean, like… undercover?" Well, that ruled him out. Gus might not have met all of those presently in the Moonlight Haven Coven, but he knew at least half of them and saw them as friends. He didn't feel comfortable spying on his friends.

"Yes, I suppose that word fits." Juliette nodded. Her eyes glowed with interest, but she sat still, visibly determined to maintain her composure. "Hollister is taking a break from coven work and taking a vacation in DC with his nephew, so there's room for a new member. Someone… vigilant."

Gus worried his bottom lip. "I can't go undercover. Most of them know me, and I have issues with the, um, implications. And… that probably excludes Niall too. His name and face have been in the papers."

Juliette sighed. "Yes, I'm aware." She looked uncomfortable, so Gus suspected whatever she had in mind to suggest, it would be a doozy. "I'd like you to ask Niall's father, Owain."

Gus blinked and then blinked some more. "Owain?"

"Yes. From what you've told me, Owain is an ex-police officer and an ex-soldier. He'd be perfect for the part. No one would suspect him of being—"

"Of being a plant?" Gus cringed, skeptical. "But he's not a Wiccan."

Juliette shrugged. "I've taken strays and neophytes on before, you know." She gave him her all-knowing look, the one that told him she knew that he knew she knew best. "Besides, I've wanted to meet him ever since you told me about him." She dipped her head to put the water bottle back into her bag, but behind her brown tresses, Gus could see a fierce blush forming. He had to bite his lip not to grin. Well, that was a whole other ball game.

"Okay, I'll talk to Niall and ask his dad," Gus offered. "But I can't promise anything. He is retired, you know."

Juliette smiled, and there were the dimples once more. "Yes, of course. I was just hoping he might like to help." She threw the bag over her head to her shoulder and stood. "I've gotta get going. I've got dinner plans with Joy. See you later. Call me." She waved her hand and was out the door while the echo of her words still lingered in the room.

Gus sighed. Juliette was interested in Owain? That was a curveball. Still, he was certain Juliette wouldn't make up a petty theft just to meet a man. Gus's stomach rumbled, and a weakness washed over him. His blood sugar was low. He put the ledger and the receipts into a desk drawer, packed up his stuff, turned off the lights, and left the shop, remembering to lock the door.

Chapter 2

"OUCH! SHIT. Fuck."

Niall groaned painfully as he tried to dislodge his drenched overcoat from his broad shoulders. But that damn goon he'd tried to ambush in the alley behind the pharmacy had been surprisingly nimble, despite his massive size, and the plank he'd used to deck Niall had been rather sizable as well.

Some days he really hated his job.

"Boy, you sure know how to make a memorable entrance." Niall looked up and saw Gus smirking at him from behind the counter, his curly blond hair a mess and his green eyes twinkling. Delicious smells drifted from the kitchen, and Niall was so hungry he couldn't see straight.

"Shut up," he muttered, finally managing to get rid of his coat. It flopped to the floor with a moist smack and lay there in a wet heap. "Dammit." He added a couple of choice curses under his breath but picked up the soaked garment, kicked off his shoes by the door, carried the coat to the small bathroom by the entrance, and hung it behind the door with a hanger. Cold droplets fell onto the linoleum, a dripping sound echoing in the tiny space.

Squaring his shoulders to get rid of the kinks, Niall turned around and found himself face-to-face with his boyfriend, who held a steaming cup of coffee in his outstretched hand. *Oh, is that cinnamon I smell? Yum.*

With a relieved sigh, Niall grabbed the cup and took a huge gulp. The bitter flavor barely registered on his tongue as he savored the heated liquid going down his throat, warming him from the inside.

Only when half the contents were gone did he say hoarsely, with heartfelt gratitude, "Thanks, babe."

Gus smiled. "Bad day at the office, dear?" A chuckle escaped his lips, and his shoulders shimmied from poorly suppressed laughter.

"Cut that shit out. I'm in a foul mood." Niall drank the rest of the coffee and decided to forgive his boyfriend for being an ass.

"As opposed to your otherwise sugary sweet mood?" Gus knew him too well. *Dammit.*

Niall growled. "Shut it. C'mere and gimme a kiss." He puckered up and waited. With a soft smile, Gus leaned in. Warm lips that tasted like pineapples pressed against Niall's. Gus must have been dipping into the fruit bowl again. There was never anything left but apple cores by the time Niall got there.

But they weren't living together, so it wasn't Gus's responsibility to ensure Niall ate his vegetables and fruit.

Sure, over the course of the past several months they'd been dating, a chunk of Niall's things had migrated to Gus's place, the spacious apartment above his shop. Niall had a shaving kit, a toothbrush, and some underwear, plus a couple of T-shirts and sweatpants tucked into one of Gus's dresser drawers. But did they officially live together? No.

Niall went with the kiss, pressing closer to Gus, who was warm and sweet scented and half-hard from what Niall could tell. The intermittent poke of Gus's sizeable erection against Niall's upper thigh was a godsend, washing away Niall's aches and worries. He slanted his mouth to delve deeper into Gus's, their tongues slipping and sliding against each other, leisurely tasting and touching. He nipped at Gus's full lower lip, sucking on it gently.

Gus rocked against him, sighing and whimpering. His arms wound around Niall's neck and shoulders. They were only an inch or so different in height, so their bodies fit together perfectly as far as Niall was concerned. He was getting aroused, and he started grinding against the lean, lithe body in his embrace. They began to grope and squeeze, their kiss turning hungrier and needier, and their coordination dwindled as they both sought leverage, friction, and that blissful blend of pleasure and pain.

A bubbling sound rose, followed by hissing. Something pouring onto the hot stove?

"Oh no, my noodles," Gus mumbled into the kiss, only partially intelligible.

Niall let him go, and with his cheeks flushed, his eyes huge and dark, and his lips swollen from nibbles, Gus dashed toward the kitchen. Niall let out a breath, ran tired fingers through his hair, and turned to the sink to wash his hands.

His reflection spoke of a man not getting any younger, which was ridiculous since he was only thirty-one. Yet belying his still-young age, his dark hair lay limp on his head, his grayish stubble was strong, his blue-gray eyes were weary and bore a few more lines around the edges than before, and his slightly hunched stance gave him an unkempt, even shaggy appearance. Of course, his run-down clothes—old suit and tie—didn't do him any favors either.

Oh, who cares? No gay fashionistas in this house.

Sighing, Niall splashed water on his face to wash away some of the dirt and grime the streets had rubbed off on him. Being a PI wasn't glamorous. He never met any drop-dead gorgeous femmes fatales, let alone hommes fatales, and neither did his typical clientele rub noses with the chic upper class. His usual jobs consisted of long, boring stakeouts to catch suspected adulterers in the act, lost or stolen vehicle locates, and endless paperwork, not fancy soirées with swanky socialites, cocktail parties at the governor's mansion, or lustful early morning hours spent cruising posh nightclubs.

"Hey, lazybones," Gus called out from the kitchen, his tone more teasing than serious scolding. "You coming or what? Dinner's ready."

Niall smiled despite his fatigue. Gus was a ball of energy, and with his mere presence, he lent some of it to Niall.

After quickly drying his face and hands, Niall went to find Gus. The blond beauty with his curly bangs, green eyes, and delicate features was the spitting image of a California surfer. Except they lived in Seattle, in the great wet Northwest. Well, Niall lived in Seattle, while Gus lived and worked in Tacoma, a port town by the Puget Sound about thirty miles south of Seattle. Gus's long, lean body was surprisingly strong, although right now, in white denim shorts and a light green T-shirt, he looked almost dainty. As usual around the house, Gus wore nothing on his feet as he padded around, filling the table with food and drinks.

The moment Niall saw the dinner amassed on the dining table by the window that looked out on the street below, however, he almost forgot his boyfriend's existence.

"Are those steak fajitas?" Niall asked, his stomach protesting the wait as he stood in place, staring and licking his lips.

Gus chuckled. "They sure are. Steak fajitas with chimichurri sauce and fresh herbs. Sit and dig in." He turned back to the kitchen, hollering over his shoulder, "Want a beer?"

"God, yes!" Niall sat down, grabbed one of the fajitas from the platter, and put it down on his plate, reveling in the mouthwatering scents of parsley, cilantro, peppers, garlic, lemon, and lime. The beef had its own meaty aroma, which Niall inhaled. "Fuck, that's good." Then he chomped into his first fajita, herb leaves spilling out of his mouth and dropping onto the plate.

Gus chuckled, sitting next to him. "Easy there, buddy. No need to choke on it. There's more. I made six, just in case you were hungry."

"Mmm-mmm-mmm…" was Niall's muffled reply. The food tasted so good he had no words. It took Niall two whole fajitas before he could concentrate on other things on the table. He saw Gus with a white bowl of green noodles. "What's that?" he asked, mainly to be polite to the person who was kind enough to feed him virtually on a daily basis.

Gus swallowed his mouthful and gulped half a glass of ice water before replying. "It's creamy zucchini noodles with avocado. Why? You want some?" He shoved a forkful of something green and slippery in front of Niall, grinning.

Niall backed off, grimacing. "Get that veggie crap away from me. I'm a carnivore, not a bunny."

Gus chuckled and continued eating. "My poor Tigger. Not feeling bouncy today?" He pouted playfully and made a face, and Niall couldn't help but laugh. "So, your coat was soaked and dirty. Is it raining again? Want me to wash it for you?"

"No and no. I can do my own laundry, thank you very much." Niall didn't want to get used to someone doing things for him. As much as he cared for Gus, loved him even, he didn't wish to grow accustomed to having Gus do domestic chores for him.

"It's no trouble," Gus said.

"When you wash my stuff, it comes off smelling like flowers," Niall deflected, even though he probably shouldn't have sounded so gruff.

Gus gave him a funny look, his brow furrowed but a weird smile curving the corners of his lips. "Yeah. That's called laundry detergent. But for you, next time I'll go to the waterfront with your clothes and beat them with rocks. How's that?"

Niall lowered his head, hiding his grim expression, and muttered something close to an apology. He'd been in the Army, after all, so he lived simply. Minimalist decor in his apartment, with little furniture and few personal items, meant he didn't need to clean often, let alone do the laundry every other day—or let his boyfriend do it and end up with clothes smelling like a bouquet.

Thankfully Gus saved the moment from getting any more awkward. "How'd your coat get in that condition anyway?"

Niall straightened up a bit, snatched a third steak fajita onto his plate, nibbled on the edge, and then said, "I had in a run-in with that suspect in the pharmacy robberies. Caught up to him in the back alley. Had a bit of a fistfight. Then he got the drop on me, hit me on the back with a plank, and down I went."

"Oh my God, are you okay?" Alarmed, Gus visibly checked Niall's face and body for signs of distress, scrapes and cuts, bruises and contusions.

"Yeah, yeah, I'm fine." Niall smiled to reassure Gus, and Gus did give a thin smile in return. Clearly he wasn't convinced. "I was in the Army, remember? I can take care of myself."

Gus pouted and bit his lower lip. "I never said you couldn't." His pitch rose, and Niall foresaw a fight brewing. But Gus forked some noodles off his plate and stuffed them in his mouth, perhaps buying time. Niall didn't want them to argue. "Why aren't the cops trying to catch this guy? I mean, it's their job."

Niall shrugged. "Cases like that are low priority for them. If there was money or drugs missing from the pharmacies, then yeah, the cops would investigate faster, with greater resources. But this jerk only steals Band-Aids, who knows why, so he's not at the top of the list. Weirdo...." He continued eating, savoring each bite and washing them down with swigs of beer. "In any case, I got a good look at the dickwad. I gave Hughes a pretty good description, and he got a hit in the NCIC. The cops know who the perpetrator is and where he lives, so an arrest is up to them. They should have him in custody by now."

Gus harrumphed. "You could have told me from the start you closed the case."

"It ain't closed till I see the idiot's face behind bars. And besides, I work for the owner of the pharmacy, not the cops." Wanting to improve the mood, Niall decided a little praise was in order. "These fajitas are really yummy. I must say, for a guy who doesn't eat meat, you sure cook it real well."

To Niall's surprise, Gus grinned at him broadly. "But Niall, I *do* eat meat. Didn't I prove as much last night?"

Niall's eyes widened. Gus didn't always engage in sexual innuendo or sexy banter, but when he did all bets were off. A slow smile spread to his lips. "Yeah. You're right. Now how could that have slipped my mind? Hmm. Maybe I require a reenactment." He waggled his eyebrows even though his meaning was clear enough on its own.

With a wicked smirk, Gus slid down slowly from his chair until his blond head disappeared under the table. Then warm hands landed on

Niall's thighs, and he spread his legs. Deft fingers rubbed Niall's growing erection and then unzipped his fly. A hot, wet mouth pressed against Niall's boxer briefs, tracing the firm outline of his cock. His hips bucked.

"Shit, yeah," Niall moaned, letting his head fall back as he relaxed.

Gus mumbled something under the table, but Niall couldn't hear it with blood roaring in his ears. A hot hand wrapped around Niall's dick and pulled it out from beneath the fabric. Then lips sealed around Niall's cockhead, and a nimble tongue licked around the glans and dipped into the slit, causing Niall's prick to spill precome into Gus's hungry mouth.

"Fuck, so good," Niall whispered, his head swimming in chaotic bliss.

Gus kicked the blowjob into high gear. His lips seemed to travel the length of the shaft and still suckle on the head, while his tongue laved and wet all of Niall's cock and still managed to tease the slit until Niall lost his mind. It had been a long day, and Gus's touch was perfect.

The second Gus's left hand began to pump and his right to fondle his balls, Niall succumbed to his cresting orgasm. Waves of pleasure thrummed through his body, washing away every tired thought and relaxing every taut muscle. His head vibrated along with the tune Gus was humming around Niall's prick as he continued to swallow Niall's load and still suck and lick like he wasn't planning on stopping at all.

Finally Niall threaded his fingers through Gus's hair, urging him off while he panted and slumped, boneless. It was a miracle he didn't melt into goo and glide off the chair. "Gus, babe, too sensitive."

Once Gus licked Niall's dick clean, he tucked the limp member back into Niall's underwear, zipped him, and wiggled his way up from under the table. As he adjusted himself in the chair, Gus carded a hand through his mussed-up curls and wiped the corners of his mouth.

Niall stared at Gus with half-lidded eyes. Gus's cheeks were pink, his dick-sucking lips swollen and red, and he sported a just-fucked look, even though he hadn't been. *Fuck, he's so super hot.* Niall wanted to return the favor and shifted with the intention of blowing Gus's mind as well as his dick.

"Niall, we need to talk," Gus said suddenly.

Stopping midmotion, Niall held his breath, worried now. "What?"

Gus squirmed again in the chair, and judging from his appearance, he clearly had an unattended erection hidden under the table. Niall wanted to take care of his boyfriend's predicament firsthand. But then Gus locked gazes with him as if heralding a serious discussion. *Shit.* They should have had that talk before Gus sucked Niall's brain through his dick.

Gus took a deep breath and recounted his meeting with Juliette. Niall listened through the whole thing without interruptions. But when Gus ducked his head and mentioned Owain being the one to go undercover, casual and cool as a cucumber, Niall had to interject.

"You know my dad's retired," he informed Gus firmly. Gus nodded but said nothing, obviously waiting for more. Niall didn't disappoint. "He was a cop, sure, but he doesn't do that shit anymore. Frankly, I'm a little offended Juliette would even have the balls to suggest such a thing." Gus nodded again, quiet, staring at his plate, worrying his bottom lip. Niall had to ask. "Is that why you gave me head? To get me to go along with this plan of yours?"

Niall knew he'd gone too far when Gus went rigid and his eyes flashed and then went bleak. Gus stood, his back ramrod straight, and left the room without a word or a backward glance. A few moments later Niall heard the bedroom door snick closed quietly.

"Shit." Niall shook his head, angry at himself for being so cruel, and shoved his plate aside and let his head fall on the table, banging his forehead on the hard surface a couple of times for good measure. "Stupid, stupid, stupid…."

The problem was, crystal clear in hindsight, as always, Niall knew very well that Gus would never do anything like what he had accused him of doing. Gus could be stubborn about doing things his own way. But being deliberately devious and exploitative? No.

Niall had two choices. He could leave Gus's place and let his words fester and likely ruin the future of their relationship, or he could man up and try to explain his reasoning or… well, really the only sensible option and the right thing to do was to apologize. Perhaps with a dose of groveling on the side.

Hating how he'd ruined the good mood and the afterglow of a wonderful blowjob, Niall made his way down the hall to Gus's bedroom. The door was closed, and no sounds came from behind it. Niall pressed his ear closer, thinking he'd hear if Gus was crying. But all was quiet.

Gently he knocked on the door. "Gus?" He waited but to no avail. "Gus, I'm sorry. Can I please come in?" He swore he heard a soft noise, like the movement of fabric or rustle of clothes, but no one bid him enter or opened the door. "Gus, I didn't mean it." He rubbed his forehead, sweaty and furrowed, uncomfortable in this anxious situation, sharing his feelings with an inanimate object, only hoping someone he cared about was listening on the other side. "I know you'd never do anything like that. I'm just kind of overprotective when it comes to my dad. He doesn't need it, but I can't help it."

After a moment of silence, while Niall was preparing another round of apologies, the door opened a crack. Niall couldn't see Gus but sensed his presence behind the door.

"Gus, I really am sorry. I was an ass." Niall prayed he was getting through to Gus. He wasn't good at this sort of thing, mending fences, which probably accounted for why he'd never been in a serious relationship.

Then Gus came into partial view, a mere shadow. "No, *I'm* sorry," Gus said, surprising the hell out of Niall. "It was childish of me to run away and lock myself in my bedroom instead of staying put to have an adult conversation. Guess I overreacted and behaved immaturely, like a child having a temper tantrum. It won't happen again."

Now Niall felt even worse. "Look, please let me explain." He took a breath and swiped a hand across his forehead. "This whole thing just brought up old memories. Residual childhood fears, you know. My dad was a cop, and I remember being a kid, eavesdropping when I should've been in bed. How Mom always worried when Dad went to work, wondering if today was going to be the day when he didn't come back, and some police officer, a total stranger, would come to our doorstep to deliver the news. For a long time, it was my fear too, subconscious even as a grown man. All those nights spent worrying, yeah, they left their mark on me, like a looming darkness." Niall nodded to himself, acknowledging the anxiety he'd felt for so long. "When Dad finally retired, I just felt so fucking relieved, like a weight had been lifted from my shoulders."

Gus let out a half sob, half exhale. "And I brought it all back by suggesting your dad could go undercover at Juliette's coven."

Niall scraped nervously at the door frame with blunt fingernails, needing something to do with his hands, and a sliver of white paint peeled off. "Yeah, I guess so. My mom's gone. Dad's all I've got left." He shrugged, aiming for an appearance of nonchalance but knowing he would fail. His mother had died long ago, but he still feared the prospect of losing his father. It was a child's fear but one that easily carried into adulthood, unchanged.

Suddenly he had arms full of an apologetic Gus. "I'm sorry, Niall. I shouldn't have pressed." Warm breath fanned over Niall's neck, and Gus's scent filled his senses. Gus shivered in Niall's embrace.

Niall hugged Gus and planted a reassuring kiss on his neck. "Look, it's okay. I swear. I should've explained the whole thing better, or even started to explain. I was mean, and I shouldn't have been. Forgive me?"

Gus nodded several times. "Yes." His hold of Niall tightened. "I'll tell Juliette that—"

"Wait." Niall pulled back to see Gus's face and eyes. "Listen, I'll ask my dad first if he's interested. I worry about his safety, but honestly, I'll worry whether he's tracking down a thief or taking a stroll through the park. And…." He swallowed hard, calming himself. "I know he misses it. Being a cop. Sometimes." He offered Gus a soft smile, and Gus returned the gesture. "There's no harm in asking, right?"

Gus shook his head and blinked hard. "No, no harm." His eyes glistened a bit, but Niall pretended not to see it. No self-respecting man wanted to be called out as a crybaby.

Niall cleared his throat and took a step back, clapping his hands together and raising his voice in a theatrical show of enthusiasm. "Well, now that's sorted, how about we get back to our meals, yeah?"

Gus chuckled. "Yes, let's." Before Niall could retreat, Gus took his hand and squeezed gently. "Thanks, Niall." He looked like he had more to say but in the end only gave a small smile as a peace offering.

Niall accepted it with a nod. They'd had their first domestic tiff but survived relatively unscathed, so from his point of view, it was a win. Side by side and hand in hand, they returned to the table and their interrupted meal. Later, once they had sated their bellies, they took a dirty shower together, to their mutual satisfaction, and then went to sleep in the same bed, cuddling each other.

Next day Gus washed Niall's coat.

Chapter 3

"SO, EVEN though I'm not a witch, you want me to go undercover in the, uh... what was it, a coven?" Owain sounded uncertain of his interpretation, and Gus could relate. Faith was a tricky thing. No two people in the world believe exactly the same things. And pretending to believe while trying to do covert surveillance sounded potentially hazardous to Gus.

"Wiccan, not witch, and a coven, yeah." Gus worried his lower lip as he sat with Owain at the dining table in Gus's apartment the day after Gus and Niall had had their first tiff. Niall sat on the opposite side but was not contributing anything to the talk. "If you have any questions, I'm happy to help."

Owain shook his head calmly. "I can do my own research, thank you. I'm not that old yet. I can still work a computer." He winked at Gus, who smiled back. "Besides, I think I got the gist of this dilemma. It's in the bag. Petty theft, ten or so suspects, undercover spy needed."

"Yes, that about sums it up." Gus liked Owain and didn't want him to get into trouble over this. That's why he'd offered his aid and expertise.

The former homicide detective had just passed his sixtieth birthday in the spring, but he was fit and strong. Niall had told Gus that Owain ran track and lifted weights still, which accounted for his athletic appearance. His black hair did have streaks of white, showing his age, but his blue eyes burned with vigor. He wore simple slacks, a sports jacket, and a gray Henley shirt. The only difference between him and Niall was that Niall's pants were jeans and his jacket leather.

Owain rubbed his jaw, and his ever-so-light stubble made a soft scratching sound. "I don't mind helping out," he finally said, his gravelly voice the result of a past smoking habit. He locked gazes with Gus. "Will you be there?"

Gus nodded. "Juliette usually prefers to have twelve participants, mostly for logistical reasons. Traditional covens go for thirteen people present at any given ritual, so for the upcoming esbat, Juliette's going to make an exception to her own rule. With us there it'll be thirteen."

Niall chuckled, addressing his father. "That's Gus-speak for yes, he'll be there."

Gus blushed but didn't take offense. Good-natured banter showed him how well Niall knew him and how much he cared. "Right. We'll both be able to attend. It'll be day after tomorrow. Midnight isn't always feasible for everyone, so Juliette tries to aim for moonrise. Hope that's not a problem?"

Owain grinned. "Nope. The old folks' home doesn't have a curfew." Niall laughed, and so did Gus, because of course, Owain didn't live in a nursing home.

"Well, that's super," Gus said, going along with the joke. "But I meant do you think you can learn the basics of Wicca by then?"

"Dad's got a great memory," Niall interjected, fiddling with a coin, flipping it through his fingers like an illusionist.

"I'm sure he does," Gus said in a complimentary manner, smiling. "In any case, Juliette will introduce you as a neophyte to Wicca, so as long as you know the basics and appear to share those ideals in a manner consistent with a believer, you'll do fine."

"Being excited about nature is a good thing, yeah?" Owain commented. "I can handle that. I've recently started recycling too." His jesting turned the possible dangers of the situation into ones Gus felt they could handle. "You gonna be there too, Son?"

Niall quirked an eyebrow and faced Gus. "I don't know. If I'm spotted hiding in the bushes, would I have to fear a, yelling; b, being chased; c, guns; or d, horrible curses?"

Gus rolled his eyes. "Would you please take this seriously, numbskull." Niall cackled at Gus's scolding tone of voice. "And if you *are* discovered by any of us, you aren't doing your job." He flicked a tongue at Niall, who just grinned wider. "A-ny-way," Gus went on, focusing on Owain. "I'll give you a couple of books to read and a few websites to peruse. We'll meet here, then fetch Juliette from her house and proceed from there to Jason's house." Gus turned his attention to Niall. "Did you look into the coven members to see if any of them have a record, like I asked?"

Niall nodded, fumbled in his jeans pocket for a notepad, and flipped it open. "The host of the evening, Jason Upton, has several arrests for speeding and driving under the influence, all paid for. Aeryn Newton, the lawyer, has been the target of several lawsuits, most settled by her firm or dismissed by a judge. The only one with an extensive criminal record is Sydney Keen, the journalist. She's been arrested on numerous occasions at environmental demonstrations and rallies, and a few include charges of assault against an officer. Seems like a passionate lady."

"An anarchist?" Owain asked.

Niall shrugged, flipping the notepad closed. "These days it's hard to say. It's not like the environment can carry on without help." Gus beamed, so proud of his enlightened boyfriend that he vowed to surprise Niall in some pleasant way in the near future.

"And anarchy comes in several shapes and sizes," Niall continued. "Corruption in politics isn't exactly unheard of, least of all when big corporations with their big money come into the picture. Speaking against corruption can easily earn a person the label of anarchist, and undeservedly so."

Gus had a total fanboy moment then, staring at Niall in awe and arousal. "I'm going to bake you a cake," he declared, earning curious looks from Niall and Owain. "Just a thought."

Owain smiled like the cat with the cream, as though he knew exactly what Gus was thinking. "Well, give me the literature you think I need, and I'll get out of your hair." He stood, and Gus dashed to his study to fetch some good introductory books on Wicca.

A few minutes later, he returned to his guests and extended Owain a pile of books. "I'll want these back," he said solemnly. *"Buckland's Complete Book of Witchcraft*, by Raymond Buckland, is great—a wealth of information there."

"Aha." Owain seemed amused and bemused, and yet accepted one book after another.

Gus kept shoving volumes into Owain's lap. "Scott Cunningham's *Wicca: A Guide for the Solitary Practitioner* and *Living Wicca* are excellent, as he writes well and clearly. For basic info also, here's *Wicca for Beginners* by Thea Sabin and *The Craft* by Dorothy Morrison. Margot Adler's *Drawing Down the Moon* and Janet and Stewart Farrar's *A Witches' Bible* require a bit more in the basic knowledge department but they're also fine sources of info. Gerald Gardner's *Witchcraft Today* can be useful, but you should take the contents with a grain of salt, so maybe that book's not necessary. I've added it anyway."

"Um, thanks." Owain seemed overwhelmed by the growing number of texts, so Gus decided enough was enough.

"Well," Gus said slowly, keeping the rest of the books to himself. "There are notes in the margins and pieces of paper probably inside all of them. Plus, I'm pretty sure there are several useful websites mentioned here and there, like Witchvox and Wicca.com." He backed off, certain he'd drowned Owain in information. "I'm sure you'll find at least some of that beneficial." Then he quieted, running out of breath. His excitement did sometimes advance in leaps and bounds, much to the bemusement of others.

Niall came to stand at Gus's side. "You might have noticed, Dad, that Gus is into this big-time." It wasn't said in a malicious manner. Gus heard the underlying humor in his boyfriend's tone and leaned closer. Niall wrapped an arm around Gus's shoulder, an act of intimacy Gus hadn't expected from Niall, at least not in front of his father.

Owain still had an amiable smile on his lips. "Good night, boys." He tucked the books under his arm, inclined his head slightly as a farewell, and left. Gus followed, locking the door once Owain had left, then crossed to the window overlooking the street and watched until Owain got into his car and drove off.

Staring into the night, Gus got a sudden chill, and he hugged himself for warmth. He had an unpleasant, sinking feeling in his gut, portending something terrible. He didn't prescribe to psychic powers or clairvoyance, but his instincts had never let him down yet. Well, once, when he'd made an error in judgment and almost gotten strangled to death by a murderer. Most of the time, though, his intuition served him well. Especially on the plus side, since it was thanks to his hunches Gus had met Niall.

A strong, warm body pressed against his back and an arm wound around his middle. "You okay?" Niall's coffee-scented breath tickled Gus's ear and cheek.

Gus nodded. "Owain is a good man. And he can certainly take care of himself."

Niall kissed Gus on the neck, giving him goose bumps and generating heat in his groin. "Yeah," Niall agreed. "I guess I have nothing to worry about. I mean, before he retired he was a cop for nearly forty years. He doesn't need me to watch over him."

Gus leaned into Niall, swaying gently. "I don't think he minds." Gus turned around in Niall's embrace to see his man's smiling face. "You gonna take me to bed now?"

Niall quirked an eyebrow, sporting a wicked smile. Then he crouched, put his shoulder against Gus's abdomen, and lifted him off his feet in a fireman's hold. Gus started to protest, weakly, but a smack on his butt silenced him. As he was carried to the bedroom, Gus thought his life couldn't get much better than this.

Twenty minutes later, as Gus was screaming his head off, caught in the pure pleasure of climax, Niall proved him wrong.

TWO DAYS later on the first full moon night in June, Gus drove his white Smart Fortwo with green stripes through the busy Seattle streets. Evening was falling, but they still had time before sunset. The sky was cloudy, with rosy hues, golden slivers, and darker blue patches here and there. He gripped the steering wheel too hard, but he couldn't let go. Why he worried so, he couldn't say.

"Babe, take it easy, okay?" Niall rested his left hand on Gus's right on the wheel and tenderly pried his death grip to a more relaxed one. "Deep breaths now."

Gus nodded frantically. "I don't know why I'm so freaking nervous. Maybe 'cause I feel like I'm playing spy, and someone could get hurt."

Niall patted his hand gently. "We're talking about a few hundred dollars. I seriously doubt anyone in the coven would be crazy enough to resort to violence over it. Come on, now. Just calm down."

The car fitted only two, the driver and a passenger. Gus could talk about anything and let his anxiety show because Owain wasn't with them. He was following in his own car, a black Nissan Juke, with Juliette. Gus took a couple of deep breaths, trying to calm his nerves.

"I'm gonna give the whole thing away," Gus said, hoping he didn't sound as whiny as he suspected. "Owain's gonna be in big trou—"

"First of all, my dad can take care of himself," Niall cut in, sounding infuriatingly cool and rational. "Secondly, Gus, I've never known you to shy away from confrontation or be afraid of anything or anyone. You'll do fine."

Gus nodded, licking his dry lips, and trying to find solace in Niall's faith in him. "So, remind me again. Where will you be?"

"Nearby. I promise. You won't see me, but I'll be there." Niall took one of Gus's hands in his and lifted it to his lips, placing a soft kiss on his knuckles. "Plus, I'm armed. Just in case. My dad knows what to do in a crisis and how to take someone out, even if he's unarmed and the other person isn't. Honestly, babe, you're overreacting. Everything's okay."

Gus needed the reassurance and the guidance. He'd been in a pickle twice before. First time, a murderer had tried to choke the life out of him. The second time he'd actually jumped onto the back of the murderer who had tried to kill Niall. Naturally, while both had been heroic acts, sort of, they didn't exactly improve his track record for getting into trouble and in harm's way. And besides, it was easier to jeopardize one's own life than someone else's, least of all his lover's father's!

By the time they pulled to the curb a couple of blocks away from Jason Upton's upscale estate in Bellevue, Gus still hadn't worked out all his issues. But when Niall gripped his chin, turned his head so they faced each other, and kissed the bejesus out of him, Gus got control of his nerves. He wagered no one could be anything but mellow after that talented, hot, and slippery tongue delivered its comforting and arousing message.

Gus sighed when Niall pulled back with a grin. "Not so scary anymore, is it, babe?"

Gus shook his head slowly, his head fuzzy with red, horny images. Snapping out of the daze, he blushed and chuckled. "I'm being ridiculous, aren't I, with all this needless worrying?"

Niall scrunched his nose cutely. "Just a tad." Then he grew serious. "I'll be close by, so no fretting, okay?" Before Gus could comment, Niall suddenly shook his head and laughed. "What am I saying? I know you. You'll be fine." He rolled his eyes, kissed Gus quickly, and stepped out of the car, closing the door quietly. In a heartbeat Niall had vanished into the trees on the waterfront side of the road.

Inside the car Gus smiled goofily at no one in particular. If Niall had faith in him, the least he could do was have faith in himself. Gus checked the rearview mirror to see if Owain was still there and saw his black Juke in a holding position right behind Gus's parked car. With a wave, he put the car in gear and continued down the street toward Jason's luxurious estate.

TO SAY that Jason Upton lived in the lap of luxury was no exaggeration. Flanked by Juliette and Owain, Gus spent the better part of a minute staring at the entrance alone.

The majestic mansion was as white as pure driven snow. High arches and tall pillars gave the three-story stucco building a Mediterranean appearance. The vaulted front door was framed by cypress trees and columns on either side, with decorative carvings of what looked like a coat of arms. Through the glass doors was visible a winding staircase made of light cherrywood and cast iron, illuminated by a chandelier. Though further views beyond the foyer were obstructed, the gleam of the marble floors and the brightness of the interior were discernible.

"This Upton has deep pockets," Owain commented on Gus's right, whistling low at the sight.

Juliette chuckled. "You haven't seen anything yet, I assure you." Her knowing look was accentuated by the mischievous glint in her eyes. Her gaze flickered over Owain, who smiled at her. Gus watched with amusement as Juliette blushed and ducked her head.

Ah, romance is in the air.

"We gonna stand here gawking at the place much longer or brave on inside?" Owain said, a teasing note to his deep voice.

Both Gus and Juliette laughed, and together they headed for the door. A tall man with gray hair, an impeccable suit, and gentlemanly manners opened the door before they had a chance to knock or ring the bell.

"Good evening, gentlemen and lady," the butler said and bid them enter with a sweep of his arm. Gus had never been to a place with its own butler—or servant of any kind—and he wasn't sure he liked the idea of being waited on in his own home. Guess that ruled him out of ever owning a luxury estate, complete with a staff.

"Mr. Upton and the other guests are out in the back garden," the butler told them.

Gus tried not to let his mouth gape as he walked through wide-open spaces, over gray marble floors, and past white pillars in the kitchen, dining room, and living room.

At least Owain was on top of things, as he whispered inconspicuously to Gus, "When I'm the focus of attention, you pay attention to people's behavior and to what they say. I'll do the same when everyone's looking at you."

Gus nodded, still befuddled by his lavish surroundings. "Okay."

"You do the same, if that doesn't bother you," Owain said to Juliette, who nodded, all solemn and proper. Then she blushed and again ducked her head, and Gus was back in the game with a smile on his lips.

Finally the three of them were ushered outside onto a large patio with several white lounge chairs and big white parasols. From there they entered a vast, lush garden with colorful flowerbeds, a three-tiered fountain, high hedgerows bordering the yard on either side, several tall trees dotting the ample, well-maintained lawn, and a pebbled beach culminating in a pier with a white motorboat moored to it at the far end. Beyond it, the dark blue waters of Lake Washington rippled gently, and the Seattle skyline, with its skyscrapers, and the Olympic Mountains, with its mist-covered peaks, provided a breathtaking backdrop.

"Lifestyles of the rich and the… who's the owner again?" Gus snorted sarcastically.

"I don't think money is a problem for Jason," Juliette commented, equally ironically.

"Think we should rob them?" Owain asked, surprising Gus and Juliette with a wicked wink. His jaw dropping practically down to his knees, Gus ogled, wide-eyed, not having expected Niall's father to know the lyrics to a Good Charlotte song. Next to him, Juliette did pretty much the same.

Then, as if sparked by some collective instinct, all three of them started laughing.

"Hey there, comedians!" a blond, tall, lean, and lithe man called out to them. He wore fitted black jeans, a black turtleneck shirt, and a black blazer, with a black leather belt and black canvas shoes. He even had a black signet ring on his right-hand index finger. As Gus approached, he almost drowned in the darkness, as though the man's attire sucked in all the light like a black hole. Gus tried to morph his instinctive grimace into a polite smile as he made his way to the man who had to be their host for the evening.

"Hello, everyone," Juliette greeted all those present with her typical cheer. She moved to the man who had hollered at them and waved Gus and Owain closer. "Owain Wallis, meet Jason Upton."

Jason and Owain shook hands briefly. Gus noted that Jason didn't seem particularly interested in Owain. That was kind of odd since Owain was completely new to the group and thus should have garnered at least a modicum of curiosity.

Then Juliette gestured between Gus and Jason. "Gus, this is Jason Upton. Jase, this is Gus Goodwin."

"Ah, the prodigal son returns." With a model-perfect smile above his trimmed goatee, Jason shook Gus's hand, his grip far tighter than necessary, as if he was trying to prove something.

Gus tried not to wince at the nearly bone-shattering grip—or Upton's impolite words and their unpleasant implications. "Nice to meet you." He wasn't being exactly truthful, but he suspected neither was his host.

Jason gave him a leisurely once-over with an arrogantly quirked eyebrow, and he kept hold of Gus's hand. "I've heard much about you, Gus. Juliette's prodigy. The one everyone else in the coven has to measure up to."

"Now, Jase, you know that's not true." Even Juliette's ever-present, kind smile faltered, and Gus felt the mood chill. His quick glance around showed that, thankfully, none of the other guests seemed focused on them. Instead, they chattered animatedly in small clusters.

"In the circle," Juliette went on, "everyone is equal, and I do not ever practice picking favorites."

Jase chuckled as though it had all been a giant joke. "Of course, of course. Come now. This is a party. No pouting." He finally released Gus's hand with a salacious wink Gus really didn't like. In fact, he didn't like much about this latest addition to the coven.

"Let's get some drinks, and later hopefully see some skin in the circle." Jase laughed as he moved off.

Juliette inched closer to Gus with an apologetic, even embarrassed, look on her face. "I apologize for Jase. He can be, um…." She seemed to have trouble finding the right word.

"A bit of a sleaze-bucket?" Gus finished for her in a subtle whisper. He especially did not appreciate Jason's insinuation that rituals done naked, or skyclad, somehow led to wickedness or orgies, or to the million other lewd practices the prejudiced ignorant drew from ritual nudity.

Juliette pursed her lips and slapped Gus's arm, but he barely felt it because her reproach was far from profound. That told him she agreed with his judgment of Jason's character. "Hush, you. He's, well, an acquired taste."

Gus grimaced. "Sorry, Jules, but he gives me acid reflux." Jules burst into helpless laughter but for the sake of decorum at least tried, if somewhat ineffectively, to muffle it behind her hand. "Let's go meet the others, shall we, dear?"

Gus watched with no small amount of amusement as Owain gallantly extended his hand and Juliette hooked her arm under his. Together, with Gus following leisurely and aimlessly after them, they ambled toward the rest of the members of the Moonlight Haven Coven for the meet and greet, knowing the night was just beginning.

Chapter 4

"Gus. I've missed you, Grasshopper." Tom hugged Gus warmly, and Gus returned the gesture, happy to see his friend again.

"Me too. We really need to find some time to see each other more often." Gus pulled back, smiling. "I've missed you too, Master Jedi." He bowed playfully, earning a chuckle from his friend. Since the inception of the coven, the members had given each other nicknames to mark the love, trust, and friendship they shared.

Tom Hardy carried himself like the soldier he'd been, back straight and always poised for a fight, even though he walked with a bit of a limp on his left leg due to an unfortunate encounter with a bullet. The fact he was in his forties changed nothing, as he was in excellent shape, muscular and bulky. His dark hair sported a buzz cut, and he wore formfitting, dark green cargo pants and a matching rugby shirt. His eyes were lighter green, offering a fascinating contrast that beckoned one to take a closer look and admire the sight. He commanded respect. But despite his long career in the army, Tom was a sweetheart, the kindest man Gus had ever known.

"What's new with you?" Gus asked.

Tom shrugged. "Same old same old. One day at a time."

"Yeah. Me too. You still on disability?" Gus tried to keep the pity out of his voice. He wished Tom could find meaning in his life beyond spirituality, so he didn't mean his question in a negative way.

Thankfully, Tom knew him well enough to know what Gus meant, and he smiled ruefully. "Yeah. I've applied for a couple of jobs at the unemployment office, but so far… zilch."

"I'm sorry." Gus wanted only the best for his friends, along with everyone else in the world.

"It's okay. Times are tough all around. I'm fine with it. The disability income isn't much, but it's enough for my needs." Tom shrugged, but Gus suspected he wasn't as nonchalant as he appeared.

"*All* your needs?" Gus winked salaciously.

Tom chuckled. "You randy young buck," he jested. His eyes darted briefly over to Alec, and melancholy longing briefly showed on his face. But he simply smiled again, brave if a bit fake. "I'm not as horny as you." Gus blushed, his thoughts immediately veering toward Niall and all the wondrous things they did together in the bedroom.

"So, what have *you* been up to since I saw you last, Grasshopper?" Tom asked, calm once again.

"Yeah, that's what I'd like to know." A woman's authoritative, surprisingly deep voice startled both men. The woman who approached chuckled evilly. "Boy, you two are jumpy." She punched Gus in the arm, far harder than Juliette had earlier.

Gus rubbed his arm, where a bruise would undoubtedly form. "I was just peachy before you came along, Ballbuster."

The woman laughed, a metallic tone to her voice. "Oh, don't be such a baby."

Gus giggled. "Me? Careful, Aeryn, or we'll go back to calling you Babycakes."

"You wouldn't dare." Aeryn Newton growled, a scary sound that might have sent chills down the spines of even the bravest men.

Aeryn was only in her midtwenties and already quite the ballbuster, reflected in her nickname in her successful and notorious career as a defense attorney. A tall and thin but busty brunette, she epitomized beauty designed by the hands of men. Her long fake lashes could have fanned fires; her little button nose was quite pert; her glistening lips were twice the normal size for women; and her heels were so high she teetered on the precarious risk of permanent injury. Her dark burgundy cocktail dress matched the hue of her lip gloss, and her silk stockings glimmered in the last rays of the setting sun.

Along with everyone else in the coven, Gus knew her ultrafeminine appearance hid the iron power she wielded with authority at work and play alike.

"We'd never," Gus swore solemnly to Aeryn, hand on his heart. To be honest, none of them would have dared call her a sweet endearment for fear of severe bodily harm.

"Perish the thought," Tom echoed, with a scout's honor gesture.

Aeryn studied them with narrowed eyes, like a prowling predator in view of her prey. All of a sudden she burst into hearty laughter, and Gus and Tom joined in. "Love you, guys." She pointed squarely at Gus's chest, her look threatening. "But you? I've talked to the gang, and there's a consensus." Gus feared the worst, eyes wide, breath lodged in his throat. "No more being a stranger, got it? No more missing coven meetings. And would it kill you to call any of us once in a while?"

Gus sighed in relief and smiled. "I promise. I've missed you guys too." Then he sensed Owain coming to stand at his side and recalled their clandestine mission for the evening. "Oh, guys? I'd like you to meet Owain Val—"

"Wallis. Owain Wallis. Nice to meet you all. I may have just met Gus on the ride over, but he speaks very highly of you all." Owain shook first Tom's, then Aeryn's, hand with a courteous smile as they introduced themselves to him. Gus prayed his expression didn't betray how he'd nearly misspoken, especially after the lecture Juliette had given him outside the mansion about remembering Owain's pseudonym.

Tom seemed guarded as he studied Owain but still nodded. "Thanks. You too."

Aeryn, however, assayed Owain in a different light. In an instant, she put on her feminine wiles. "Very nice to meet you too… Owain." She batted her eyelashes and gave him the kind of look that would work on any man. She held onto his hand longer than Tom had and smiled seductively.

As Owain smiled back congenially, Gus moved off, letting Owain take the reins and be the focus of attention. This would be Gus's opportunity to see what he could learn about people he already thought he knew well and others he knew next to nothing about.

The setting sun cast its bright orange-tinted rays onto the white stucco walls and pillars of the mansion and turned them golden. A night breeze rustled the leaves of the bushes and trees. Gus moved among the chattering folks, listening to pieces of conversation and trying to use them to ascertain what lurked beneath the surface.

Of the group, Jason Upton was the easiest to interpret.

Owain had joined him as he spoke to Tom, Juliette, and another man whose pretty face Gus remembered. He was Alec Hope, Jason's boyfriend. He was short and slender, almost delicate. His black hair was cut in a trendy, hipster style, and his attire confirmed it. The word Twink was emblazoned on his white Henley in large rainbow-colored letters, and had his jeans been any tighter, he probably wouldn't have been able to move at all. Just as Gus recalled, Alec was extremely beautiful.

But Gus noticed quickly how unbalanced Alec and Jason's relationship was.

"What do you do?" Owain asked Alec politely, smiling.

Alec beamed, obviously pleased by Owain's interest. "I'm a nurse at—"

"Alec is a wonderful nurse," Jason interrupted him, talking to Owain. "I simply adore him in those dark blue scrubs. Always makes me wanna play naughty nurse."

Owain nodded but turned his gaze right back to Alec. "You like the work?"

Alec nodded, his smile genuine and wide. "Oh yes, it's the best to be able to help—"

"My little Alec has saved the lives of many of Seattle's most prominent people," Jason cut in, his voice louder than Alec's, drowning him out. Alec bit his lip, and the eager light in his green eyes dimmed as he ducked his head. Gus wondered if he was embarrassed or angered by Jason's constant interruptions and belittling. "But enough about that," Jason droned on, oblivious to his boyfriend's state of mind. "So, Owain, what do you think of my place? This estate cost nine million dollars. There are seven bedrooms, nine bathrooms, a sauna, a solarium, a hot tub, a pool and wet bar, a wine cellar, state-of-the-art high-tech cabling, and…." On and on he went.

Forming an opinion of Jason's personality wasn't hard at all. He was an arrogant, conceited ass, and who knew where his money really came from. Gus couldn't even venture a guess. As minutes passed in Jason's self-indulgent soliloquy, Gus's dislike of him grew.

He decided to take action. Inconspicuously, Gus moved behind Jason's back and took a hold of Alec's arm, gently drawing him away. "Hi, Alec. I don't know if you remember me from last Yule, but I'm Gus Goodwin."

Alec's bright smile did funny things to Gus's insides, even though he was happy in his relationship with Niall. "Gus. Yeah, I remember you. Well, vaguely, just like the rest of the night." He offered a sheepish smile and the cutest conspiratorial wink.

"Ah, yes. Jules's mulled wine. You too, eh?" Gus chuckled, and Alec joined in. "So, you live here with Jason?"

Alec's smile faltered slightly as he glanced over his shoulder at his boyfriend. "Yes."

Gus's instincts told him not to press, but he was on a mission. "Like it here?" He hoped his tone conveyed his sympathy.

Alec looked down at his feet, fidgeting and twirling his Tequila Sunrise. "It's beautiful here." He again glanced at Jason, who was busy praising his wealth and success to an obliging Owain. "Jase is rarely here. Work is his first love." Alec muttered so low under his breath that Gus almost didn't catch him adding "And only love."

Gus veered away from the depressing subject. "You like being in Jules's coven?"

Alec looked up, smiling again. "Yes. No doubt about it. Not all covens are the same. I'm something of an eclectic, so I haven't always fit in with the more traditional covens. But Jules is great. She's supportive of everything I do. She says my spiritual growth is her number one concern. I know she exaggerates, but it's wonderful to feel welcome."

"I know what you mean," Gus said, happy and grateful. "Jules helped me a lot when I came into the Craft. I'd read all the books and scrolled through all the websites, but I still kind of felt like the odd man out, you know. Jules helped me see what I believed was fine, even if it wasn't a hundred percent the same as everyone else. She showed me a coven can be composed of different points of view, and that's okay."

"Yes, that's true." Alec nodded firmly, showing a glimpse of the intelligent young man underneath his boyfriend's thumb. "My parents weren't crazy about me being gay. But when I told them I was a witch too…. It didn't end well. I was sixteen then. For the next two years, I lived on my friends' couches, until I got into Nursing School at the University of Washington. I was lucky. I got a scholarship, and in my second year I snagged an internship which turned into a job."

"You chose a good career. Nurses are always needed, if not appreciated as much as they should be, which is a crying shame if you ask me. The most needed people in society never earn the kind of money they deserve."

Alec smiled, a dreamy look on his face. "Yeah. But I'm not in it for money. I love it. It's all I've ever wanted to do. To help people."

"That's amazing and very admirable," Gus said, in awe of someone so young committed to such a challenging profession.

Alec shrugged modestly. "I just do what I can to make a difference. My faith adds to that, letting me gain insight into the spiritual side of being a nurse. It's like a light at the end of the tunnel, you know, 'cause in my job I see so much pain and suffering. It's good to see an upside."

Gus nodded. "So, you have a nickname yet?" He grinned wickedly.

Alec laughed, a bubbly joyous sound, and his cheeks flushed. "Sunshine."

Gus laughed. "How fitting. I was sure it'd be something like, oh I don't know, Angel or Candy Striper."

"That last one was my fave, but I lost my vote," a soft woman's voice said behind Gus.

He swiveled around and came face to face with a friend. "Joy!" Gus hugged her, and she hugged back tighter. "How are you, Kitten?"

Joy kissed his cheek before withdrawing. "I'm fine. I'd be six feet under if it weren't for you." Since she'd survived a murder attempt—being buried alive at Olympic National Park—her nickname in the coven had been changed from Hot Lips to Kitten, the woman with nine lives. Catwoman was unfortunately already taken by a comic superheroine.

"You've cut your hair," Gus noted in surprise. Her hair had been longer before.

Joy brushed a hand through her extremely short brown hair. "I felt like a change, you know, after I got a new lease on life. Well, after that, plus once I started working for Jules."

Joy Bennett was delicate, with a willowy, average-height body, hazel bedroom eyes, and full, pouty lips. Unlike Aeryn, though, her beauty was all natural. After several months of being held captive by a cruel man, she had appeared dangerously wan and frail. She looked much better now, healthier and stronger. Even her skin had a golden, sun-kissed hue. She wore several earrings, a variety of necklaces and rings, and her bare arms showcased tribal-style henna tattoos.

"It looks good on you, Joy. Your hair, I mean." Alec pointed at Joy with a smile.

"Yeah, totally." A new voice came into the scene, one from a man so young he was really a boy. This had to be Matty Osborne, the college kid. Gus introduced himself, and Matty confirmed his identity. "Nice to finally meet you, Gus. Juliette speaks highly of you, and so do a lot of the others."

Gus prayed sincerely that Jason wasn't right in his characterization of him, that the newer members had to prove themselves to Juliette, to outdo Gus or fill a void he'd left behind. "I've had the privilege to know Jules for a good many years. But you all get to spend more time with her than I do, so I'm rather envious of you."

"You own the occult shop in Tacoma, right? The, uh… Four Winds, or something?" Matty seemed interested, so Gus told him about how he'd worked in the shop, The Four Corners, as a teenager and then in his twenties bought the place from the former owner, Mr. Hennessey, who had retired to Florida. Matty was so intrigued his eyes were wide with enthusiasm. "So, you became a shop owner while you were still in college?"

"My last year, yeah. The balancing act was hard, plus I had a lot to learn, like how to do the books, how to refill purchase orders, how to be able to afford festival sales, and so on. I sure wouldn't recommend the experience to just anyone."

Matty nodded, listening intently. "Wow. That's off the hook, man."

Gus smiled, hoping the gesture appeared only a little amused. The kid was nineteen, after all. Gus assumed he'd soon be lost in teen jargon he had no clue how to interpret.

Matty Osborne was of average height, a gangly, lanky boy whose slight hunch alluded to hours spent in front of computer screens. His shoulder-length hair, which could have used some serious trimming, was auburn, and he had orange-brown freckles on his face. His brown eyes were like the rest of his face, unremarkable but kind and open, and he had braces. Every emotion he felt was clearly evident in his expression. His slacks were tight and drooped quite low on his hips, and his worn, dark blue T-shirt had the words "Computer Nerds Like To Plug It In" emblazoned on it in white.

In essence, Matty looked like a typical teenager.

"So, what's your coven name?" Gus asked, curious. No derogatory names qualified, not even if self-nominated. Humiliation had no place in the circle.

Matty quirked a flashy grin. "Pinhead. You know, a computer nerd in the slang of like minds." He shrugged but also seemed proud as a minor blush colored his cheeks. "I like it. Works for me." His gaze drifted to Joy, who was talking about some savory appetizers in the kitchen with Alec. Matty quickly lowered his voice. "Do you know if Joy is seeing anyone?"

Gus honestly couldn't see Matty and Joy hooking up, let alone in a relationship, but stranger things had happened. "I don't think so. But I'm not sure. You should ask her yourself."

Matty shifted his weight from one foot to the other, clearly nervous and smitten. "Girls like that wouldn't give guys like me the time of day."

"Oh, I wouldn't be so sure. Many geeks I've known ended up with the hottest ladies." In truth, Gus only knew one guy like that:

Damon, who was in the high-tech business and dated supermodels and A-list ladies. Then again, he made millions in a year, so perhaps not the best real-life example. But Gus liked Matty and tried to give him something to hope for. In his case he sure hoped nice guys *didn't* finish last. "Joy's seen a lot of action in a short while. She might like a guy who's calm and soothing."

Matty frowned, as if bewildered at the mere notion, or maybe doubting the label "calm" and how it would fit him. In any case, after a second or two, his furrowed brow smoothed and he nodded to himself. "I'll try that. Thanks, Gus."

"Any time." Gus hoped he had made a friend of Matty, the computer geek. He might seem awkward and shy, but he was smart and opinionated, in a good way. Gus glanced at the young girl he assumed was Pine Seed Tash. "I would've figured Pine Seed was more your type."

"Why? 'Cause she's closer to my age?" Matty shook his head and glanced at the girl in question, his face scrunching as though he was chagrined for some reason. "No, thanks. Piney's not for me at all." His gaze returned to Joy and relaxed. "Joy's not that much older than Piney. Plus, she's a woman, not a girl." He turned up his nose.

Gus thought there was something going on between Matty and Piney. Still, he changed the subject to avoid alienating the kid too early into his mission. "What kind of computer stuff you working on?"

Matty's grin reappeared and widened; he was clearly psyched about the possibility of chatting about his love interests. "Careful, man. Once I get going I might not stop."

Gus laughed. "I don't mind. I may not have a lot of free time these days for games, but I'd like to hear what's good."

"I play all kinds of games. I wish I could become a game designer. That'd be awesome!" His eagerness and genuine enthusiasm were catching, and Gus found himself smiling at everything Matty said. "I like strategy games and puzzles most of all. At the moment, I'm super excited about the twentieth anniversary edition of *Gabriel Knight* by Jane Jensen. I had to try the *Witcher* games too. The books were great! I mean, how freaking awesome it'd be if we were monster hunters too? I still play *Skyrim* and *Oblivion* from time to time, modding the hell out of them whenever and wherever possible. A few weeks back I was kinda wigged out, but in a good way, about *The Room*. God, that was one hellish, mind-bending freak show of a puzzle game. Loved it!"

As Matty went on and on about cool games he'd encountered recently and since he'd first gotten into gaming, Gus tuned in to only about half of what he heard. He was also paying attention to what he *didn't* hear. Niall had to be amazingly well concealed since there was no sign of him. All around Gus echoed the chatter of like minds, distracting him, old friends and new gathered together to celebrate the full moon.

Then someone tapped lightly on his shoulder. Matty quieted and moved off, while Gus twirled around and came face to face with a woman he hadn't met before. "Hi. I'm Kerry Pryor." She extended a hand in greeting, though her gaze flicked over to Matty's retreating back.

Gus shook her hand. "Hi. I'm Gus Goodwin."

Her smile was barely there, sort of shy. "Yes, I know. Juliette has told me many things about you." She glanced over her shoulder at Juliette, her gaze full of fondness. "She has been like a mother to me, as well as a mentor." Her voice was so soft it was only a decibel or two above a whisper, as though she had never raised her voice in her entire life.

Gus surreptitiously checked her out. Kerry was of average height, slim, and dowdy in appearance. Her upbringing in a conservative household had obviously affected how she presented herself, which basically seemed to consist of trying to blend in while drawing as little attention as possible—the classic wallflower. Her sand-colored hair was in a slack ponytail, revealing her sculpted, oval face, and her big, gray eyes faded behind gray upswept glasses. She wore a plaid (gray-checkered) wool sweater dress, which made her appear dull and colorless—despite the dress being formfitting.

In any case, her appearance made it difficult to form an opinion about her personality. She could have learned to hide herself in a restrictive home environment, or perhaps she didn't care how she looked, or maybe gray was simply her favorite color. Gus suppressed a cringe at the difficulty of making guesses about a person who held so much back.

"I'm ashamed we haven't met before now," Gus admitted. "I used to be involved a lot in Juliette's coven. But work and stuff has eaten up my time. Anyway, how do you like this coven?"

Her smile didn't widen with warm thoughts, and Gus had to wonder if this woman had ever burst into spontaneous, boisterous laughter in her life.

"Juliette has a way of making everyone feel welcome," Kerry said. "I have missed feeling a part of something like a family." Her eyes grew sad and wistful. It seemed to be her defining feature, the melancholy in her gaze. "My parents...."

"You don't have to tell me if you don't want to," Gus assured her. "I don't wish to pry."

Kerry nodded, still dispirited. "I grew up in a conservative, highly religious household. I was never physically abused. My parents were oppressive, though, narrow-minded and intolerant. Anything new upset their world view. They were always cold and repressed, except in church." Her voice took on a bitter undertone. "There they would listen to the fire-and-brimstone preacher and shout and clap like mad. The preacher's sermons validated their points of view, I guess. They lived life in the past, homeschooling me. I didn't get into a real school until junior high, where I learned my parents' way of life was small and sheltered—in a bad way. I didn't even know there were such things as prophylactics, or women with careers and freedom outside the home, or places where the cultural and religious norms were stark in their difference from what I had been taught as the truth."

Gus felt a surge of sympathy. "I'm so sorry to hear that."

Kerry shook her head slowly. "Thank you. But I've made my peace with the past. As soon as I was old enough, I left home and traveled across the country to the most distant point from my home town. Here, to Seattle. I have never regretted that choice." She cocked her head as if curious. "What are your parents like? Do they approve of your spiritual conviction?"

Gus smiled and nodded. "They do, yes. They didn't get it at first, but after I explained the major tenets, they kind of understood. These days it's old news. They live in Portland now, but I try to talk to them once a week at least. I'm an only child, so I suppose they pampered me growing up." Gus decided to change the subject, his goal being learning about others, not them learning all about him. "You're working for a… congressman, or something?"

"An ex-congresswoman, actually," Kerry replied, sotto voce. "She owns a pioneering green-tech company now, and she's quite the businesswoman. I admire her greatly. As a boss, she's tough but fair. You have an occult shop, is that right?"

"Yeah, that's right." Gus narrated his usual sales speech about The Four Corners. His mind really didn't need to focus on it much anymore, so he let the words flow on their own while glancing at the other folks present. Kerry was nice, her quiet voice soft, feminine, and appealing.

Joy and Alec were discussing the proper preparation of apple pies. Tom and Aeryn argued about adequate mood setters for the upcoming coven Litha sabbat, and Owain was still listening with apparent interest to Jason's monologuing about his property, stock portfolio, and the fabulous luxury vacation spots he'd visited. Farther away, a tiny group consisting of Rodney, Sydney, and Pine Seed seemed focused on setting unlit candles on the ground for the esbat circle. Gus knew Rodney and Sydney from that group, but not Pine Seed.

But Gus didn't have a chance to make any observations about them or speak to any of them as Juliette demanded their attention by raising her voice above the din. "Good evening, dear friends. The sun has set, and the moon is rising. Shall we begin?"

Gus took a deep breath and steeled himself for whatever might come.

Chapter 5

"WELCOME, FRIENDS, to this, our circle, on this hallowed night when the moon shines her power and casts her beauty down upon us, her followers."

Gus shivered. Juliette had mastered the creation of a potent voice that carried effortlessly and ominously through the sanctified space.

They settled at regular intervals and within touching distance of each other around a circular perimeter marked by unlit candles. Owain found his place among the others, taking up a position between Tom and Joy. Apart from Tom and Owain, the rest of them were spaced man, woman, man, woman, and so on.

Gus let his mind drift, gathering within him the energy of the night and the moon. Like the others, he too had cleansed himself with a ritual bath prior to the actual ceremony now commencing. As he had done physically in the water, he now added the mental element. He visualized purity as a bright white light. It was a conscious act of discarding worries, fears, doubts, all that was negative, outside the circle and centering his mind on the ritual alone. He prepared for the encounter with the divine.

Though he had meditated during the cleansing preritual bath, Gus realized much of his thought lingered on the case he was supposed to be solving. The notion that one of these good people around him, his friends, could be guilty of theft left him unsettled and unable to reach the core of serenity. Gus still prayed the ritual would not go awry because of him.

"Come, friends." Juliette spoke with a smile, standing at the northernmost point of the circle. "Take hold of your implements, and let us purify this, our circle, of negativity. Please, come and travel with me *deosil*, erect our proud temple, and cleanse our sacred space from darkness."

Where everyone stood just outside the circle of unlit candles, on the ground lay items to be used. The directions Juliette gave were meant to describe what would happen shortly, not orders to carry out right at that moment. Gus stood to the right of Juliette, Tom, Owain, and Joy, at the westernmost point of the circle. Juliette and Gus both picked up brooms, or besoms as they were called in the Craft.

Juliette addressed Gus. "Come, Gus, and sweep the circle with me." Gus smiled and nodded, readying himself for the first phase of the ritual. One by one, Juliette advised everyone, with individual phrases telling them to gather their tools and purify the circle. When she had spoken to all present, she bid Tom closer from her immediate right. "Come, High Priest, and join me in this, our circle, and consecrate our implements of this night of magic."

Silently Tom ambled next to Juliette, and they both faced north together. There, by the inside edge of the circle, stood a makeshift altar trunk with a blue and silver altar cloth depicting three phases of the moon—waxing, full, and waning. The altar was jam-packed with items to be used during the ritual, the feminine objects on the left and masculine on the right. Not all were used in the ceremony but leaving the circle once the ritual began broke the sanctity of the situation. Only a counterclockwise, or widdershins, cut with an athame, a black-handled ritual knife, could create an opening to enter and exit through. To call it a circle was misleading anyway since it was, in fact, a sphere, the sacred space reaching high above their heads and deep beneath their feet.

Juliette touched a lit brown taper to one of the candles on the altar—the Fire candle, Gus knew, the color of orange for flames and with silver ribbon around it for the moon. With her arms wide and high before her, she said reverently, "I bless and consecrate this element of Fire so that it may illuminate our hearts, minds, and souls. Let darkness wither and be cast out. Blessed be."

Everyone in the circle repeated out loud "Blessed be." Owain said the words after the others, but Juliette's encouraging smile told him and the others that it was fine to proceed at one's own pace. It wasn't a race to perfection.

As the night around them grew darker, Juliette beckoned Joy closer. "Blessed Maiden, light the fires in the circle so they may shed their light upon us and this, our circle."

Joy held a special Maiden candle in her role as the High Priestess's assistant, and with it, Joy lit six other candles on the altar and then sauntered around the circle clockwise and kindled the candle markers of the circle, all except for the ones at the cardinal points. Once Joy was done and had resumed her place, Juliette and Tom knelt by the altar, he to her right, and bowed their heads briefly.

Tom held up a cup of salt and dipped the tip of his athame in the substance. "I bless and consecrate this element of Earth so that it may grant us power of purpose and steady our feet firmly on the ground. Blessed be." Others repeated the last words.

As Tom put his athame back down on the altar, Juliette held up a bowl of water in one hand while slowly plunging the point of her athame into the liquid, and said, "I bless and consecrate this element of Water so that it may wash away our doubts and fears and leave us cleansed of darkness. Blessed be." After everyone spoke the final two words as well, Juliette rested her ritual knife on the altar as Tom had done.

Tom used the consecrated Fire candle to light an incense burner, and said, "I bless and consecrate this element of Air so that it may blow away our worries and wraths and leave us light and pure. Blessed be." Everyone repeated the words, and Owain was on time with the others. Tom then sprinkled three pinches of salt into the water bowl Juliette held and respectfully said, "As water has purified our bodies, so shall salt purify our spirits in this, our circle."

Excitement over participating in a group ritual poured over Gus, who began to feel the connection to the others as a sense of sanctity descended upon him. This moment when the parting from the mundane world began had always held profound meaning for him. In the circle, they would all step over a hallowed threshold and encounter the divine, nature, and magic. To him, this instant defined what it meant to be a Wiccan and to enter into a joyous union with gods and goddesses.

Gus held his broom tightly and waited for Juliette to give the cue. When she nodded and started to go around the circle clockwise, sweeping gently with her broom, Gus followed suit. It was more a visualization exercise than actual cleaning. As mirror images, they walked the line once and then resumed their former positions, placing the brooms on the ground outside the circle.

Then, as if by some mutual and magical consensus, they began to sing. It was a slow, monotonous chanting, more sounds and reverberations than actual, intelligible words. The melody rose and fell, a low background hum. Owain watched what was happening, curiosity imprinted on his face, and Gus could relate. The first time he had witnessed and been a part of a coven ceremony, he had felt like coming home. It was a potent moment, and the memory would remain with him till the end of his days.

Tom stepped forward, raised the God's sword toward the sky, and declared, "I conjure this, our circle, to be a place of power and magic, of peace and joy, of love and friendship." As Tom spoke, he ambled around the perimeter, drawing the sacred circle in the air and continuing to voice the prayer. "In the name of the Lady of the Moon and the Lord of the Sun, I declare this, our circle, to be a threshold between worlds that shall contain and direct the magic sought here. Blessed be." All those present repeated the final blessing.

By the time Tom was finished, he had circled the boundary and drawn the line with his sword. He placed the sword back on the altar and resumed his place on the right side of Juliette.

Aeryn stepped forward, accepted the saltwater bowl from Juliette, and started her own cycle, starting from the east and moving sunwise. She strewed the saltwater around the circle in Tom's footsteps and echoed his declaration verbatim. Once she had made her rounds, she passed the bowl on to Jason, who stood on her left. He sprinkled some over himself and then passed the bowl to Pine Seed, who stood on his left. She repeated the sprinkling, and so the saltwater bowl traversed through the hands of the participants, clockwise, until everyone had been sparged.

Jason moved forward next, took the incense burner and a feather from Juliette, and he too walked around the circle, fanning the incense along the perimeter while reciting the same words as Tom and Aeryn before him. Once he was back in place, he handed the items to Pine Seed, who fanned the incense toward her, and then passed them along, sunwise.

Gus stared at Pine Seed with some admiration. From her name alone, he had expected a hippie flower girl. Instead, he got a punk-rock chick with electric blue hair, piercings and tattoos, heavily made-up eyes, skin like fine porcelain, and wearing tight pink fishnet stockings, a green tube top, and a yellow miniskirt. Definitely not what Gus had pictured beforehand. Her black leather combat boots added to her mesh of clashing styles and colors, creating a unique combination for a unique personality.

As the incense made its rounds, Gus made another startling observation. Out of all of them, the best singers by far were Pine Seed and Alec. Their voices rose above the din in perfect harmony, a sweet cadence to both of them, waving about and bringing a melancholy mood down upon the circle. Gus lowered his own voice to a near whisper to better appreciate the performance of natural singers. Either one of them surely could make a successful career in singing.

Slowly all their voices ebbed and flowed until they vanished altogether. It was time to draw down the moon and do magic.

ALL THE coven members faced east and held up their athames. Owain had one as well, one given by Gus before they'd arrived on the scene. Gus relished the silky strength of the black-handled knife he owned, having used it in all rituals he'd participated in since becoming a Wiccan. It belonged to him and was dear to him.

The eastern sky was dark blue, with billowing clouds forming ominous shapes behind the white mansion. Yet the silver disk of the moon floated high in the sky. An hour had passed since sunset, and the moon rose ever higher. Their ritual would be over before the moon hit its zenith. The waves lapped gently against the shoreline, trees creaked and rustled in the strengthening wind, and a low hum of distant traffic reminded them they were in the city still.

Jason stood in the east, so therefore he was the one to call the eastern quarter. With a surprisingly solemn look, he raised his athame high and declared, "Guardians of the Watchtowers of the East, spirits of Air, I call upon and welcome you to this, our circle, to witness and guard our rites on this full moon's night in the name of the Lady and the Lord. Blessed be." As he spoke, quite pompously, he drew a pentagram in the air with his athame, and Joy in her Maiden role knelt next to him and by lighting the yellow eastern-cardinal-point candle, paid homage to the old ones.

People recited, "Hail and welcome!"

Everyone turned on their heels and faced south. The tall trees and hedgerows hid what lay beyond, leaving only the roofs of a few nearby mansions flashing in the night when light hit them. It served as a reminder that their nighttime ritual was hidden from possible onlookers.

Kerry Pryor stood at the southernmost point. She raised her arms above her and said in a voice as quiet as the breeze, "Guardians of the Watchtowers of the South, spirits of Fire, I call upon and welcome you to this, our circle, to witness and guard our rites on this full moon's night in the name of the Lady and the Lord. Blessed be." Her voice grew stronger as she went on until Gus caught a glimpse of the strength within this woman. Gus had to admit the potential duality intrigued him. As Kerry drew the pentagram in the air with her knife, Joy knelt by her side and lit the red southern-quarter candle, and people hailed and welcomed the guardians.

People turned again and faced west. The dark blue, open waters of Lake Washington undulated restlessly. Beyond, the Seattle skyline was as impressive as ever, with its flickering lights and shadowy shapes of skyscrapers. A faint residue of the setting sun still clung to the cloud rags hovering above the horizon.

It was Gus's turn since he stood at the westernmost point of the circle. He raised his arms, and his mind invoked images of blue seas. With years of practice and the fortitude of faith, he said, "Guardians of the Watchtowers of the West, spirits of Water, I call upon and welcome you to this, our circle, to witness and guard our rites on this full moon's night in the name of the Lady and the Lord. Blessed be." He drew the pentagram in the air before him and observed Joy lighting the western-quarter candle, which was blue, and hailed and welcomed along with the others.

One last swivel and everyone faced north. More trees swaying in the wind, the foliage rustling and shimmying, and flowers lit by lanterns on metal poles cast curious lights and shadows everywhere. Thrushes, herons, and kingfishers sang in the night, far away.

Juliette raised her athame high and said, "Guardians of the Watchtowers of the North, spirits of Earth, I call upon and welcome you to this, our circle, to witness and guard our rites on this full moon's night in the name of the Lady and the Lord. Blessed be."

"Hail and welcome!" Gus echoed with the others. He closed his eyes tight and focused on feeling the change in the air. The circle was now sealed for the night. He envisioned a beautiful, bright woman with long flowing hair, dressed in silver and blue, walking quietly among them, gently brushing against them, passing on her blessing. No longer did he recall his task for the night. The ceremony had become alive for him and all that mattered.

As he opened his eyes, serenity in his soul, Gus watched Juliette stand by the altar, her face aimed skyward, her gaze directed at the moon. She held a wand in her right hand and her athame in her left, crossed over her chest and pressed against her bosom. As she spoke, Gus could tell Juliette had slipped into her spiritual subspace, as she called it, a trancelike state of concentration and holiness.

Her voice was beckoning, soft at first, rising in pitch and strength as she proceeded. "Luna, high queen of the night; Aradia, radiant in your beauty bright; Diana, shimmering goddess of the moon's might; Hecate, come and shine upon us with your light. We call you and invoke you, to bless and guide what we do, on this nighttime dark and gloom, that our circle may flourish and bloom."

As Juliette alone recited the invocation to the Goddess, the others began to hum. To Gus this phase always reminded him of the Hindu Om mantra, but in their case the constant ebbing and flowing noise was part sacred hymn, part a mere low, soft croon. No specific words, sacred or otherwise, were uttered by anyone. The droning tune continued as Juliette went on.

Gus closed his eyes and let the tingling sensation whisk him away toward the moon and the stars. The air crackled electrically as they all began to fall into a spiritual frame of mind, lost in the ritual. Gus swayed with the sound within that began to morph into a purr of pleasure, rocking back and forth on his heels, allowing the chant to lift him and oscillate inside him.

"Oh moon, symbol of the mother," Juliette proclaimed, her voice potent, reaching all of them with ease, causing Gus to shiver. "Universal and constant, the shifting phases, the changing tides, the flow of women's bodies, the passion of lovers entwined. In the deep dark of night, you shine down upon us and keep us safe with your light and love. I pray to you, oh queen of witches, come and teach us your magic and your might. I beseech you, oh divine mother, join us here, in our circle, on this brightest night."

Entranced, her eyes closed, Juliette danced in place, her feet unmoving, only her hips spinning, her arms following the rotating motions. Gus had opened his eyes to see it, how the high priestess drew down the moon, taking in the power and light and beauty of the moon goddess. Gus could swear he sometimes truly witnessed a profound change in Juliette as she personified the moon goddess.

In his role as the high priest, Tom knelt in front of Juliette, his intention to give her the five-fold kiss. In this coven, this practice was performed during the invocation to show the love the coven members had for both their high priestess and the moon goddess, now that she was a bit of both. Here, the rite was also performed clothed.

All of a sudden, a man shouted, "Upton, take your damn freak show someplace else! People are trying to sleep here!"

Everyone started at the sudden outburst, and a blinding beam from a high-powered flashlight aimed in their direction. Gus blinked in the harsh light and brought his hand up to shade his eyes.

An angry, bearded man in a dark blue pajamas, bathrobe, and slippers stood by a small wood gate hidden in the hedgerow, now visible because it had been swung open. Apparently it connected Jason's estate with his neighbor's land. An awfully furious neighbor's land.

Jason rushed closer to the man but managed not to break the circle by stepping past the candle perimeter. "Mr. Abrams, I sent you a note a week in advance, informing of our intentions of having a nighttime get-together. Are we blasting bass and drums? No. Are we drinking to excess? No. Are we using high-powered tools in mad revelry? No. Are we engaged in a nude spectacle of wild orgies? No. We're minding our own business in relative quiet. The only one making noise here is you. Now, I'd appreciate you be on your merry way. And may I suggest earplugs for your nocturnal convenience? Good night."

The man, Mr. Abrams apparently, fumed, his face darkening—probably reddening, in fact, but it was late at night so colors bled away. He pointed a finger at Jason. "Now you listen to me, you little twerp. If you and your merry band aren't done in an hour, I'm calling the cops. Mark my words." Muttering quite unseemly invectives under his breath, he retreated through the gate, slamming it closed hard to make his point.

Jason resumed his place in the easternmost spot. "Sorry about that, guys. Abrams is on a rant about something or other every week, I'm afraid. I did my due diligence and informed all my neighbors of this soiree, so if any of them had any complaints, they had plenty of time to make them known." He squared his shoulders and threaded a hand through his slick hair as if grooming himself back to his cool state of being. "Let's just get on with things." Suddenly he cast all of them a knowing look and a wink. "Besides, I have a big surprise for you all before the night is out. It'll blow you away."

Gus gave Juliette a questioning glance, but she met his gaze with as much confusion as he felt. What did Jason have planned? Most of the time, after an esbat ritual, they were mentally and physically exhilarated, yet exhausted, and didn't want an after party. But Jason was the host of the evening, so if he had something in the works, it would be rude to wave their good-byes on their way out.

In any case, the drawing down the moon was a bust. The circle might have been intact, but the mood was broken and Juliette back to her old self. They would have to start again, or forget the whole thing and move on with the ritual without invoking the Goddess again.

Then, in a blink of an eye, night turned into day.

A DEAFENING boom and a flash of blinding light struck his senses deaf and dumb.

Gus flew in a short arc through the air, as though a missile made of stormy air had hit him square in the chest, like an invisible punch by a vengeful deity or a supervillain. He landed on the ground with a hard thud, his head banging on the ground. His lungs burned, and his body ached all over. He gasped for breath purely on instinct.

Something hot rained down on his face, drops of liquid and specks of dirt. A coppery taste and smell filled his senses. Blood? His ears were ringing, a constant high din he couldn't turn off, and though he blinked, everything was a blur. He couldn't tell if his eyes were open or closed. His eyesight was fuzzy and gray, and nothing made sense.

He smelled burning, and flickers of the lawn on fire appeared in his field of vision. His head swam, dizzy and overwhelmed. He trembled uncontrollably, but he had no strength to get up.

A shifting shadow loomed over him. A face that was familiar somehow, but his rattled brain wasn't providing any recognition. The man—for it was surely a man—must have said something because his mouth was moving. *Damn, what a sexy mouth.*

Gus fell back on the ground though the man was trying to pull him up. He felt limp and boneless, slack like a bag of potatoes, the way he felt when waking during the night and having no control over his body for a while, the remnants of sleep clinging to him and dragging him under.

He tried to speak, but he had no idea if he succeeded because his ears were still ringing badly. But the effort proved too much for him, and Gus's mind went blank as he plummeted into the black depths of unconsciousness.

Chapter 6

"YOU OKAY, Son?" A warm hand rested on Niall's shoulder, a gentle squeeze to show much-needed comfort and unwavering support.

Niall squared his shoulders and straightened his back, his face a mask of determination and fortitude. "Yes." Then the futility of what he was trying to accomplish washed over him, and he slumped, defeated and weary. "No." He brought his hand up to touch Owain's, as though he could gain power from him through osmosis. "Gus…. Dad, I'm scared." It wasn't an easy admission, but if he couldn't trust his father, then who could he trust?

"He's alive. He's strong. He'll pull through, Son. You just gotta believe." Owain pulled a chair closer to Niall and the hospital bed. "Have faith."

Niall stared at the motionless body on the bed, wrapped up in bandages and appearing so frail. It tore Niall apart at the seams, even though according to the doctors, Gus had been moved to this regular room because, in their professional opinion, he was out of the woods, not unconscious from the concussion, but merely asleep. Niall wasn't going to be convinced until Gus woke up and spoke to him. Niall's eyes itched with unshed tears, and his lungs burned from the heavy weight settled around his heart.

Gus will pull through. He has to. He just has to.

Niall swallowed hard, feeling helpless and in pain. He could still hear it, that awful whoosh, like a back draft or a gust of wind, when the explosion detonated. He had been blinded by the flash for maybe five, ten seconds. At the time it had felt like an eternity as he had scrambled to get to Gus, panicked at not finding him immediately. It had looked like a battlefield: burning fires, pieces of earth scattered around like dusty rain, and people lying in moaning, shaking heaps—or not moving at all, bloody and burned.

Niall shivered at the memory, so vivid before his eyes whether open or closed.

From outside the room, at the nurses' station nearby, a TV blasted the morning news. "…questions as the police continue to investigate the shocking bombing at a neopagan ritual in Bellevue last night after sundown. The vicious attack has left two dead and eight injured, two seriously. The neopagan community is in an uproar. Our own Jane Little is at the scene, following the case as it unfolds—"

Owain got up and closed the door, blocking out the droning noise of the news. The night had ended and the sun had risen hours ago, but Niall hadn't slept a wink. He couldn't think; he didn't know how to act, what to do, how to be. All he did was stare unblinking at his friend, partner, and lover lying on a narrow hospital bed, unconscious and wounded.

When Owain sat next to him and hugged him, Niall let him. His body shook, and he allowed himself to shed a couple of tears before the masculine instinct to regain control reasserted itself and he drew back, wiping his tired, wet eyes.

A knock came from the door, which then opened a crack. Juliette peeked through, her face riddled with scratches and bandages. "Hi. Can I come in?" Her voice lacked the luster of life it usually sported.

Niall beckoned her in with a wave of his hand, grateful they could bring in a few more visitors. Had Gus still been in the ICU, the protocol would have been different. "Yeah, yeah. Come on in."

Juliette slunk in, quiet and unassuming. Her gaze was aimed at the hospital bed also. "How is he?" She stepped closer, brushing against Gus's hand above the covers. That single gesture revealed in spades how much she loved Gus, and Niall could relate.

"He hasn't woken up yet," Niall replied, his voice hoarse and craggy. "While they were treating him, they kept him awake because of the concussion. Once he threw up and was patched up, they finally let him sleep. That's when he was transferred here from the ICU. That was hours ago. No news or change since."

Juliette nodded, her gaze never leaving Gus. Her jaw quivered and tears slid down her round cheeks. "I've just been to the m-m-m-morgue." Her voice slipped into a hiccup, and her body trembled as she cried silently.

Owain quickly moved to her, putting his arm around her shoulders and whispering in her ear softly. Niall couldn't hear him, but the effect on her was visible. She nodded and sniffled, but the tide of sorrow seemed to diminish. Finally Juliette turned into Owain completely, and he hugged her to his chest.

Without intending to, Niall smiled. He wondered what Gus would think if his mentor and Niall's father became an item.

His smile vanished. Gus wasn't there to appreciate the growing affection between Jules and Owain. His body lay in bed, but his mind was who-knew-where.

Slowly Juliette's hushed words began to seep into Niall's awareness. "At the morgue I identified P-P-Piney and M-M-Matty's bodies.... They were so young and had so much potential. They had their whole lives ahead...." Her voice disappeared under audible gulps as she seemed to fight her instincts to lament.

Niall closed his eyes. Pine Seed and Matty were dead as they had been the closest to the explosion. Aeryn, Rodney, Sydney, Alec, Gus, and Juliette received minor injuries in the blast, Jason was still in intensive care, and Kerry was in a coma due to a massive head wound. The whole situation was more than a tragedy; it was a disaster.

Another knock came from the door, and without waiting to be bid entry, Aeryn and Alec slipped in. They were both bruised and battered, shell-shocked, covered in bandages like Juliette, and Aeryn needed crutches to get around as her left leg was encapsulated in a white cast. Still, she looked as high-spirited as one could in the midst of such a horrible event. Alec put on a brave face, but his nerves were clearly frayed.

"Hey," Aeryn said breathlessly. Niall quickly shoved a chair toward her, and she sat on it, exhaling deeply and grimacing. "God, I need more time at the gym."

Juliette and Owain had stepped apart. She blew her nose in a handkerchief and asked, "Where's Rodney?"

"Harvard went home as soon as they discharged him," Aeryn replied, her naturally low voice so husky now it sounded like she smoked five packs a day. Niall assumed Harvard was Rodney's coven name. "You know how, um… delicate he can be. Disasters of any variety bring out all his insecurities. But he made us swear we'd inform him as soon as there was news." She locked gazes with Niall, who believed she did so to avoid looking at her friend on the bed. Her holding onto her own arms as if to an anchor and fidgeting about nervously confirmed as much. "So, is there any news?"

Niall shook his head. "Gus is asleep. The doctors are watching him closely in case his condition worsens. They said it might take a while for him to wake up, like the whole day maybe. All we can do is wait and see." He sat back down in his chair and resumed his silent vigil over his sleeping boyfriend. Had he thought for a second that a kiss might wake him up, Niall would have slobbered all over Gus till he dripped saliva.

Aeryn looked at Gus, frowning in bafflement and sadness. "It's weird he hurt his head so bad, considering me, Kerry, Rodney, and Alec were much closer to the, eh... zero point."

A heavy, loaded silence fell in the room. The clock ticking on the wall was loud.

Juliette broke the mood suddenly, causing most of them to jump. Of course, none of them had gotten any rest that night. "Where's Syd?"

"She stayed with Tom," Aeryn said quietly, a depressed expression on her face. "Tom got hit in the face by something flying through the air, like a piece of shrapnel or debris or something. They had to put stitches in him. The cut was pretty deep from what I heard. He has to wear one of those eye patches for a week at least. Syd stayed to help him get around. They might stop by before going home."

"I don't mean to butt in, but bed is probably where you all should be right now." Owain sounded logical and calm, and Juliette's tiny nod indicated her agreement.

Niall, however, didn't feel calm in the least. But he did want these people to leave, for a while anyway. "Yeah, you all should go. I'm gonna stay and call or text Jules as soon as things change. For better or worse." His voice cracked on the last word. The mere possibility was enough to drive him insane. He'd just found Gus less than three months ago. He wasn't ready to concede to the notion Gus might—

No! Gus is stronger than anyone I know. He'll make it. He'll be fine. 'Cause I love him, and we're gonna be together. Niall nodded frantically to convince himself. As he stared at Gus's closed eyelids and slowly heaving chest, Niall wasn't entirely reassured.

"Niall is right," Owain cut in, his voice smooth as silk, authoritative without sounding gruff or aggressive. "None of you have eaten since last evening or rested in twenty-four hours."

Aeryn suddenly growled, causing everyone to face her. Her expression was wary and a bit angry. "I may not speak for everyone, Mr. Wallis, was it? But you just showed up last night. We don't know you, and we're sure as hell not taking orders from you. And come to think of it, I personally find it pretty fucking suspicious that our coven takes a literal hit the very night you appear on the scene for the first time. Just who the hell are you, and how do you know that guy?" She thumbed in Niall's direction.

Niall had known this would come up. He just wished it hadn't happened now when Gus was injured. A part of him understood Aeryn's position. She and Gus hadn't spoken in a while, so she, like the others, might not know Niall was Gus's boyfriend.

Juliette tried to intervene. "Aeryn, that's incredibly rude and—"

Owain silenced her with a touch on her arm. "No, it's okay. I understand." Speaking to Aeryn, he said, "I'm Owain Valentine, and that gentleman is Niall, my son and Gus's…." His brow furrowed and he glanced at Niall with a slightly baffled look. "Is boyfriend still a word you people use?"

Niall actually chuckled then, a weird bark of amusement combined with a breath exhaled. "You people? Dad, really. Yeah, Gus is my boyfriend." He knew his father hadn't meant gays but young folks.

"I was hurt when the… b-b-bomb went off," Alec cut in, frowning and doubtful. "But I'm sure I saw *you* there. Right after it happened." He pointed his finger straight at Niall.

Niall hesitated. He was a private investigator, after all. Unless his client—in this case Juliette—gave him permission to divulge details about his mission and who hired him, he wasn't allowed to go blabbing information to anyone.

"Niall was there because of me," Juliette said out of the blue, her voice steadfast and her back ramrod straight. Aeryn and Alec focused on her but didn't seem to understand what was happening. "I asked Niall to observe our esbat last night and for Owain to participate."

Aeryn gave her a disbelieving sneer. "Why?"

Juliette took a deep, calming breath. "Niall is a private investigator and Owain an ex-police officer, so I believed they were the best for—"

Aeryn tried to climb back on her feet, awkwardly with the crutches. But her anger was evident as her cheeks grew red and her eyes blazed. "Best for what, Jules? Did you know this was going to happen? The bomb?"

"No! Of course I didn't!" Juliette snapped, her furious voice rising in shock and alarm. "How could you even suggest such a thing? That I'd ever endanger any of you is unthink—"

"Then what the hell is going on?" Aeryn had gotten up on her feet, shouting in fury, but at least she wasn't advancing on Juliette. Her cast might have had something to do with that.

"Someone's been stealing from the coven funds, okay?" Juliette stopped abruptly, her chin trembling and her eyes glimmering moistly. She swiveled around sharply and hugged herself. It was easy to see she was crying from the shaking of her shoulders and back.

"Come now, young lady," Owain said soothingly, patting Juliette on the back. "Let's all take a deep breath and regroup. We're all friends here."

Aeryn said nothing, but neither did she offer comfort to Juliette. She only plopped back down on the chair and breathed heavily, the fight leaving her.

Alec wasn't quite at the point of detente yet as he asked, his voice incredulous, "You thought one of us was a thief, so you hired these men to investigate us?" He ran a hand through his hair, obviously exasperated and confused. "A ritual is sacred. You enter the circle with perfect love and trust. You don't bring in… spies under false pretenses to watch us at our most private moment, in communion with the divine. How could you?"

"Juliette never meant it to hurt any of you," Niall cut in, his voice harsher than he had intended as he stood up, getting more upset by the minute and gathering righteous indignation like a lightning rod. Niall could see the perceived breach of trust, but honestly, who told even their closest confidants every single thing? It was reasonable to assume everyone held onto something private and kept some things a secret. "She just wanted to know how come money's missing from the coven funds, that's all. Whoever is responsible, that person is stealing from all of you. If you can't understand why she'd want to find the culprit and learn the truth and the reason why, then you aren't worth a—"

"Son." This time Owain's voice was commanding, an order to cease and desist. Niall shut up, sighed, and sat back down heavily, rubbing hands across his face, feeling dead tired. "We are all in shock, tired and hurt. Let's not say anything we might want to take back later." As sensible as Owain's speech was, Niall just wanted everyone gone so he could give Gus 100 percent of his time and focus.

The door swung open, no knocking preamble. A nurse, a stout older brunette with wire-rimmed spectacles, called out adamantly, "This is a hospital, not the mall. Take this racket outside." She stepped aside and pointed toward the reception area and the waiting room beyond, glaring at them all.

Niall's cheeks heated with embarrassment. But he wasn't ready to leave Gus's side, so he said, reluctantly, "I'd rather stay, if it's all the same to you. He'd want me to be here when he wakes up." He couldn't glance at Gus on the bed, or he'd start crying again. But he lifted his chin in defiance, ready to duke it out with the nurse.

Despite her indignation, she regarded him with sympathy. "Talk with your friends. I need to take Mr. Goodwin's vitals anyway, and recheck his bandages. You are… immediate family?"

Niall didn't hesitate. "I'm his boyfriend and in-case-of-emergency contact, along with Ms. Hayes there." He nodded toward Juliette, who shared a glance of agreement with the nurse.

The nurse pursed her lips, apparently being a strict adherent of hospital policies when it came to visitors. Nonetheless, she showed grace and mercy as she said, "It'll take me about ten, fifteen minutes to do the checkup. Come back afterward, but only if you behave." Her stern look passed over each of the current occupants of the room, who all probably felt adequately scolded.

One by one, in a slow, mournful procession, they vacated the hospital room and moved off to regroup at the designated waiting area, where ugly and uncomfortable, putrid-green plastic chairs awaited them in rows. Yet none of them sat, except for Aeryn with her cast.

But before they got the chance to resume their argument, a man joined them, his expression grim. The bald, pudgy man in the wrinkled old suit and tie was none other than Homicide Detective Virgil Hughes, who was Niall's good friend and Owain's former partner in the SPD.

"Hughes, good to see you." Owain clasped Hughes's hand and shook it firmly. Both men smiled and nodded to acknowledge the bond they had formed so many years ago. Niall found himself slightly envious of their lasting friendship. That was the problem working alone as a PI. Of course, if Gus had been awake, he would have made for an excellent, if unofficial, partner.

"Owain. Niall." Hughes's bushy eyebrows indicated his moods far better than any other expression. Well, that and his huffs. His gaze landed on the closed door to Gus's hospital room, and a worried frown appeared. "How's the kid?"

"Still out of it," Niall replied. "He had a concussion from the blast, plus an assortment of cuts and bruises, just like the others. But he's resting now, so that's a good sign." He returned his focus onto Hughes. "Any news on what the hell happened over there?"

Hughes rubbed his chin, glancing at the other people in the waiting area sharply before saying, "The tests are ongoing but… it looks like an IED was used."

A shocked gasp escaped Niall's throat, mixing with similar sounds from the others. Chills ran up and down his spine. "An IED? Are we in a war zone now?"

"What's an IED?" Alec asked, bewildered.

"It stands for an improvised explosive device," Owain replied matter-of-factly. "It's basically a homemade bomb." He looked at Hughes questioningly. "It was buried, was it?"

Hughes nodded grimly, making a chewing motion with his jaw, a remnant of his time as a cigar smoker. His wife had convinced him to stop. For the most part. "Yeah. The point of origin seemed to be between the… um, the two deceased victims."

"Oh my God." Aeryn looked sick, and Alec reached for a chair and collapsed on it, his face as white as a sheet. "Someone tried to blow us all to kingdom come. It's a hate crime."

"I urge you all not to jump to conclusions at this stage in the investigation," Hughes cut in, his tone demanding obedience.

Aeryn chuckled dryly, a bitter sound. "And to think we cared about a thief among us."

"What's this?" Hughes demanded to know.

Niall and Owain both started to speak, but Juliette got there first. "I hired Niall and his father, Owain, to be present last night because a few hundred dollars had gone missing from the coven cashbox. The only people who knew I kept money there were those in the coven." Pressing a trembling hand over her chest, she appeared fragile and worn. "I had no idea I'd be placing people in danger…."

"Don't be daft, MC," Aeryn snapped, an affectionate smile on her lips to cushion the blow. "You'd never hurt anyone on purpose. You're our wise and courageous leader, dammit."

Alec ambled in front of Juliette, an ashamed redness creeping up his face. "Jules, I'm sorry. I said stupid things. I…. With Jason and…. I was just overwhelmed…." Tears glimmered in his eyes and he kept gulping to be able to speak.

Juliette pulled him into a fierce hug. "You're all so dear to me. Never doubt that, Alec. Ever."

Hughes cleared his throat at the emotional scene, pursing his lips in distaste at public displays of affection, especially during an open inquiry. He never strayed from professionalism. "Well, now that everybody's friends again, could someone fill me in on this theft?"

"The overall sum gone missing in the past two months is \$317.69," Juliette replied as she broke the hug with Alec, who shifted to the side awkwardly but was noticeably lighter in spirit. "As for who is the culprit, that was what last night was supposed to help us out with."

"Oh, who bloody cares about a few bucks when it's obvious who tried to kill us?" Aeryn said abruptly, silencing everyone in the room. "It was Jason!"

"No, it wasn't!" Alec shouted back.

"Oh, don't be such an innocent," Aeryn scoffed and scrambled to get back on her feet. "Jason admitted it himself."

"When?" Alec cried out, so upset he was shaking, his hands fisting at his sides.

"Just before it happened," Aeryn replied. "He said he had a surprise for us. One that, and I quote, would blow us all away, unquote." She looked at everyone straight in the eye, as if challenging anyone to disagree with the accuracy of her memory. "Jason *did* say it. I heard it, and I'm positive I'm not the only one."

"No...." Alec's small voice faded away as he seemed defeated by the memory. No one was disputing the statement. "He couldn't have.... I mean, he was hurt in the explosion too. He's in surgery right now! Why would he blow himself up? It makes no sense!"

"Ehem."

The cough from the doorway startled everybody.

The newcomer was no one Niall had met during the case, and he therefore wondered who the heck he was. Tall and thin, the handsome man wore a fancy business suit, probably Hugo Boss, with a dark purple silk tie and luxury leather shoes, and he had an expensive wristwatch plus an honest-to-God cane with a silver handle.

His long black mane was in a stylish ponytail, tied with a black silk ribbon, and Niall could have sworn the man's slightly up-slanted, almond-shaped dark eyes sported gray eyeliner. With his high cheekbones and narrow, sculpted face, he was quite beautiful in a manly fashion. Niall was reminded of an Asian version of the vampire Armand from the film *Interview with the Vampire*, based on a book of the same name by Anne Rice.

"*Pardonnez moi*," the man said suavely in French in a deep and reverberating voice and then continued in English with a charming French accent. "Please, allow me to introduce myself. I am Guilbert van Es. You may call me Gil. At your service." He bowed theatrically, reinforcing

Niall's image of a creature centuries old. "Please, do excuse me, but where might I find Jason Upton?"

Niall stared at the man's eyes and couldn't tell what color they were. A starry darkness swirled in their unfathomable depths, almost giving Niall vertigo. "What do you want with Jason?" he asked to break the mesmerizing silence, again making everyone jump.

Mr. van Es smiled charismatically. "I was to meet with him last night at his mansion in Bellevue, but alas, my plane, it was delayed. When I arrived at Monsieur Upton's estate, *mon Dieu*, there were police, ambulances, and media everywhere. I was informed there had been an accident and directed to come to this hospital. And, *voilà*, here I am." Gil van Es spoke with silent *H*s and purring *R*s and shushing *S*s. It was really quite sexy, if a bit theatrical.

"You were supposed to meet Jason Upton last night?" Hughes asked, flashing his badge at the charming intruder, his face like an impending gale, suggesting he didn't appreciate these surprises making his job more complicated. Yet his tone remained composed.

"Ah, *oui*, you are *absolument* correct. I came last night at Monsieur Upton's request to hold a séance." Van Es offered everyone a dazzling smile, one that could have melted even the coldest of hearts. His hand vanished into his inside breast pocket and produced in a flash a calling card with gilded lettering. "Guilbert van Es, psychique extraordinaire" it read.

It seemed Jason's blow-your-minds surprise wasn't meant to be taken literally after all.

Chapter 7

"JASON INTENDED to have a *séance* after the esbat ritual?" Juliette sounded and looked outraged. Gus had told Niall quite a bit about his mentor, and therefore Niall knew Juliette viewed certain spiritual things in a conservative light. Séances were apparently an affront to her beliefs. She looked at Alec, her eyes ablaze. "Did you know about this?" Niall cringed. Juliette really shouldn't have been the one to cast any stones. She'd kept secrets too.

Alec shook his head, studying Mr. van Es warily. "No, I didn't. Jase doesn't always tell me everything. I think he knew I would have opposed this, so he didn't tell me." Directing his words to the questionably esteemed French medium, he added, "Not that I have anything against psychics, you understand, but esbat rituals aren't séances."

"Nor should they be," Juliette cut in, her lips an angry white line.

"*Je suis désolé, Mesdames et Messieurs*," Mr. van Es declared, a hand on his heart as he bowed so deeply it was as if he were bent in half by a force outside himself. "I did not mean to cause such distress, of course." A dramatic expression of horror arose on his handsome features. "If Monsieur Upton had not been so adamant about me coming here, I would not have. The cards, *mais oui*, they warned me not to arrive."

Niall wasn't the only one in the room staring dumbfounded at the curious man.

"Say again?" Hughes asked, visibly baffled and getting agitated.

Gil van Es nodded, the anguished expression vanishing in an instant to be replaced by enthusiasm. "I have many abilities of the paranormal kind." He actually winked then, causing Niall to suppress an inappropriate chuckle behind a cough. "One of my talents, *mon cher*, are the cards."

While Hughes growled at being called darling in any language, Mr. van Es produced a splayed deck of beautifully drawn Tarot cards in his hand with a flick of his wrist. The magically gifted Mr. van Es seemed to be quite adept and nimble with his fingers, Niall concluded and grew more certain they were in the company of a confidence trickster.

"My cards," Mr. van Es said with flourish, chin up, "were given to me personally by Aleister Crowley himself—"

"That's impossible," Aeryn interjected, sneering sarcastically. "Crowley died in 1947."

Gil van Es smirked. "I did not say he was alive when he gave them to me."

While everyone again ogled, their mouths hanging open, Hughes snapped himself out of the stunned state. "Yes, well. So Mr. Upton, one of the injured parties, hired you to perform a… a séance, is that right?" He grimaced while saying it, his opinions on the matter clear as day. Niall smiled a little, also of the same mind.

"*Vraiment, c'est ca!*" Mr. van Es snapped his fingers. "He wrote to me and asked me to contact a certain deceased acquaintance of his, known by a mysterious name, Scire. I was to receive further information upon my arrival at his château."

Juliette stepped forward, shock evident in her face and posture. "Jason told you to use the séance to contact… the Scire?"

Niall had to intervene, if only to satisfy his own curiosity. "Who is this person?"

Juliette paled slightly. "It was the craft name of Gerald Gardner."

"The creator of the Wiccan religion?" His eyebrows practically rising to his hairline, Niall whistled. "Wow. That was unexpected." Then he frowned. "I was under the impression Jason wasn't all that into Wicca."

Alec nodded, looking as depressed as a whipped dog. "He wasn't. It only mattered to him because it was what *I* believed. I had no idea he would… that he was planning to… that he could do something so…." He struggled to finish, finally giving up, letting out a deep breath and slumping on his seat.

"How exactly was Jason supposed to accomplish this séance?" Aeryn demanded. "I thought to conduct such a… thing you needed something from the deceased person. Did Jason own something that once belonged to Gerald Gardner? Alec?"

Alec looked utterly confused. "Not that I know of. But he told me so little of his life and what he did." He looked down, wrenching and twisting his hands nervously as if in deep emotional distress. Niall thought he understood: Alec was a kind of a male version of a trophy wife for Jason. Who Alec was at heart didn't seem to matter, at least not to Jason.

"Was there an artifact belonging to Gardner that Jason intended to give to you to use?" Niall asked Mr. van Es.

Gil van Es nodded, disinterested. "Oui. Monsieur Upton spoke of a special book."

"A book?" Juliette interceded, seeming both furious and confused. "What book?"

Mr. van Es shrugged as though indifferent, checking on the condition of his manicured nails. "*Malheureusement*, Monsieur Upton did not elaborate." He checked his watch and a crease appeared on his brow. "*Je suis désolé*, but I must return to my hotel, for I have—"

"Absolutely not," Hughes cut him off, in full-on detective-running-the-show mode. "No one leaves yet. Everyone will kindly tell me who you are, where you can be found, and how you can be contacted, what was your role at that ritual and why. Plus, I want to know who decided who was standing where during the ritual, and who determined the exact spot of the ritual?" His suspicious gaze moved from one person to the next, earning looks varying from bewilderment to outrage.

Niall had a hunch this part of the investigation would take a while, and he realized he needed a whiz badly. "I'm gonna get some coffee and fresh air, okay, Detective?"

Hughes nodded at him and focused on Juliette who looked utterly dismayed. But one gentle touch on her arm from Owain and she calmed down. Niall left the room pondering whether his father and Gus's mentor might end up a couple. Sure, she was in her forties and he in his sixties, but after reaching a certain point in the aging process, trivial issues like that began to matter less and less. Or so Niall assumed.

He passed the nurse's station, and after a jerky nod as a quick greeting, he received a couple of sympathetic, even pitying glances. Keeping his head down, Niall hastened his pace toward the elevators.

That was when a familiar black feather boa and heavily made-up, upward-slanted eyes made an appearance in his field of vision. Quickly the apparition disappeared around the corner.

"Hey! Stop!" Niall ran after him, wrath in his mind, adrenaline in his speed. Now it all made sense. He'd returned to wreak havoc on his and Gus's life again.

As NIALL rounded the corner to the hall leading to the elevators, he saw the elevator doors sliding closed, a taunting face vanishing from sight. Niall ramped up his momentum and did indeed manage to shove an arm through the opening. The automatic doors slid wide, revealing the person Niall had known he'd meet again one day. He just hadn't counted on that being today.

Niall jumped aboard. The doors slid closed and the elevator jerked into motion. It was empty of occupants except for the two of them, so Niall hit the emergency stop button, and the elevator screeched to a halt. The lights flickered for an instant but stabilized.

Niall growled, leapt toward the young man, grabbed his shirt, and shoved him against the wall. "If I find out you did this, Autumnsong, I will kill you. Mark my words."

The drop-dead-gorgeous Asian twink with hazel eyes quirked an eyebrow, as cool and haughty as ever, and removed Niall's hands from his shirt with surprising strength. "Blowing people up is boring, Valentine. And I am *not* boring." He straightened his rumpled clothes and locked his gaze with Niall's. "Besides, I am the last person you should go about accusing of such horrendous deeds. After all, I am indebted to both you *and* Goodwin for ridding the world of the likes of Florian Talbot."

Niall had his suspicions. He recalled the image of Autumnsong in the distance at the place where Florian Talbot had tried to kill Niall and Gus. And he'd done nothing to aid either of them. "Why are you here, then? Satisfying some morbid curiosity?"

Autumnsong's beautiful face revealed little of what he felt, if he felt anything at all. Niall had his doubts about that too. "Believe this or not, there are those who have a vested interest in Mr. Goodwin's continued health and security."

"Just who would those interested parties be?" Niall tried not to get upset again, but this young man, who may or may not have been a Satanist, really pushed his buttons.

Autumnsong's lips curled up in a half smile. "Who was that foreign dandy who came into Goodwin's room?"

"Guilbert van Es, or Gil, as he prefers to be called. A French psychic."

Autumnsong frowned. "Gil van Es? Never heard of him." Then, suddenly, his frown disappeared, and he chuckled. "How droll." Before

Niall could ask what the joke was, Autumnsong continued. "What did he want? I was under the impression Ms. Juliette Hayes doesn't believe in… psychic abilities."

"One of the coven members invited him." Niall wouldn't usually have given this much away to someone as suspicious as Autumnsong, but he had a feeling the young man would have found out what he wanted regardless of Niall's input. Better to be the one doing the telling—and having the chance to observe his responses. "Jason Upton. Apparently van Es was supposed to do a séance to conjure up Gerald Gardner's spirit from the great beyond." He sneered.

Autumnsong's eyes flashed intently. "Invoking the spirit? While not unknown to the world of Wiccans, still seems like an odd way to spend a leisurely moonlit evening."

Niall scoffed. "The whole arrangement was a surprise on Jason's part." He grew glum and bitter. "That was before the bomb, of course."

"You think the two are unrelated events?" Autumnsong inquired.

Niall stared at the young man dubiously. "You don't?"

Autumnsong shrugged. "I have no idea. I wasn't there." He seemed to briefly get lost in thought. "Séances require a personal item from the dec—"

"Yeah, I know. Apparently Jason had a book by Gardner."

This time the flash of interest in Autumnsong's eyes, paler than his skin, was intense. "What book?"

It was Niall's turn to shrug. "Don't know. Jason didn't tell anyone about any of what he had planned. The only mention he made was to van Es, saying the personal item was a book. Well, a *special* book."

Autumnsong's eyes narrowed. "Valentine, do yourself a favor and find out if Upton meant a book *written* by Gardner or a book simply *owned* by him." The hard-as-nails look in his predatory gaze told Niall the question was important. Not like he hadn't already figured that one out for himself. Autumnsong shoved a hand down the front pocket of his remarkably tight black jeans and produced a simple calling card with only a number on it, no name. "When you have an answer to that question, call me. Day or night."

He pushed the stop button, and the elevator started moving again.

By the time the ding indicated they'd arrived at the ground floor, Niall still had no clue what more he should ask Autumnsong. The young man was trouble with a capital *T*; that was the foremost thought in his head.

"I hope Goodwin pulls through," Autumnsong said as he swiftly rounded Niall to get out of the elevator car. "Let me know, will you, Valentine?" Just before he dashed off, he glanced over his shoulder, his gaze downcast, less secretive and more... empathetic. "Either way it turns out." His meaning was clear. Niall nodded, and Autumnsong faded into obscurity amid the masses in the hospital lobby.

Sighing heavily, Niall decided he needed a drink.

Luckily for him, there was a bar across the street, likely designed to cater to the needs of many a woeful traveler like him.

NIALL WAS on his third drink of scotch on the rocks when Hughes sat next to him on a barstool, huffing as his slightly outward-protruding belly hit the counter.

"Who makes these seats, dammit? Are they for toddlers for fuck's sake?"

Niall chuckled a time or two but then let his blues carry away the notes of happiness. "You interviewed everybody?"

Hughes asked for a soda, which meant he was still on the job. Of course, he would be. Tragedy might have struck, but it was only midmorning. "Yeah." He flipped open his notepad. "The location for the circle was Jason's idea, since the estate was his, and he knew the right spot. Even ground or some such. Not anymore, though." He laughed weakly, but the sound quickly died down. "The places people took in the circle were ones they'd used before. The only two differences were Gus in place of one—" He checked his notes. "—Hollister Baines, accountant. And then Owain made for an uneven thirteen, which from what I gather is a lucky number for witches." He shrugged and downed a gulp of his soda, grimacing. "Eww, foul...."

"Any news from forensics? About the... device used?" Niall found it hard to say the word. *Bomb.* A simple word but.... As though if he said it, the whole thing might happen again, or at least replay before his mind's eye, showing his boyfriend almost getting killed.

"Preliminary findings arrived from the bomb squad as I was walking down here." Hughes checked his notebook. "There was no timer, apparently. The device was activated by remote."

Surprised, Niall quirked an eyebrow. "Range?"

"Not much. About twenty-five yards." Hughes grunted in displeasure as he shoved his notebook back in his inside breast pocket.

Niall understood why, growing more depressed. "So… one of the coven members, then."

"Seems so." Hughes sipped his nonalcoholic beverage with clear distaste. Niall wondered why he even bothered. "Considering the amount of media coverage and outrage on the rise in the Wiccan community, I'd say we're gonna get conclusive results relatively soon. Of course, it might be that by tomorrow the feds will come swooping in and take over the case. Bunch of bumbling idiots…." Niall nodded vaguely, knowing the backstory behind Hughes' behavior. One of his nephews had striven to get in the FBI but hadn't made the cut. Regardless of the reasons why, the decision had earned Hughes's wrath. That, plus average street-cop pride, and you got this—general rambling on the inefficiencies of law enforcement agencies that *weren't* the police department.

"You're gonna keep me in the loop. Right?" Niall's tone rose at the end but he wasn't asking, not really.

Hughes half snorted, half chuckled. "What do you think?" His piercing gaze landed on Niall. "That's gonna be a two-way street, Junior. Got that?" And that wasn't a question either.

Niall grunted. "You need to ask?" His head started swimming as the whiskey kicked in. He was well aware getting drunk was a bad idea at the moment, but his head was filled with dark, gruesome sights, sounds, and smells. Death had crept too close for comfort.

"Your dad was asking for you back at the hospital." Hughes gave him a candid once-over. "You up to going back? Gus might wake up any min—"

"I can't go back yet. Soon. Just… not yet, okay?" Niall hung his head, stared at the bits and pieces of what used to be peanuts, smeared wet circles from bottles and glasses, and chinks and cracks in the wooden counter. He gazed at them unthinking, as though the answers to the mysteries of life were written there.

Naturally, they weren't.

Hughes slapped him on the back, hard, though it was probably intended as a hearty pat on the back. "Chin up, Junior. Gus is a fighter. Been in tougher scrapes than this. If you don't trust that, you're doing him a disservice."

Niall felt lousy, and for the second time inside a week, he banged his head on a wooden surface. "We had a fight."

"When?" Hughes sounded confused, which Niall could relate to.

"Gus suggested that Dad go undercover in the coven to find out who was stealing from the till." Niall plonked his head on the counter. "I was dead set against it." Another bang. "I said nasty things to him." Yet another slam on the wood. "I was a piece of shit. And now my Dad's injured, and—"

"What are you talking about? He's fine." Hughes sounded like he was about to lose his patience any second. "Barely a scratch on him."

"Yeah, but...." Niall buried his face in his hands, slumped over the counter like a wet dishrag. "But he is hurt a bit, and it could've been much worse. When Gus wakes up... he's gonna feel so guilty for putting my dad in danger. I know he will. As soon as he wakes up.... Dad might be okay, but Juliette's hurt, as are his friends. Two are lying dead and cold in the morgue. I mean, what if...?" He could scarcely say the words, having to push them out past the emotional lump lodged in his throat. "What if he doesn't wanna wake up? Why would he? Everything's fucked, and—"

"That's the stupidest, most ridiculous thing I've ever heard you say." Hughes rumbled on like a freight train, huffing and puffing as he went. "Nothing is fucked. Yeah, okay, two people are dead. Shit happens. The important thing is that Owain and Gus are alive."

"Yeah." Niall felt like sobbing but was too much of a man to resort to that in public. "But he's gonna wish—"

"Then I'll haul both your asses to the morgue and show you just how damn lucky you two are. Now quit your damn bellyaching, Junior, and get back to the hospital. Pronto. Your man's waiting." Hughes tossed the last drops of his drink down his gullet, stood up, and loomed over Niall like the shadow of death, or maybe vengeance and righteous indignation. "Did I stutter, kid?"

Grumbling under his breath, Niall got up, paid his bill, and followed Hughes back to the hospital. Inwardly he kept grumbling all the way there. Hughes was a father figure to Niall as much as Owain was, even though only the latter was his biological kin. In any case, both acted the same when it came to Niall: overprotective, slightly patronizing, and prone to lecturing.

Right then, though, he considered all those good things. Indifference would have felt far worse.

As they approached the door to Gus's room, cozy chatter filled Niall's ears.

And a familiar, if slightly rusty, voice said, "Where's Niall?"

The last few steps between Niall and Gus became meaningless as Niall rushed to Gus's side, kissed him, and embraced him hard enough to cut off breathing and circulation. But Niall just couldn't stop, not if his life depended on it. Gus hugged him back, though more weakly.

"God, Gus, you have no idea how much I fucking love you," Niall murmured in his ear, desperate to keep his man close. But Gus's blond locks smelled of dirt and smoke, his skin of disinfectants and blood, and as Niall pulled back, those green eyes were huge and haunted.

Gus's voice was small and frail. "Niall, what happened?"

And wasn't that the billion-dollar question. Too bad Niall didn't have the words.

Chapter 8

"WOULD YOU please fucking sit down already?" Niall's agitated voice lowered, taking on a note of danger.

Gus growled back in response, hobbling toward the kitchen. "I have a sprained ankle, Niall, not a broken leg. I'm supposed to move around normally." He enunciated Niall's name clearly and slowly to show his boyfriend that his constant hovering was neither necessary nor asked for.

"You had a concussion for fuck's sake." Niall obviously wasn't about to back down. He followed Gus to the kitchen, right on his heels like a bird dog. "And that means taking it easy." Gus tried to open the fridge and pull out items for preparing food, but Niall slammed his hand on the door, shoving it closed and almost cutting Gus's arms in half. "It's only been two days, Gus. You need to rest and recuperate. That's what the doctors said."

Gus resisted the urge to roll his eyes but the growl escaped nonetheless. "I did rest, dammit. I rested the whole day yesterday. I need to do something, Niall, or I'll go out of my mind. I'll get cabin fever and hunt you all over the apartment with an axe."

Niall harrumphed. "You got an axe to grind, eh?" Gus glared at him furiously but only earned a flicker of a grin in return. Niall was trying to bring humor into their argument, Gus concluded and smiled a little himself.

"Look, babe," Niall continued. "All I want is for you to be okay. And right now that means resting. Is that so terribly bad of me? To wanna see you get better?"

Niall's frustrating point of view made Gus cringe with guilt. "I understand your point, Niall, I swear I do." Gus closed the gap between them and hugged Niall's waist, pulling him close. Niall's fresh, spicy aftershave turned Gus on, and he did a little swing of his hips. Maybe if Niall was aroused, he'd forget to lecture Gus. "You know, there's a pretty great muscle-friendly exercise we could do. Best of all, we can do it lying down." Waggling his eyebrows, Gus brushed the tip of his nose against Niall's.

Niall rolled his eyes but grudgingly let himself be held. "You really think that sweet-talking my ear off is gonna work?" Gus kissed Niall, mostly to shut him up. Well, perhaps half. "Mmm, how right you are." Niall tilted his head and fused their mouths together.

Gus slumped against him, grabbing the back of Niall's shirt for leverage and to keep the man near. Moaning, Gus relished Niall's taste, the tiny tang of coffee and scrambled eggs he'd had an hour ago mixing with his natural flavor. He sucked on Niall's tongue, getting hungrier by the second.

Niall moved forward, pushing Gus back until his hips bumped the kitchen counter. He wrapped his arms around Gus and started to slowly grind against him, almost causing sparks to fly. Gus wound his arms around Niall's neck and followed suit until they were dry-humping one another and getting hot and sweaty and needy.

"You said something about a bed," Niall murmured into the kiss.

"What's wrong with the kitchen floor?" Gus muttered in reply.

Niall grunted. "Nothing wrong with the floor, babe. Less-than-young knees, however, protest the idea." His lips traveled to Gus's neck to lick and suckle at the sweet spot beneath his ear by his jugular.

Gus chuckled breathlessly. "How about fucking me against the counter?"

Niall froze midkiss and he stared at Gus with widened eyes as though he was doubting his hearing. Then his eyes narrowed dangerously, and Gus's breath caught in his throat. Next thing Gus knew, he was spun around fast and shoved onto the clean and polished counter, his chest plastered over it. Niall divested Gus of his pants, bunching them uncomfortably around his shins, and they were soon followed by his underwear.

When Niall's rough hands caressed and squeezed Gus's buttocks, his dick rose to join the party. Gus chuckled to himself. Like they hadn't fucked just last night. Well, made love really, as Niall had been ultracareful with Gus, ensuring at even the hottest, wildest moment of abandon that his ankle and head were safe and sound.

A heated, wet tongue swiped over Gus's entrance as Niall parted his ass cheeks and dove right in. Gus groaned, groping for purchase over the fake marble counter but finding none. He rested his flushed cheek on the cool surface and let himself be pleasured. Soon Niall's insistent fingers probed Gus's twitching opening and slid in next to his tongue, thumbs spreading Gus to ready him for Niall's dick.

"Niall, come on," Gus urged. His cock was by then rock-hard, wedged awkwardly between his hipbone and the edge of the counter, sending frissons of delight and discomfort over him, one after another.

Laughing like the devilishly cruel sexual fiend he was, Niall licked his way up from Gus's crack, lapping around each nub of his spine up to his nape, then sucking hard on the side of his neck, leaving his mark. "Patience, beautiful." He bit the softer junction of neck and shoulder, making Gus quiver with want.

"I need it, Niall, please." Gus twisted his head to catch a half kiss from Niall's lips.

Niall rubbed his erection into the crevice of Gus's buttocks, up and down, driving Gus insane. Then the weight on Gus's back left him, giving him cold shivers and goose bumps. But soon Niall returned, his dick gloved up and lathered richly with lube, which accounted for the splashing sounds Gus heard. Nimble fingers coated his opening and channel with lube.

Once Gus was adequately prepped, Niall pushed past the easing ring of muscles and in all the way in one slow, slippery slide. Once Niall was fully inside Gus, they groaned aloud at the same time. Niall's jeans scraped against Gus's thighs, which meant he had only lowered them down to his thighs, not removed them entirely. The touch was a bit coarse and kind of erotic, giving Gus yet another sensation to swim in.

Gus whispered, "You do know I did this to shut you up? In part, that is."

Niall chuckled. "You think I don't know you by now, babe?" He kissed Gus's nape, a soft and tender brush of lips that Gus felt all the way down to his curling toes. "At times you can be so infuriating. Especially when it comes to your health and well-being." Niall snaked his hands from Gus's hips to grip his buttocks and then moved them slowly up his back until he wrapped his arms around Gus's chest and waist, keeping them locked front to back.

Gus tilted his head to expose his neck for Niall to ravage, which he did with his mouth, sucking and licking and nibbling. Gus moaned. "That, *oh*, doesn't mean I don't value those things. I, *uh*, I just need to feel useful, you know."

"You're most useful when you're at one hundred percent, Gus, not teetering on the brink of passing out." Niall started to move within Gus, leisurely little thrusts in and out, giving Gus all the time he needed to adjust, which he appreciated the hell out of.

Gus wanted to argue his point some more, to tell Niall that it was *Gus's* friends who had died in that bombing, which meant Gus needed to be involved in the investigation. He did have an axe to grind with whoever blew apart his sense of security and peace of mind when it came to his spirituality and friends.

But when Niall kissed his neck lovingly and rocked his cock back and forth, his pace quickening as desire built, Gus couldn't bring himself to speak his mind. Niall understood; he had lost friends too, in the war, right there on the gory battlefield, so Gus couldn't very well blame Niall for being inconsiderate and ignorant.

No. Gus would politely ask to be involved. After their bout of lovemaking.

Throwing all his issues to the wind, Gus let his mind go blank of worries, sorrow, pain, and guilt. Niall held him close, their skin touching, their heartbeats syncing, their rhythm matching. Soon all the words they exchanged between them were pleas for faster, harder, deeper, and more, more, more, and oh yeah, ohmygod, oh please.

Niall caressed Gus's nipples, twisting them just a little past the edge of pain, and then slid his hand down to grip Gus's aching, hot, hard cock. Gus panted and moaned, needing the sheer blinding force of climax to wipe his thoughts away. Niall fisted Gus's dick, jerking him off with a flick of his wrist at every upturn, causing his thumb to graze and press on his slit until Gus was dripping precome by the bucket loads.

"Mmm, that's what I like," Niall murmured, his fist pumping faster as he ground inside Gus, claiming him with his prick. "My pretty Gus, shooting like a rocket, yeah."

Had he been more coherent or rational, Gus might have objected to being called pretty. As it was, though, all he heard was an endearment, which ratcheted his arousal to heavenly heights.

Niall pounded furiously into Gus, ramming his cock deeper with every single thrust, until Gus saw stars and his cock burst forth splashes of creamy white droplets. He groaned heavily, his body wracked by spasms of pure pleasure. His balls pulled up so tight he felt his body might just suck them in permanently. It sure helped that Niall nailed Gus's sweet spot with every nudge, over and over, sending waves of delight through Gus's body.

Niall grunted hard, stilled for an instant, and then Gus felt heat fill his ass, even through the latex. He really wished he could feel Niall's dick inside him with nothing in the way, but they hadn't had the exclusivity talk yet. The health situation was implied in their trust in one another every time they had sex, but they still used condoms.

Niall's hips stuttered, and his hold on Gus trembled. Their sweat mixed, and they both panted hard as they came down from orgasmic heights. "Fuck, I love being inside you," Niall said in a whisper, his hot, moist breath fanning over Gus's neck and upper back.

Gus chuckled, out of breath. "Not as much as me, trust me." They both laughed, and the relaxed mood returned. Sure, they argued at times, but they could still talk about stuff that bothered them and try to fix things. Staying together was worth it.

Then Niall had to go and spoil the whole thing. "You're still gonna get your ass to bed, babe. You mark *my* words." With a low, victorious chuckle, Niall pulled out slowly, discarding the spent condom, and left Gus to ponder what tricks he'd have to resort to next time since apparently sex didn't erase Niall's memory.

NEXT MORNING Gus snuck into the kitchen of his apartment as quietly as he could on his tippy-toes. As he brewed his morning coffee, with cinnamon and cardamom, he asked himself how this situation had taken place, mostly without his consent.

In effect, Niall was now living at Gus's place, in his apartment above his occult shop.

He had no real response. As he stood by the coffee machine, watching hot water drip, Gus knew he didn't really mind Niall living with him. After all, if their relationship was getting any more serious, moving in together was the next logical step.

Still, shouldn't they have discussed it together instead of simply letting it happen while Gus was recuperating? Was this a real move, or one just born out of difficult circumstances? Once Gus had healed enough, as he already felt he had, was Niall going to go back to his own place? And was that what Gus wanted?

He poured coffee into his mug and took a sip, blowing gently on the heated liquid. He had no reply to offer to the nagging part of him. Then again, perhaps thinking about such deep issues at seven in the morning wasn't the brightest idea. His brain sure hadn't kicked into gear yet.

A pair of strong, warm arms wrapped around him. "Mornin', babe." Niall kissed Gus's nape softly, his stubble slightly burning Gus's skin. A mellow warmth seeped into Gus's heart. His boyfriend was great, no doubt about that. "Made any coffee for me?"

Gus scoffed playfully. "Of course. What kind of an ogre do you think I am?" As Niall reached for the coffee pot and his cup, Gus asked, "So, what's on the agenda for today?" He really hoped Niall wouldn't exclude him. This case was personal, to the highest degree, and the only way for him to cope was to be a part of finding out who was responsible for the bombing and the death of two innocent people.

Niall took a huge gulp of his coffee and smacked his lips, sighing in satisfaction. The look of rapture sure suited him. "Hughes is coming to pick me up in an hour. We're gonna head out to interview Rodney Easton and Sydney Keen. Hughes interviewed everyone else yesterday. Jason is also awake, I hear, so we're gonna see him too, at the hospital." After another sip, he asked, "Is there gonna be some kind of, uh… memorial service for Matty and Pine Seed? I don't know how Wiccans, um… do that." He sounded more confused than weirded out by the topic.

Gus turned away, not wanting to seem weak with emotion, not even in front of Niall. "Wiccans tend to honor the dead during Samhain. But that's months away. I haven't talked to Jules yet, but I imagine she'll arrange something soon." The pain and sadness were fresh on his mind and heart, and he felt the anguish in his chest as a heavy weight, bending him and pulling him down like an undercurrent.

A touch on his shoulder was comforting. "I'll go with you, Gus, if you'd like. I mean, if it's not inappropriate or intrusive. I'll hold your hand the entire time, I promise." He slipped his hand into Gus's and intertwined their fingers.

Gus had never loved Niall as much as he did at that exact moment.

The doorbell at the side door rang. "That'll be Hughes. I'll go let him in," Niall said.

But Gus held onto Niall's hand, stopping him. "I wanna come along."

Niall locked gazes with him, quirking an eyebrow. "Okay."

Gus groused. "Look, my ankle is fine, and so's my head, so I really don't need to rest anym—wait, what?"

Niall laughed. "Considering what we did yesterday right here in the kitchen, yeah, I'd say you're fine. So go and get dressed, babe, 'cause you sure as hell aren't coming with us in your jammies." Niall nodded toward Gus's pajama bottoms and T-shirt.

Gus blushed, ducked his head, and rushed out of the kitchen to the bedroom to change.

"HEY, YOU two," Hughes said joylessly as Gus and Niall entered his car. He looked tired and annoyed, so Gus muttered only a quick good morning and settled in place on the backseat. He appreciated Hughes not coming in a police car. The bars would have made him uneasy.

Niall sat on the front seat and was less formal and considerate. "Damn, Virg. You look like warmed up baby puke." Gus rolled his eyes and sighed at his boyfriend's indelicate comment.

Hughes grunted. "Yeah, you'd be too if you knew what's been happening. DHS has stormed in to run with the possible terrorism angle, and the feds are poking their noses in about the hate crime aspect. They've pretty much taken over those sides of the investigation and left us plain old cops to do the grunt work, like gather evidence and interview the victims and witnesses, such as the disgruntled neighbor, Mr. Abrams."

Niall sighed as Hughes started the ignition and steered the car into motion and onto the streets. "That blows. Just what the hell are they doing anyway, if interviewing people is beneath them?"

Hughes shrugged and made an angry noise in his throat. "No clue. But whatever it is, they ain't sharing. Blast them all to hell." After a deep exhale, he added, "Still, I hope they do find something to justify their interference. They've got better resources and more manpower, plus their connections reach higher up than ours, or mine." He glanced at Niall inquiringly. "I bet you have a bunch of your own questions for these people, so by all means, ask away if you need to. You too, sunshine." He looked at Gus via the mirror.

Gus felt a twinge of pain, sorrow, and loss. "That's Alec's coven name. Matty's was… was Pinhead." He swallowed hard, fighting the emotions threatening to reemerge. "I don't know what Pine Seed's name was. God, I should know that. How could I have been so remiss—"

"You weren't, you aren't," Niall cut in, his voice sliced with anger. Gus understood it was hard for Niall to see Gus beaten by loss. "You didn't even know her."

Gus nodded, staring at his hands, wringing them, searching for that physical pain that would diminish the mental strain and hollow feel in his heart. "No. I didn't get a chance to…. Now it's too late. But Matty was wonderful, funny, and smart." A tiny chuckle escaped his mouth without his noticing it. "I think he had a thing for Joy."

"Huh." Niall offered no judgment in his tone. "Wasn't he a teenager? Pine Seed seemed more his age group."

Suddenly Gus recalled the oddness of a moment past. "Funny, but I didn't remember until just now. I don't think Matty liked Pine Seed. When I talked to him, Matty seemed to dislike the girl. When I asked him, he just said Pine Seed was not at all for him. He seemed… resentful."

Niall glanced at him over his shoulder, frowning. "Did you find out what the beef was between them?"

"No, the ritual started before an opportunity presented itself." Gus stared out the car window. Rain made striations on the cold surface, trickles of a small downpour common in the Northwest.

"Hmm. Guess we'll find out the truth eventually." Niall sounded confident, as though solving the case were a foregone conclusion. Gus envied his certainty.

"So, where are we going to first?" Gus asked, wishing to steer the conversation toward something useful.

"Rodney Easton's home," Hughes replied. "He wasn't at the hospital for more than a quick checkup and with only a couple of minor bruises. I have questions for him." Again, he took a glimpse of Gus via the mirror. "What do you know about him, Goodwin?"

"Rodney? He's a retired professor. He went to Harvard, which is his coven name too. He's brilliant, but he couldn't hack the tenure track. The pressures made him burn out, and he quit his job. Like Tom, he's living off disability, I think, only of the more mental kind."

"What was his field of specialty?" Hughes asked.

"He has several doctorates. Philosophy, art history, bibliography, antiquities, and the like. I'm not sure about all of them. He's always been academically oriented. Once he was ambitious, too, but not anymore. Not since his… breakdown."

Gus hated the idea that someone he had known for years could not only steal from the coven, but actually try to kill their friends. For him, it was an impossible notion, not simply because he abhorred killing, but because he believed he was a relatively good judge of character. How could someone pull the wool over his eyes and deceive him so. He shuddered at the mere possibility.

Yes, today could prove to be beneficial for the case but detrimental to Gus's sanity.

Chapter 9

"RODNEY, ARE you home?" Gus knocked on the white front door of a suburban one-story house. Niall watched his boyfriend's growing concern and nudged Gus aside to bang on the door harder. Gus glared at him. "You'll wake the dead with that racket."

Niall didn't get a chance to respond as shuffling and rustling could be heard behind the closed door, then locks clicking, and finally the door opened a crack.

A man with a haggard look on his face stared at them warily. "What's this all abo—Gus!" The man's expression softened and he cracked a smile. He opened the door wider as well. "I'm so glad to see you." He stepped outside and hugged Gus.

Niall might have felt a spark of jealousy if the man hadn't appeared so old and worn. Which was odd since Gus had told Niall that Rodney was in his late thirties. But this worried man could have passed for fifty.

In every respect, though, he matched Niall's mental image of a university professor to a tee. Dressed in beige slacks and a matching-colored cardigan over a white dress shirt, Rodney had brown eyes, sand-blond hair with a slightly receding hairline, a well-trimmed graying beard, and a hunched posture. How on earth could this man be in his thirties? If occupation stress had done this to him, then stress was definitely something to be avoided at all costs.

"Rod, can we come in?" Gus asked as he separated from Rodney, whose welcoming, happy face immediately evaporated. He quickly glanced behind him, and Niall didn't imagine him paling.

"This, uh, isn't the best time," Rodney hedged, nervous now.

Gus frowned, clearly baffled. "Rod?"

Rodney seemed incapable of saying no to a confused Gus, which was something Niall totally could relate to. "Oh, very well. Please, come in." He stepped aside to let the three men pass him, but Niall observed him glancing anxiously at a half-open sliding door off the living room. "I'll make some tea. Or do you gentlemen prefer coffee?"

"I'd like tea, if you don't mind making some," Gus said, his usual friendly, open smile in place, and Rodney returned the gesture. "Can I help in any way?"

Rodney hesitated, blinking hard, but then smiled again, though the gesture appeared forced. "Of course. Follow me."

As they disappeared toward the back of the house and presumably the kitchen, Niall wasted no time. Silently he dashed toward the half-open door and slid it open. A low whistle came from Hughes behind him.

The room, which looked to be a study, was a mess. Books, folders, and papers lay on the floor in heaps, and the dark wood desk was in an equally disheveled state. A few of the smaller bookshelves were tilted over, partly collapsed on the floor but held up by brown leather furniture. The dark red rug was littered with stacks of papers, the flower vase on the one upright dresser had fallen on its side, droplets of water still dripping from its mouth, and every drawer in the room had been opened.

"This room's been ransacked, and with a heavy hand too," Hughes commented in his typical laconic manner.

Niall nodded. "This is no spring cleaning, that's for sure." He scanned the room with a careful eye. "I wonder what they were looking for?" A thought occurred to him. "Rodney Easton's a specialist in books and antiques, right?" Hughes nodded, waiting for Niall to make his point. "We know from Mr. van Es that Jason Upton had a special book he'd intended to use in the séance. One either written by or belonging to Gerald Gardner, the creator of Wicca. What if Upton gave the book to Easton for… appraisal or provenance?"

Hughes grunted. "If it was here, I doubt it's here anymore." He also studied the room with a sharp eye. "See any safes or secure hiding places?"

Niall was about to comment with a negative when an outraged shout stopped him.

"What an earth are you doing in there? I didn't give you permission to search my house!" Rodney was so angry he was shaking and red in the face. "I must ask you all to leave." Gus, standing behind Easton, seemed unsure of what to do, frowning in bewilderment and a moderate amount of shame and embarrassment.

Niall knew Hughes could not really refuse. They didn't have a search warrant or any evidence of wrongdoing by Rodney Easton. Hughes would be required to obey the law.

But Niall was a PI, not a cop, and he didn't take orders from anyone, not even Gus's friends. And certainly not when two people were dead and two others still in danger. "Sure. We'll leave. I only have one question: did Jason Upton give you a book for appraisal of authenticity or provenance? Oh, better make that two questions: who broke in here and ransacked your study?"

Rodney paled and broke out in a sweat, his fear palpable, and when he spoke, he stammered. "I, uh, I... I don't have to answer your questions." He straightened his back and pointed at the door, adamant and, for the moment, in control of his emotions. "I demand you leave at once."

Niall and Hughes had no real leg to stand on, but Gus was another story. He moved closer to Rodney and spoke in a soft, baffled, irresistible voice. "Rod, what are you doing? These men are trying to find out who killed Matty and Pine Seed and tried to kill all of us. Why are you acting this way?"

This time Rodney clearly had an internal struggle going on: on the one side, his self-preservation, and on the other, his loyalty to his friend. Finally he made his decision, exhaled deeply, and slumped. "I'm so sorry, Gus. I really am. I didn't know that... that horrible thing was going to happen. If I had, I would never have...."

Gus seemed about to collapse or start screaming or crying. Niall readied himself for any contingency. But Gus only asked, his voice cracking, "The bomb.... That was you...?"

Rodney looked up, appalled and horrified. "No! Absolutely not!" He closed his eyes and obviously fought for control. "Please, let's sit down in the living room. I'll tell you what I know."

Rodney and Gus sat on the couch, and Niall and Hughes commandeered the two armchairs by the coffee table. The tea was forgotten.

"Last week," Rodney began, "Jason called me and told me he'd bought a book that he wanted me to take a look at. Naturally I agreed. As you may be aware my, um, occupational situation isn't stellar these days." He chuckled briefly in a self-deprecating manner.

Gus rested a hand on his arm, sympathy visible on his expressive face. Niall admired his boyfriend more every day. "Don't worry, Rod. Something will come along. In the meantime, if you ever need anything...."

Rodney patted Gus's hand in fatherly way. "You're a good man, Gus." Perhaps he was prompted by Gus's empathy, but in any case, Rodney seemed fully invested now in disclosing what he knew. "I have no knowledge of when or how Jason procured the book. He gave it to me at his house last week."

"Can we see it?" Gus asked enthusiastically.

Rodney fidgeted in discomfort, bowing his head in shame. "I... I can't. It's been stolen. Two days ago, I returned home from the hospital. I'd been too far from the blast to sustain any real injuries, so I felt confident enough to go home."

"You found the place in this disarray?" Niall asked.

"Oh, no, no." Rodney shook his head. "Everything was fine. The book was where I'd left it. The mess you saw, that happened yesterday. I left the book in my safe."

"We didn't see a safe," Hughes cut in, his professional eye sharp as ever.

"It's not in my study, no, but in my bedroom. I might not hear if someone came into the study at night, but I'd certainly wake up to someone in my bedroom." Rodney nodded to himself, as if to confirm his reasoning for the safe's placement. "In addition to Jason's book, I keep many valuable things there." A sudden wave of depression gave him a haunted look. "Yesterday I went to the Seattle Central Library to do some research, and I took my notes with me. I spent most of the day there. When I returned, my study was a mess and the safe upstairs cracked open. The book was gone."

Gus squeezed his arm comfortingly. "I may not know Jason very well, but he seems to me the kind of person who insures everything, even his gold fillings. The book must be insured. I wouldn't worry. I'm sure the police will find it."

Niall and Hughes exchanged glances. Gus's optimism was nice but not necessarily all that realistic. The truth was, stolen goods weren't always recovered, not even if the culprit was caught and found guilty. Niall decided to move the conversation along to the most important question. "What was this mysterious book anyway?"

Rodney looked at them all in turn, solemn and dead serious. "It was a *grimoire*."

"WHAT THE hell is a grimoire?" Hughes insisted, a frown marring his forehead.

Thanks to his time with Gus, Niall had a hunch about the answer, to some degree anyway, but he wisely chose to let his more expert boyfriend explain. Gus and Rodney had an established rapport.

"It's a book of magic," Gus explained. "It's a kind of a manual for ceremonial magic, how to cast spells and conduct rituals, how to create magic objects and charms, how to see into the future, and how to summon supernatural powers, such as spirits and divinities. In a general sense, all books on magic could be construed as grimoires."

"Exactly right," Rodney agreed, seeming pleased and proud with Gus's accuracy, as though they were a teacher and his most promising disciple. "The word originally described books written in Latin, which only scholars and clerics spoke. That made them magical in the eyes of the common man. As public fascination in all things occult grew during the nineteenth and twentieth centuries, the word began to be associated with only books of magic."

"In Wicca, a grimoire is known as a Book of Shadows. The phrase was invented by Gerald Gardner," Gus added.

"So, this Book of Shadows is like… like some kind of *The Wicca Code*?" Hughes offered succinctly, referring to Dan Brown's bestselling thriller *The Da Vinci Code*.

Gus chuckled and Niall smiled. "Not quite," Gus said, obviously trying not to give in to the temptation to laugh his ass off. Niall had to admit he had the same problem. "The first draft of Gerald Gardner's Book of Shadows was called *Ye Bok of Ye Art Magical*, and it borrowed from a lot of grimoire sources, like the *Key of Solomon*, and others. The draft was discovered posthumously from among his papers in the, uh… in the Museum of Witchcraft on the Isle of Man, I think. Currently it's in the possession of… of…. Damn, I can't remember."

"The Wiccan Church of Canada," Rodney filled in politely.

"Yes, well, as fascinating as that sounds," Hughes cut in, rolling his eyes, "what's so special about this particular book?"

"Yeah. Is it something Gardner himself wrote or something he just owned?" Niall had to ask since Autumnsong had suggested this was an important question. Plus, he was now intrigued himself to learn the answer.

Gus gave him a curious look but quickly looked away again. Niall wasn't ready to tackle the inquiries his boyfriend would undoubtedly soon unleash upon him. Niall's own fault since he'd decided not to inform Gus about Autumnsong's visit to the hospital ward.

Rodney frowned, apparently lost in thought. "Gardner's biography and bibliography are well known by the Wiccan and neopagan communities. It would be quite astonishing to discover something new from him."

"Astonishing but not impossible?" Niall concluded.

Rodney seemed opposed to the mere notion. He looked offended, as though Niall had put his professionalism and reputation into question. "I am a scholar, Mr. Valentine. Nothing is impossible to a scientist. That said, not all things are likely or probable." He sighed impatiently and started again, calmer. "While Gardner was an innovator to an extent, he was also a difficult person to be around in his later years, courting media attention and revealing secret aspects of Wiccan practices to outsiders. Plus, most of what he wrote were bits and pieces borrowed from other literary sources, like Margaret Murray, Aleister Crowley, Charles Godfrey Leland, and Robert Graves, just to mention a few. None of it was original except for the compilation and embellishment of material. Gardner claimed he was a Doctor of Philosophy and that there was a continuing, unbroken line of witchcraft from ancient times. Of course, that was all hogwash."

"Wiccans these days ignore the whole origins debate and focus on the beliefs," Gus cut in. "That whole topic is ripe for differences of opinion, so no one I know engages in it. It's a dry well as far as the truth is concerned."

"Indeed," Rodney agreed with a curt nod. "Plus, what Wiccans see as the Gardnerian Book of Shadows these days was radically rewritten by Doreen Valiente, who was Gardner's High Priestess, at least until their falling out."

"Oh?" It seemed despite himself Hughes was getting as interested in this as Niall was.

Rodney replied quickly. "In the 1950s, Gardner created his own version of so-called Wiccan Laws, which drastically undermined the power of the High Priestess while increasing the power of the High Priest. Also, the gender inequality placed men in the position to oust female members who were too old."

Niall scrunched his nose. Owain had taught him long ago about gender equality. There was only one difference between the genders according to Owain: men were stupid and women were crazy, but women were crazy because men were stupid. Niall had rolled his eyes back then and did so now. Nonetheless, in his world view men and women stood on the same level.

"Of course, today the Wiccan Laws are completely different," Gus said. "There is only one law, and that's the Rede." Hughes was obviously about to ask, but Gus got there first. "It's a simple rule of ethics and morality, basically stating that if it harms no one, do what you will.

There's also a karmic thing happening, but the Rede is the fundamental rule for Wiccans."

"Yes, yes," Rodney said, dismissing Gus with a wave of his hand. "There's also the Charge of the Goddess to which many Wiccans adhere. It speaks of the Great Mother mythical figure from many different religions, but also functions as a moral compass with its words, like keep your highest ideals pure and to strive for them throughout your life, not just when it's convenient."

Hughes rubbed his forehead, looking bewildered. "So, what does all that have to do with the missing book? You've seen it, Professor. Is it this... *Book of Shadows*, or grimoire, or what have you?"

"Sorry. We got a little sidetracked," Gus spoke in a hushed tone, blushing apologetically.

Rodney chuckled. "Yes, yes. Rambling is a sign of the academic mind-set."

"Modern Books of Shadows are no longer just the one for the whole coven," Gus said. "Any Wiccan or neopagan can have their own grimoire. Some traditional covens do have a single book for all coven work, but even the individual members can keep their own personal and private versions."

"Gardner kept one for his entire coven, though, right?" Niall asked. Gus and Rodney both nodded. "But it's not this missing book?"

Rodney shook his head furiously. "No, no, no. Absolutely not." He brought his hands up in a surrendering gesture and cooled off. Niall thought that for an academic, the man sure had a short fuse about some things. "Jason gave it to me for appraisal. He told me the book had once been in the possession of Gerald Gardner. But the grimoire wasn't written by him."

Gus appeared baffled. "You had the book for a couple of days. How old was it? And if Gardner didn't write it, then who did?"

Rodney puffed his chest and seemed to be about to start a long lecture. Niall cringed, hoping his instincts were wrong. "The book was bound in leather, with parchments pages. I have a doctorate in the study of books and antiquities, so a careful study of the ink used, the condition of the parchment, the binding technique, and—"

"No offense, Professor, but could you cut to the chase?" Hughes interrupted, and Niall could have kissed him.

Rodney pursed his lips in obvious dismay but nodded reluctantly. "Long story short, I determined the book originated from the sixteenth or seventeenth century." Gus gasped, and Niall started to think Autumnsong had been onto something with his intense focus on the book's origin. "But—" Rodney paused for effect, causing Niall to grind his teeth anxiously. "—the most startling discovery was *who* I believe wrote the grimoire."

"Who?" Gus asked, holding his breath. Niall was pretty sure they all were.

Rodney beamed as all focus was on him. "John Dee."

GUS LET out a shocked gasp. Niall and Hughes looked at each other in confusion. It was Niall who asked, "Who?"

Gus bubbled out information so fast Niall had a hard time following him. "John Dee was a famous adviser to Queen Elizabeth I. In addition to mastering several sciences, like mathematics, astronomy, and navigation, Dee was also a noted expert in the occult and magic. He devoted a huge portion of his life to the study of Hermetic philosophy, angel summoning, and divination. During his lifetime, he assembled one of the biggest libraries in England, if not the biggest. He even coined the phrase 'British Empire,' being the first person to use it."

Rodney nodded enthusiastically. "Yes. Dee even wrote a Hermetic book and created a new Cabalistic symbol to describe the mystical unity of all of creation."

"Okay, okay." Hughes raised his voice and put up his hands to stop everyone. "That's all really fascinating, I'm sure, but let's get back on track, shall we? So, if this Dee guy wrote this stolen grimoire, that's important how? Is this Book of Shadows worth a lot of money?"

Gus shook his head, frowning. "Gardner was the one to call his grimoire the Book of Shadows. Back in Dee's time, that phrase didn't even exist."

Hughes growled low. "Fine. Is this *grimoire* worth big bucks or not?"

Rodney scoffed in disbelief. "It would be priceless. The monetary value would be in the millions to a collector, and invaluable to scientific organizations, museums, and the like."

"Then why the hell didn't you put it in a safe place?" Hughes argued, his eyes ablaze.

Indignant, Rodney turned red-faced. "I did! I put the book in my safe. That's why I went to the library, to try to confirm my suspicions of the manuscript's origins. My appraisal was in its initial stage, so naturally

I kept the book with me to study it. And no one besides me and Jason knew I even had it."

"Okay, let's all calm down," Gus interjected in a soothing voice. "If we start arguing, we're not gonna get anywhere." He turned to Rodney, a question on his face. "You sure Jason didn't tell you anything about where or how he obtained it?"

"No. He was remarkably secretive. He's usually the one to advertise everything related to money, privilege, or simply owning something no one else has. He's the worst kind of *nouveau riche* dunce!"

Rodney snorted in a manner that might have been construed as snobbish, but Niall let it pass. After all, his own opinion of Jason was leaning toward the negative end of the spectrum too, so he couldn't really judge. Owain had told him what he'd discussed with Jason at the esbat, which wasn't all that congenial, plus Niall had been in a position to hear fragments of conversations while he was hiding in the bushes that night.

The question was what did the stolen book have to do with the bombing or the theft from the coven cashbox? They could all be totally separate crimes, even though the timing did lend itself to doubt. And Jason Upton seemed to be at the heart of it all. Jason had purchased the stolen book, perhaps by questionable means, and the bomb had detonated on his estate, exactly where the ritual circle was. His role in the minor theft, if any, was still unclear.

Rodney seemed to realize he might have come across as callous and insensitive since he added swiftly, "I don't mean Jason is a bad person, by no means. I do hope he comes through all this with his health intact and gets his life back in order."

"We all wish for that, I'm sure," Gus said with a rueful smile. Niall wanted to console him on the spot but it was the wrong time and the wrong place.

Hughes snapped his notebook closed and straightened up. "I'm gonna send a couple of officers here to take your statement about the burglary and all that you know about the stolen book. From the state of your study, would I be right in speculating they got everything related to the grimoire?"

Rodney nodded, looking miserable and defeated, slumped and heavy. "Yes. All I have are the notes I took with me to the library and the notations I made there. I'll get them for you." He stood and hurried to the kitchen for his satchel.

Niall glanced at Hughes. "Think he's good for the theft or the bombing?"

Surprisingly, Gus said nothing and gave away nothing with his blank expression.

Hughes sighed, tucking his notebook in his inside jacket pocket. "Nah. I don't think he's got the skills to make a bomb, nor do I think he'd be street-smart enough to fake a burglary. He did try to get rid of us instead of showing us the ransacked study."

Niall hummed in agreement. "I don't get those kind of vibes about him either. What's next?" He asked, but he already had a hunch.

"Jason Upton," they said in unison.

Chapter 10

THE MOMENT Niall, Gus, and Hughes entered the hospital's ground-floor reception area through the sliding doors from the parking lot, Niall's cell phone beeped. He fished it out of his jeans pocket and read the mystifying text.

"GR FL. M WC. ASAP."

Niall stared at the screen, feeling like he had to be on a candid camera reality show. He looked up and scanned his surroundings with a wary eye. The ground floor men's bathroom was just to the right of the entrance. At least, that's what he assumed the text alluded to.

He called out to Gus and Hughes. "You two go on ahead. I gotta, um, take a whiz."

Hughes grunted something, and Gus nodded to him. Then they walked off toward the elevators. Niall walked toward the men's room, slowly rushing. There was a piece of cardboard hanging by a string on the handle, saying "out of order" in block letters, and a plastic bucket and a mop beside the door.

Vigilantly, Niall glanced around, but no one was paying him any attention. Why should they? It was a busy hospital. So he quickly ducked in, closing the door behind him. His hand went to his gun in its outside belt holster.

A pretty Asian face peeked out from one of the stalls. "Valentine."

Niall let out a breath, annoyed and still guarded, but released his hold of the handgun nonetheless. "Autumnsong. What the hell? How'd you get my cell number anyway?"

Autumnsong ambled closer, swishing his narrow hips. "It was on your PI web site." He rolled his eyes, making a *duh!* sound.

Niall steeled his nerves for another irritating talk. "Okay. How'd you know I'd be here at the hospital? Are you having me followed?"

Autumnsong sighed in exaggerated boredom. "You're wasting precious time with silly questions. So, what have you learned about the book? And to save both of our patience, just tell me. You know I'm gonna find out anyway."

Niall was well aware of that fact. Autumnsong seemed to have a finger on the pulse of the town, always on top of things, especially things hidden. Which was why Niall didn't argue the matter, only rechecked fast that all the stalls were empty. "The book is a grimoire. It wasn't written by Gardner but by John Dee. Oh, and it's been stolen."

Autumnsong's hazel eyes flashed intently and then narrowed. He was obviously thinking very hard, his brain working in such overdrive Niall could practically hear the cogs turning. "John Dee. The occultist back in the sixteenth century. Tried to commune with angels." Niall was still trying to catch up, but Autumnsong pulled out his smartphone and started to tap the screen.

Niall said nothing. There was no point. Instead he focused on observing Autumnsong in detail. As usual, the young man wore a black feather boa, had heavily made-up eyes, and wore the tightest black jeans and shirt Niall had ever seen. He was skinny yet limber, like a racing hound. Niall was certain the young man wielded a great deal of unassuming power in his lithe body.

For the first time, though, Niall noticed the guy wore a silver ring on his left thumb. The ring had a stylized letter *C* on it. Niall knew Autumnsong's possible real name was Kin, of Japanese origin, as Gus had learned by accident during the Talbot murder case. Yet he had no accent, so he must have been born or gone to school in the US.

Autumnsong shoved his smartphone practically into Niall's face. "Have you seen this symbol anywhere recently?"

Niall leaned back to see the picture better. The symbol combined two images, one of a tall letter *T* and the other the letter *E* made by a serpent with a tail going around them both to form a circle. "T.E.? No, never seen that before."

"E.T.," Autumnsong corrected, frowning.

"Phone home?" Niall finished, smiling.

Autumnsong glared at him but soon refocused on the screen. "And they aren't letters, per se, but the Ouroboros serpent and the tau cross." Niall wasn't familiar with either of the terms but he saved them in his memory for future research. "If you see this symbol anywhere, be sure to contact me immediately."

Niall growled. "You know, I'm getting real tired of this cloak-and-dagger business. I want information in return."

Autumnsong snorted sarcastically. "You're smoking something real strong, Valentine. What do you think I've been doing?" He cocked his head arrogantly and hustled to the men's room door. Before Niall could ask about the symbol, Autumnsong added over his shoulder, "I've sent the symbol to your phone. Later." Then he was gone, leaving the door to slam closed.

Sighing, Niall rubbed a hand across his face. This case was getting more complicated by the minute. He walked out of the restroom and headed for the elevators. Once he got in the car, he tapped on his phone, and Autumnsong's picture was indeed there.

"Ouroboros and the tau cross," he mumbled to himself as he did an Internet search on the words.

He learned that the Ouroboros was a serpent or a dragon eating its own tail, a symbol from as far back as Ancient Egypt, signifying cyclicality. Yet, in the combined symbol, the serpent wasn't devouring its tail, merely encircling it.

The tau cross, on the other hand, was an older form of the Christian cross and also a Greek letter of the same name, tau. The symbol was associated with the Franciscan Order and signified salvation, since in Ezekiel the tau sign was marked on the foreheads of those who were to be saved in the Apocalypse.

"What about both of them together?" Niall asked himself, his whisper echoing in the empty elevator car.

His results came back with vague conspiracy theories of Christians, Jews, or Muslims ruling the world in the dark, of the Illuminati secret society, and of TV shows where symbols that looked cool and had a rich mythology of their own were brought together in odd mysteries for the heroes to solve.

Basically, it was all rubbish.

Until Niall found an obscure article in a five-year-old broadsheet with the title, "Who are the Esoteraphim?"

Niall glanced over the subheadings and main points of the article. Apparently, the ominous-sounding group derived its name from two separate terms, esotericism and teraphim. The former described hidden knowledge held by an inner circle of privileged people or esoteric religious movements, while the latter apparently referred to religious idols, ancestor figurines, or household deities, depending on the source material.

In the article the mysterious Esoteraphim were depicted as a secret society ruling from behind the throne, so to speak, having ties to governing bodies all over the world. It seemed their tendrils reached so far that the article had only been published in this single broadsheet, secured for posterity in the bowels of the Internet, while every other method of publication had been quashed.

Niall had his doubts. Secret societies, religious or otherwise, were not his specialty. To him, they were all nonsense, even the ones that might have had a grain of truth buried somewhere. Then again, just because you were a conspiracy theorist, it didn't mean they *weren't* out to get you.

Yet the most interesting part of the article was under the headline, where the name of the writer was spelled out: Sydney Keen.

"YOU WERE gone for a while," Gus commented as soon as he set eyes on Niall.

Niall harrumphed. "The restroom was out of order. Had to look for another one."

Gus and Hughes were already in Jason's hospital room waiting for him, along with Alec, Tom, and Juliette, plus a second woman Niall hadn't met yet but had seen from afar during the esbat ritual. The average-height, red-headed beauty introduced herself as Sydney Keen, the environmental journalist. She looked like something out of a fairy tale, with long, fire red curls, large emerald green eyes behind rimless glasses, and full, pouty lips. Her long legs, big boobs, and curves to contend with an hourglass were covered by simple light blue jeans, a tight light green T-shirt, and light gray sport flats, which suggested she hadn't come here to make any feminine impact but just to visit friends in a hospital.

But Niall didn't have time to ask her anything because Jason sat up in bed, his voice raspy. "Glad the mansion's okay. Cost too fucking much." The left side of his body had burns and stitched-up cuts. He glared at Niall. "Heard you were hiding in the bushes, Valentine. What use are you if you can't even stop some lowlife from blowing up my mansion?"

"How dare you to talk to him that way?" Gus raised his voice, shaking in anger. "He saved our lives, while *you* had a bomb in your garden, which led to two of our friends dying! How dare you even—"

"Gus, don't." Niall placed a hand on Gus's shoulder, pulling him near, hoping to cool him off with a soft, low voice. It worked since Gus fell silent and turned away, his face still pulled and distorted in righteous indignation. Niall didn't let go.

A tall male nurse with big black-rimmed glasses and jaw-length shaggy hair replaced the half-empty glass jug on Jason's bedside table with a new full one.

Hughes spoke into the silence in his professional, authoritative voice. "The bomb, as Goodwin said, was indeed buried under your lawn, Mr. Upton. Right at the spot where the moon ritual was held. Is there anyone who might hold a grudge against you? Anyone threaten you lately? Do you have any enemies?"

"Probably anyone who's ever met him," Gus murmured under his breath, crossing his arms over his chest, clearly still sullen.

"I object," Alec said out of the blue, his pretty face torn up in anguish. "Jason is a good man, and he'd never—"

"I practically shit green," Jason interrupted, again cutting off Alec like he wasn't even there. Alec's face shuttered closed. "Of course I've made my share of enemies. That comes as a balancer with making money. But no one's threatened to blow me up, Detective. However, I did inform most of my neighbors in Bellevue about the esbat, so they could prepare for chanting, dancing, moderate nudity, and whatever else we decided to do. Abrams next door, for example, doesn't like any loud outdoor activities after 10:00 p.m. He's an old fuddy-duddy."

"We've checked him out, Mr. Upton," Hughes reported. "Apart from his irritation over your wild parties at all hours, not all of them Wiccan in nature, he's got no beef with you."

Jason coughed, and reached for a glass of water on the bedside table. Alec tried to help, but Jason waved him off. Alec had an expressive face, and his breaking heart was easily visible.

After consuming the water, Jason glared at them all as though they were the culprits. "If I wanted to blow someone up, I wouldn't do it at my nine-million-dollar estate!" He coughed, his voice becoming hoarser with every sentence, and he drank some more. Jason breathed heavily and his skin, where it wasn't burned, was turning pinkish. With his other hand, he rubbed his temple like he had a headache. From Niall's perspective, Jason gave everyone *else* a headache.

"Did you hire a Mr. Gil van Es to hold a séance after the moon ritual?" Hughes asked.

Jason inhaled and exhaled several times, nodding, his face a mask of vexation. "Yes, yes, yes. He's an excellent medium. He was recommended to me."

"What about your recently acquired grimoire?" Niall asked. The tactic of changing the subject all of a sudden was a useful one because it almost always threw suspects for a loop.

Jason's eyes widened as he shot a nervous look at Niall. "W-what do you know about that?"

"Mr. van Es mentioned a special book you intended for the séance," Niall answered, not elaborating since Jason was needed to fill in the blanks. And they had a lot of blanks.

Jason blinked but relaxed a little. "Ah, yes, well, that." Then he seemed to recall what Niall had called the book. A grimoire. That could not have been a lucky guess, and Niall could see the exact moment when Jason caught on. He licked his dry lips, grabbed the water glass, and drank it down till the glass was empty. "It's a special book. One of a kind. Got it dirt cheap." He tried to wink, but the gesture turned into a grimace as he shifted on the bed, appearing restless and anxious.

"Where did you acquire it?" Niall continued to press.

Jason grabbed his stomach and appeared ill. But he still managed to grumble, "None of your business. Unless the book somehow caused the explosion, it has no bearing in this case." He swayed a bit, back and forth, and he seemed to have trouble focusing. He reached for the water jug, but his hand slipped on the handle, landing limp on his lap with a thud. If it hadn't been for Alec's quick reflexes, the jug would have fallen and shattered on the floor. "What...?" His eyes strayed around the room, as though he couldn't see, and then he doubled over, groaned in agony, and threw up on the bedcover.

"Nurse!" Hughes called out.

By then Jason was moaning loudly, his skin reddening, and he spewed more vomit all over. "I'm burning.... It hurts...," he mumbled. His eyes rolled back in his head, and he appeared to fall unconscious. But his body convulsed so hard the bed shook.

An alarmed Alec tried to stop Jason from flailing about, but Owain drew him back. An army of nurses and doctors took his place, bustling about, giving snap commands, and taking swift actions. Niall watched, holding Gus, feeling helpless and confused. The only things he understood from the cacophony going on were respiratory failure and too slow a heart rate, neither boding well.

Then one of the nurses ushered them all out of the room and drew the curtains in front of what was happening. That surely was bound to be bad news. Yet another nurse waved harshly toward the waiting area, to which the group eventually migrated, defeated. Alec was crying quietly, with Tom holding him in his arms, whispering softly in his ear. Juliette and Sydney immediately sank into the uncomfortable chairs, both devastated and in shock, if their numb staring was any clue.

One by one, the others all found a place to sit, and silently they waited for an outcome.

Twenty minutes later a doctor came into the waiting room. One look at his grim face, and it was clear the news wasn't going to be good or even encouraging. He sighed ruefully. "I'm sorry. We did everything we could." He locked gazes with Hughes. "Detective, may I speak with you for a moment in private?" After Hughes nodded, the two of them moved aside to converse in hushed voices.

Alec cried hardest, hiccupping and trembling like a leaf. Tom tried to console him but seemed unsuccessful. Niall watched them and remembered seeing during the night of the esbat how Tom had surreptitiously glanced at Alec on several occasions. His longing gaze then and mournful appearance now hinted to Niall the depth of Tom's feelings for the younger man.

Hughes waved Niall over. Once Niall checked Gus was okay, or as okay as one could be under the circumstances, sitting next to Juliette and comforting her, Niall joined Hughes. Right away Hughes said in a low tone, "Jason's death wasn't from any kind of complication from his injuries in the blast. He was poisoned."

Niall's mind went blank. Too much had happened in a short time. He tried to wrap his brain around the news but struggled. "P-poisoned? How?"

The doctor threaded a hand through his hair, peeved. "I said it *might* be poison. When I smelled his breath, or his mouth to be precise, there was a distinct odor of bitter almonds. We're conducting tests to determine if it indeed was potassium cyanide. In the meantime, I thought the police should be informed of the possibility."

"You should test the water jug as well," Niall commented. "Water was the only thing he ingested as far as we saw, and he'd probably drunk down several glasses before we got here."

"Yeah. And close down the hospital. I'm calling for backup to track down every doctor, nurse, patient, and visitor in the hospital, to secure the premises and exits, and to view all the security feeds for leads on the perp. Better safe than sorry." Hughes took out his cell phone and punched in a number, glancing briefly at the doctor while he worked. "If it turns out the poison is cyanide, the perp could still be in the building. The stuff works pretty fast, doesn't it?"

The doctor nodded. "Yes. If inhaled, lungs stop working almost instantaneously. If ingested, depending on the stomach contents, complications resulting in death can take anywhere from a few minutes to as much as twenty-five minutes. No more. And considering we were unable to revive him, that suggests the concentration of potassium cyanide in his system had to be high. I'll arrange for a lockdown immediately." He nodded to them both and rushed off.

Niall closed his eyes, feeling the hot pressure there tightening, and tried to organize his thoughts. "Unless Jason poisoned himself, which seems unlikely at this point, someone close to him did this."

Hughes nodded. "Like the bombing with a low-range remote control. Dammit."

Suddenly Autumnsong's words sprung to Niall's mind. He showed the E.T. symbol on his phone to Hughes. "Have you seen this recently on anyone involved in this case? A patch on clothing, a tattoo, or a piece of jewelry?" Hughes committed the picture to memory with intense staring but shook his head. "If you do, let me know right away," Niall said.

"What is that?"

Niall startled when Gus spoke behind his back. "Huh?"

"That." Gus pointed at the E.T. symbol on the phone screen. "I've seen it." He looked at the closed door to Jason's room. "I saw it that night, before the esbat when we were talking. Jason had on a black signet ring with that symbol."

Niall's eyes followed where Gus was pointing. Jason belonged to this Esoteraphim group that may or may not rule from behind the scenes?

As soon as that notion hit his brain dead-on, he recalled another person he needed to talk to about this exact subject.

But when he glanced at the chair Sydney Keen had occupied, it was now empty.

Chapter 11

"Is Hughes mad at us?" Gus asked from the doorway to his bedroom.

Niall already sat in bed, reading a newspaper, with only the top of his head visible. To Gus, he looked like he belonged there, in Gus's house, in his bed, in his life.

Niall looked up as Gus spoke. "Nah. He knows better than to dwell. He's got a BOLO out on Sydney Keen. The police will track her down for questioning. If not, I'm sure she'll turn up some other way. In any case, the cops recovered the signet ring from Jason's belongings in the hospital, so that part was confirmed. We'll see how this plays out."

Gus was barely listening. Niall was tucked under the covers. Gus knew he only wore boxer briefs to bed, nothing more. Behind the newspaper barrier a wide, muscular, hairy chest was just waiting for Gus to explore.

He snuck back into the bathroom, placed his wet towel on the wall radiator, and then made his way to the bed, his skin smelling of jasmine and ylang-ylang, and his mouth minty fresh. Niall was warm against him as Gus sat up against the headboard, his right side pressing onto Niall.

He watched Niall quietly for a moment. "You're squinting. Why don't you get reading glasses?"

Niall grimaced and growled at once, his tightening grip making the newspaper rustle and wrinkle. "'Cause I don't need any, that's why."

Well, that was a touchy subject. Then again, in present-day society aging seemed to be a problem for everyone, all genders included. "Okay. Sorry I asked."

Niall relaxed again, even looked a bit sheepish. "It's fine."

Gus kept his gaze on Niall. They'd only known each other for two and a half months. They cared for and loved each other and had even said the words. Gus still kept wondering if Niall would be living with him now if Gus hadn't been in an explosion.

After Gus was discharged from the hospital, Niall had already, in one day, moved in to, quote, look after Gus's health and well-being for the time being, unquote. How long was this temporal term, for the time being? A couple of days, a week or so, more than a month, indeterminate?

The trouble was, Gus was getting used to seeing Niall all the time. They went out on dates, now they lived under the same roof (at the moment); they even worked cases together on occasion. They'd become a fixture in each other's lives.

Was that the reason they were now sitting in bed, side by side, not having sex? Were they getting too comfortable, becoming domestic partners? Gus shivered at the notion that the rest of their days together would consist of this: sleeping in the same bed—but not sharing that feral passion, that wild abandon, that demanded they tear one another's clothes off, get naked, and satisfy their primal, animalistic urges, sometimes twice or thrice in one night?

Gus had been in relationships before, but he'd never gotten to the moving-in part. His past boyfriends had hang-ups about his spirituality, his shop, his reputation, his attitude, his... whatever. And Gus was no better, having dismissed boyfriends for the simplest excuses.

Niall was different, inconceivable to ignore, impossible to cut loose.

The reality of a relationship never matched imaginary scenarios. Perhaps this, lying in bed together, talking and not fucking, was what relationships turned out to be. An arrangement of comfort, companionship, and the warmth of another's touch, though not sexual.

It sounded nice. But Gus wasn't sure if this was what he wanted.

But... he did want Niall.

Gus tried for a conciliatory tone to ensure Niall would keep including him in the case. "You know, I'm all better now, my ankle and my head."

Niall kept his eyes on the newspaper but grunted a quick acknowledgment. "That your subtle way of telling me to get my lazy bones moving, pack up my shit, and skedaddle?"

"No, of course not!" Gus felt a horrible cold weight pressing on his chest at the mere thought of Niall leaving him for good. Then he saw how the corners of Niall's lips turned up. "You asshole. That wasn't nice at all."

Niall chuckled and nudged Gus with his shoulder. "Sorry. Guess I forgot you're the wicked witch of the great Northwest."

Gus sat up straighter, pissed off. "I am *not* a wicked witch."

Niall chuckled some more. "Okay. Fine." With a whisper, he added, "Glinda."

Gus's first instinct was to roll on top of Niall and show him who was boss. But then he got a better idea. "You know, I did a *Wizard of Oz* high-school play in my senior year, and I *did* play Glinda, dressed in a long pink tutu, corset, and stockings, with a glittery golden crown."

That did catch Niall's attention, and he faced Gus and quirked an eyebrow. "Huh. That must've made you popular."

Gus chuckled, since it was his turn. "Well, it did—with a certain someone."

Niall's eyes sparked and his grin widened. "Is that right? Gonna tell me?"

Gus lifted his chin defiantly. "I don't kiss and tell."

Niall had a dangerous, mischievous gleam in his eyes. "Bet I could make you tell me." Gus glared at him, warning him off. Niall merely laughed in response; not much intimidated him. "You'll tell me if and when you feel it's right." His gaze was predatory, hungry. Gus felt like a meal for a meat-eating beast. He liked it.

"Niall, I have to ask you something," he started, hesitant.

"Wait." Niall rolled up the newspaper and let it drop on the floor beside the bed. Niall appeared worried now, frowning and fidgeting as if he were nervous, which made no sense. "If you're gonna ask what I think, and hope, you're gonna ask me, I need to tell you something first. It might… change your mind."

Gus felt a chill running up and down his spine to such an extent he got goose bumps. He waited for Niall to speak, fear lodged in his throat like a tangible lump.

Niall cleared his throat, looking decidedly nervous. In Gus's opinion that didn't bode well. "I've met with Autumnsong."

Gus gasped, his eyes going round in surprise. That definitely hadn't been what he'd expected. He'd feared Niall would tell him he wasn't exclusive, didn't want it, and that he had slept with some other man while Gus had been in the hospital, or before, maybe.

"He was at the hospital after the explosion," Niall continued, rubbing the back of his neck anxiously. "He asked about the psychic, laughing at his name, and then asked about your condition. According to him, interested parties don't wanna see you get in harm's way."

Autumnsong showing concern over Gus's well-being? The thought seemed mad. Last time they'd crossed paths, Autumnsong had helped solve the case with a hint, but also stood by and done nothing when Niall's and Gus's lives were in danger. Neither Gus nor Niall knew on whose team the guy played, good or bad.

"In any case," Niall went on, apparently encouraged to do so because of Gus's silence. "He was the one who suggested the origin of the stolen grimoire was important. Whether Gardner wrote it or just owned it."

Gus recalled finding that question curious when Niall had asked Rodney about it, but he hadn't acted on the instinct. The most important question now was whether Autumnsong had told the truth or lied. Finding an answer to that mystery would tell them if they could trust the young man's meddling advice.

"He was also at the hospital when the three of us went there to question Jason," Niall said, frowning now, his eyes glazed over as if reliving the incident. "When I went looking for the men's room. I told him the book was a grimoire, written by John Dee, and that it was stolen. He in turn showed me the symbol and made me swear I'd inform him as soon as I saw it."

"And have you?" Gus cut in, feeling off-kilter, but his tone was cold and impersonal. "Kept him in the loop?"

Niall shook his head. "Jason was poisoned, and Hughes took over, so I'd wager our new best friend Autumnsong already knows about Jason's signet ring."

Gus bristled. "And while you were cozying up with him, did it occur to you that he might be responsible for the explosion, the ransacked houses, or Jason's death? Or all of them?"

Niall looked away, his jaw set tight. Guess that was an answer in itself.

The old Gus would have fled the bedroom and sought solitary contemplation in one of his Zen places, like his ritual room or the bathroom. He would have run away and left Niall to deal with his departure on his own. In short, Gus would have behaved like a child. He'd sworn to himself he'd change that habit and conduct himself in an adult manner.

Still, the secrets Niall had kept hurt Gus, somewhere in the general area of his heart. A pulse of disappointment, anger, and pain spread through him, threatening to overwhelm his better nature.

When Niall spoke, his voice was soft and beaten. "Want me to go back to my place?" He sat straight up in bed, very still, like he was waiting for the command to abandon his post and vacate the premises.

Gus wasn't ready to let Niall go or off the hook. "I thought we agreed not to have any secrets between us. Not something major, anyway."

Niall nodded slowly, slumping a bit, staring at his hands and fidgeting fingers. "Yeah, we kinda did. I know it's no excuse but… the first time I saw him, back in the hospital after I'd left your side, I assumed… I was so sure that he… that he was responsible. I threatened to kill him."

That gave Gus pause in more ways than one, and he couldn't stop the horrified gasp from escaping. "Niall…."

But Niall shook his head and raised a hand, just to make Gus stop speaking. "I didn't want you to know about that side of me. The kind of person I was. In the Army, during the war. I'm not like that anymore. Or at least I didn't think I was. Not until I saw him there." He kept looking everywhere else but at Gus, shaking his head. "Every protective instinct I had fired up. I almost lost control. I saw it in my head, you know, beating him to a pulp." He swallowed hard, Gus saw his Adam's apple jump, and he blinked furiously. "If he had done it, almost killed you… I would've killed him. Right then and there. I wouldn't have thought twice, wouldn't have felt remorse."

Gus could barely breathe. His body shook and he felt sweaty and chilled at once. He watched as Niall blinked away moisture from his eyes, turning his face away from Gus. "Niall," he whispered. Carefully he placed his hand over Niall's. Niall jumped, startled. With slow deliberation Gus interlaced their fingers—and Niall let him.

Niall bowed his head as if defeated, sagging under a heavy weight. "I never wanted you to know… that monster I could be. The kind I had been." His voice went hoarse, and he licked his dry lips. "I never wanted those two worlds to collide. That's why I don't talk about that with you, or with anyone, really."

Gus leaned closer. A subdued, bereft Niall was something that tore at his heartstrings, and he realized Niall needed him. He needed Gus to show him who he really was.

"Niall? You're the best man, the best person, I've ever known. You're good. Not evil, not a monster. I love you." He kissed Niall's cheek tenderly, trying to coax the strength of will back into the man Gus knew in his heart and soul Niall could be. The man he *was*—with or without his past and his haunting memories.

"You learned to kill in the Army." Niall went stone-cold rigid, but Gus braved on. "But you also learned to protect, to care, to have values and morals, to show kindness, to fall in love. All that makes that part of your life meaningful. It matters."

Niall let out a weak, wet, bitter chuckle. "I thought you didn't believe in killing under any circumstances."

Gus shifted closer to Niall so he was practically on top of him. "Life is complex. After everything we've been through, I've learned better than to judge things I haven't experienced. I may have some prejudices about Satanism and Christianity I'd like to get rid of, but at least acknowledging their existence is the first step." Gus rested his head against Niall's, relishing the warmth of his skin. "I can't promise you'll get over your past, your memories, the haunted way it makes you feel. But... I can promise I'll be here, right beside you, through thick and thin."

So slowly Gus more felt than saw it, Niall sat up a little straighter. He was listening, and that inspired confidence.

Niall finally faced Gus, locking their gazes. His eyes glimmered with unshed tears, and he trembled. "You mean that?"

Gus smiled tentatively, hoping the gesture instilled Niall with renewed faith and trust in himself. "Just try and ditch me, partner."

Niall chuckled for a second or two. He brushed his rough hand over Gus's cheek, the touch light as a feather. "You mean more to me than anyone, Gus."

This time it was Gus blinking back tears and letting out sniffling giggles. "Yeah?"

"Yeah." Niall leaned in and kissed him. His stubble burned a bit, but Gus didn't care. When Niall pulled back, he stared into Gus's eyes for a long time, as if assessing and memorizing everything that had happened. "I hope you feel you can still trust me. And count on me."

Gus snickered. "I can and I do." He brushed their noses together. "Autumnsong is an unpredictable variable in this equation. That said... I can't bring myself to believe he'd try to blow up anyone. That just feels too, I don't know, direct for him."

Niall nodded in agreement. "Yeah. He's more clandestine than that. And...." His eyes flashed intently. "I know this sounds weird, but I think he was actually concerned for you."

Gus frowned, weirded out. "I don't get that. I barely know the guy. In fact, I've come to believe I don't know anything at all about him, not with any degree of certainty."

Niall shrugged. "Still… you think he's lying about the importance of that symbol?"

Gus paused, pensive. "Depends. What did he say about it?"

Niall let out a disgusted, impatient scoff. "Nothing. That's no surprise. However, I did a little Internet sleuthing, and I found a secret society, called the Esoteraphim, who apparently rule the world from behind the scenes."

Gus felt a wave of disbelief wash over him, and he cringed as a result. "That sounds… kinda farfetched."

Niall agreed with a grunt. He lifted his arm and tucked Gus closer. Gus felt cherished, which was a novel emotion and a state of being he'd never associated with any man he'd been in a relationship with. "It does. Then again…. Jason did have a signet ring with that emblem on it. Makes me question a lot of things." After a brief moment of silence, he chuckled unexpectedly and kissed Gus's temple, ruffling his hair. "But not what I have with you."

Gus smiled so widely he worried his face might split. The cold weight lifted from his heart and a warm levity filled in, giving his love wings instead of chains. "Niall? Wanna move in with me?" He held his breath, waiting for a reaction, stopping everything to listen, to feel, to seek out the tiniest hint of what Niall felt about the proposition.

Gus didn't have to wait long. Niall started laughing, and he hugged Gus so tightly he almost couldn't take another breath at all. "Is that what you were gonna ask me before I told you about Autumnsong?" Niall shifted so he could flip Gus onto his back and straddle his hips to lie on top of him. A light of love glowed in his eyes, and he too was grinning from ear to ear. "Yes. Yes, of course. Yeah, I'll move in with you. I mean, shit, most of my stuff is already here!"

Niall kissed Gus deeply, his tongue sliding in and entangling with Gus's. For a while, that was all they did, and it was good. When they finally pulled apart, both men were breathless and their cocks hot, hard, and heavy in their tenting underwear.

"Gus? You sure?" Niall's earnest look, the question in his eyes, the hint of doubt still present, told Gus everything he needed to know. Gus nodded firmly. Niall nodded back, his look solemn. "I've been thinking about it too. Us moving in together. I know it may be too soon, after only a few months. But I… I wanna live with you, see you in our bed when I wake up, hold you close when I go to sleep."

"Me too," Gus confessed, his voice cracking. "I want that too."

Niall remained serious. "I've never lived with anyone before. I may not know how to do this. I may make mistakes."

Gus kissed Niall quickly, a mere brush of lips. "No matter what two people are like together, they can still make mistakes. We've already had ups and downs. If we can talk about stuff and not keep secrets, I think we're gonna be okay."

Finally Niall started smiling, shining with happiness. "Okay. Okay." He kept nodding a couple of times, as if assuring himself this was really happening. Gus admitted he felt the same, as though they were already on the same wavelength.

Dating someone didn't amply prepare one for living together under the same roof. Routines and habits would require compromises when before there'd only been one making the decisions. And real life, everyday mundane things, could make or break a relationship. Romancing and a rich sex life might take a backseat for a while to smooth out the rough edges of clashing conventions and inflexible personalities.

"You could say no," Gus offered in earnest, giving Niall a way out from his vow. "Or if you need more time to really think it over. I mean, it's a big life change."

Niall shook his head, his smile one of contentment. "What I just agreed to, I'd feel and do the same a week from now, or a month, or six months from now. Gus, take my word for it. I'm totally onboard. Let's move in together."

Gus hugged Niall, who let his weight come down on Gus's slightly slenderer figure. "I was worried you'd say no."

Niall snorted. "What man in their right mind would say no to you?"

Gus chuckled, feeling light and carefree. "It's happened. Once or twice." He leaned back on the pillow and cupped Niall's face tenderly. "Now there's only one thing to decide: your place or mine?"

Niall grinned. "Actually, there's *three* things to decide. But I'll take one off your mind right now. Your place. Even if it is all the way here in Tacoma. But Seattle's not that far away. And you've got your shop downstairs, and my place is spartan, not a real home. Just a place I go to crash. Here… this feels like… like home." His cheeks pinked upon saying that.

Gus fell deeper in love with Niall. "What are the other two things?"

Niall got a serious look. "I wanna be exclusive with you."

Gus swallowed hard, but he had no doubts. "Yeah. Just the two of us. No one else." Niall smiled happily, and Gus had to kiss him. When he pulled back, breathless and aroused, he asked, "What's the last thing?"

This time Niall's grin was downright devilish, and his white teeth gleamed in the dim lighting. "In what position and in how many ways are we going to christen this bedroom tonight to celebrate our first decision as a bona fide couple?"

Giggling like mad, Gus wrapped his arms around Niall's shoulders and his legs around his thighs and buttocks. "Since *you're* moving *in*, I think the answer is self-evident, don't you?"

After some tongue-dueling and heavy petting, Niall fucked Gus through the mattress.

Twice.

Chapter 12

THOUGH NIALL hadn't moved in with Gus yet—as they'd just decided last night—a lot of his belongings had already migrated to Gus's place. Gus had made a note of that last evening on his way to bed. The bathroom hosted Niall's shaving kit, his favorite soap and sponge, a toothbrush, plus two tubes of lube and an unopened box of condoms.

Waking up next to a man he loved was not a novelty for Gus. He'd been in love before. But Niall felt like a permanent fixture already, right at home in Gus's bed. Gus shifted carefully to be able to lie on his side and watch Niall asleep.

Niall always had his stubble, even five minutes after he'd shaved. It cast an enduring shadow on his jaw, lower cheeks, and neck. Gus brushed his fingertips over the scratchy surface, smiling like a goofball. When Gus traced the shape and fullness of Niall's thin, masculine, slightly pouty lips, Niall made a snuffling sound, stirring a bit.

Gus bit his lower lip to stop himself from giggling or saying something to wake Niall up. Yesterday had been a long day. Niall needed to get some sleep.

Yawning, Gus blinked the tears of morning dew from his eyes. He should have gotten more rest too, but his head refused to shut down after waking up to admire his dreaming lover.

Dawn colored the white drapes on the eastern-facing windows with an orange glow. It was early still, maybe half past five or so. Birds sang outside and the low hum of traffic was ever-present, so he must have left a window open a crack on the north side of the house.

Deciding to go and greet the morning, Gus started to slide out of bed, shifting under the covers furtively. Before he'd gotten anywhere, though, a hot hand with rough skin landed on his belly, caressing a bit.

"Mmm, Gus?" Niall's voice was muffled by drowsiness and pillows. "Where you off to?" The hand slipped lower to grip Gus's waist and tugged him closer. "We gonna have a mutually spectacular morning?"

Gus chuckled. "I don't think you're up for any frolicking in the sheets."

Niall grunted. "Put your hand lower and find out."

Gus touched Niall's hairy chest, feeling the muscles ripple and hairs catch. He stroked downward, petting and fondling on his way and making Niall squirm and giggle, ticklish as he was at times. Gus cupped Niall's morning wood as it rose to say hello. He fisted the growing cock and tugged at it slowly, as it was only half-hard.

"Mmm, yeah," Niall mumbled, and part of a face emerged from the soft depths of the pillow. So did a peek of a grin. "Now this is what I call a great morning."

"I'm surprised you have any stamina left after last night," Gus commented. Though Niall had morning breath, Gus kissed him anyway. After a slow, leisurely tongue-twister, only their natural flavors remained.

Niall started to tighten his hold, but Gus wiggled away, letting go of Niall's dick. "Hey, what gives?" Niall frowned, exaggerating his grumpy, pouty look.

Gus chuckled and got out of bed. "Need coffee."

Niall grouched. "Get it later. Let's—"

"Need. Coffee." Gus repeated the words with emphasis.

Niall moaned unhappily. "Man, that's just brutal." He buried his face under a pillow and continued muttering in dissatisfaction.

"Gimme five minutes, and I'm all yours," Gus said, trying to placate his frisky lover.

Whatever Niall said got lost in the sheets.

Gus rolled his eyes, caught a pair of underwear from the chair by the bedside table, and hurried to the kitchen before Niall got any more bright ideas *and* decided to act on them. He filled the coffee machine with water and grounds and left it to bubble and percolate on its own as he ambled toward the french doors.

He opened them wide and inhaled the fresh morning air. From his second-story balcony, Gus could see the manicured lawns, tiny copses of trees, and small pond in Point Defiance Park. He could faintly hear the quacking of ducks and the lapping of waves on the tiny, rocky, tree-covered island in the middle of the pond—though he might have been imagining those sounds since he'd been there often for recreation and meditation, as well as jogging and visiting the zoo. The sundry flocks of birds singing in the various moss- and fern-covered pine trees, birches, cedars, firs, maples, and oaks were louder than the noises in Gus's imagination.

The park was free and open to the public from dawn till dusk, even at this early hour, though car traffic was only allowed during the day and only on weekdays. Soon the trails and footpaths would fill up with locals and tourists alike, a lot of them on foot or on bicycles. Gus leaned on the railing, enjoying the lush sight of the verdant park. The lawns led downhill from the street to the park, and Gus remembered sitting on the gently sloping hillside last summer, catching rays and relaxing on his days off. He couldn't help wondering at how much his life had changed in the past year, in the past three months.

He smiled to himself, knowing there was a hot guy in bed waiting for him.

Suddenly he heard a voice calling to him from beneath the balcony.

Had his eyes bugged out any farther, they would have popped out of their sockets.

"THE COFFEE done yet?" Niall hollered from the bed, refusing to get out from under the skin-warmed covers. He hugged them closer, gently stroking his dick, enjoying the morning, waiting for his lover to come back and jumpstart the day in the best way a man could think of. No answer came from the kitchen. "Hey, wicked witch. You hear me? Come on already, lazyass. I got me an engine that needs to—"

Gus walked in, his appearance stern. He yanked on a T-shirt and a pair of sweats, and tossed Niall's jeans, T-shirt, and boxer briefs on the bed. "You better get up. And no, that's not a pun. We have a visitor."

While inwardly Niall groaned in frustration at not getting his usual morning sex fix, the grave look on Gus's face told him this situation was no joke. He got dressed quickly, shoving his thankfully flagging dick inside his jeans. He swore he'd get to have Gus today, even if the visitor was the President of the United States.

Gus had vamoosed again. Niall heard him puttering around in the kitchen, heralded by the sloshing of coffee. The bitter scent would soon fill the house. At least there was that comfort.

Barefoot, Niall sauntered into the kitchen—and stopped dead in his tracks to find a posh red-headed beauty sitting at the island counter, sipping coffee.

"Here's your coffee," Gus said, pushing Niall's cup toward him, his face a warning.

Niall nodded his swift thanks but beyond that focused entirely on Sydney Keen, sitting in their kitchen. His hand went for his gun belt, but the damn thing wasn't on him. Gritting his teeth over his complacency and carelessness, he stared Sydney down. "You're a wanted woman, Ms. Keen."

Behind her rimless glasses, Sydney lowered her eyelids in silent acknowledgment of the truth. "I didn't poison Jason. I swear it's the truth."

Cautiously, Niall ambled to the counter, gulped a swig of his coffee, and asked, "Then why did you run?"

Sydney shook her head, frowning in a defensive manner. "I didn't. I just left." Sighing, she added, "Well, I did kind of run. I figured something was amiss with Jason's demise. It sure as hell didn't look like a natural death to me. I heard later through the grapevine that he was poisoned, and since I'd left, I figured the cops would come looking for me."

Niall considered Sydney's denial of guilt. Surreptitiously, he scanned her formfitting trouser suit and concluded she carried no concealed weapons, at least not firearms. Because of that he let down a fraction of his guard in order to keep an open mind. "If you want me to believe you, Ms. Keen, tell me everything. Leave nothing out."

Sydney lowered her gaze to the fake marble counter, but Niall was positive she looked right through it. "This whole thing started way back when. I knew I wanted to be a reporter in high school. I was naïve, seeing the world in black and white, as though everyone was simply either good or bad and it was up to me to expose which was their true nature."

"Most people start out that way. There's nothing wrong with innocence," Gus said, his tone empathetic.

As much as Niall appreciated this quality in Gus, right now it was a hindrance. With a look he tried to encourage Gus not to interrupt again, but Gus stared at Sydney with an understanding gaze. Niall sighed and let it go.

Sydney let out a small, dry chuckle. "In college I soon learned naïveté was not a good quality to bring into journalism. I learned to be suspicious, cold-hearted, and ambitious." For a brief moment, her fragile regrets showed, and Niall made a mental note of it.

"When I was twenty-three," she continued, "I worked at a small, low-circulation Seattle newspaper and was given an assignment to do a human-interest piece on a local Wiccan high priestess. I hated those stupid assignments that were worth nothing, journalistically speaking." She smiled, and a beautiful woman appeared from behind the cynicism. "That high priestess, of course, was Juliette."

Gus chuckled. "I bet that went well." Niall suspected Gus already knew this tale.

Sydney laughed. "She wouldn't let me off easily, not in any sense. She questioned me and my questions, my goals, my job, my faith. Everything. Because of her, I wrote the best human-interest story ever. And… I found a spirituality that opened the door within me to show kindness, compassion, and love, to be one with the world in a positive way. My job sure had taught me to do the exact opposite, to see only doubts, fears, hates, and darkness. Less than a year later, I discovered environmental journalism. It fit my newfound ethics perfectly, so I never looked back. It was the best decision I've ever made."

"No more sleazy exposés, no more digging for dirt, no more compromising your moral backbone. Good choice." Gus's compliment made Sydney's eyes glimmer, and Niall had to give it to Gus for knowing how much caring and sympathy it took to get someone to talk.

"Right." Sydney nodded to herself, but then she grew serious, as though a dark cloud had passed over the sun. "I was doing a comparative piece on the way different religions viewed nature, environmentalism, preservation, and conservation laws. The perspectives of older, more established religions were well known and offered few new insights, so I decided to focus the piece on new religious movements."

"Like Wicca," Niall commented on the sidelines.

Sydney nodded. "By then it was my faith of choice, so it was the easiest to start with. I began with life-affirming new religious movements, such as the neopagan and occult movements. But… as I dug a little deeper, I soon began hearing rumors about an apocalyptic movement called Esoteraphimism."

"Apocalyptic?" Gus cut in, frowning in bewilderment. "End of the world concepts are hardly unique in world religions. Take Ragnarok, for example. But the term apocalypse suggests a Christian-based faith."

"Yes. At first I thought it was some quaint Christian denomination I hadn't heard of before." Sydney's eagerness gave way to disquiet. "Since I didn't have enough information about that unknown sect, I left it out of my new religious movements and perspectives on nature article. But, in quiet, I continued looking into E.T. under the radar."

"When you published the piece, you did it in a broadsheet?" Niall asked, curious.

Sydney admitted it with a firm, curt nod. "I offered it to my editor in chief, but he said the piece was the worst kind of fluff, with no reliable sources, no direct evidence, no substantiated names, only rumors and hearsay. In short, he told me that it wasn't suitable for the paper and to let the story go, that nothing would ever come of it, certainly nothing worth printing in a respectable newspaper."

"But you didn't let go of it." Gus smiled a little. He appreciated relentlessness when it came to freedom of speech. Niall wasn't entirely onboard or opposed to either one. To him, freedom wasn't a catchall phrase but required more deeds than words, plus a boatload of responsibility and dedication. A democratic civil society based on laws and ethics was a good start but not easy to maintain, especially if the two came into conflict.

Sydney snorted sarcastically. "Of course not. I'm a journalist. When someone tells me to bury a case, I do the exact opposite. I continued my investigation, careful not to make too many ripples. By the time I had my story, I knew it'd be hard to get out there. No respectable press would touch it with a ten-foot pole. That's why I decided to go old school. I used the broadsheet format of historical times when differences of opinion against authority and the system required new delivery methods. I used a well-known conspiracy-theory portal online as a platform to get the piece out there, making sure it was hard to get rid of without the news breaking out into more common outlets with larger audiences."

"All those safeties in place, and you still published the article under your own name." Niall wasn't sure if that made Sydney admirable or foolish.

Sydney lifted her chin defiantly, a fire burning in her eyes. "I don't hide. The choices I made were to ensure what I'd discovered would get out there, not to guarantee my personal security. The format and platform I went with has kept it floating in cyberspace to this day." Her sharp gaze landed on Niall. "Since you brought up the subject, I imagine that's how you found out about me and E.T., and why there's a BOLO out for my capture."

"Yeah, pretty much." Sydney didn't sound judgmental, or even reproachful, about how Niall had gotten her name associated with a bombing and subsequent murder inquiry, so Niall felt it was okay to tell her the truth. Besides, Niall had more questions. "So, I take it you've become something of an expert on hidden cults and weird sects during your investigation into E.T."

Sydney shrugged, but her intense gaze betrayed her journalistic curiosity. "I guess."

"Ever come across a hidden religion or secret society carrying the symbol of a stylized letter *C*?"

Sydney cocked her head, and her eyes narrowed, which told Niall she had an inkling, if not full-blown knowledge, of what Niall was referring to. She licked her lips as if contemplating what to do, buying time. Finally she said, "I'm not certain, you understand, but… I think the symbol you described refers to a secret society called the Cabal."

"The Cabal." Niall repeated the words, tasting and memorizing them. "What do you know about them?"

"They're not a religious group, as far as I know," Sydney replied cautiously, frowning as though searching for the recollection of accurate information wasn't effortless. "I have very little on them. They weren't the focus of my investigation, but the name did come up."

"With the Esoteraphim?" Niall asked. "As an ally, a rival, or an enemy?"

Sydney shrugged. "No idea. To be honest, I barely recall hearing the group's name. I can look into it for you, if you'd like."

Niall straightened up, putting on his game face. "That'll be difficult for you since the only place you'll be going is to the police. Unless you're planning on running." He quirked an eyebrow in a silent query.

Sydney stood up, her expression fierce. "I did not run last time, and I'm not doing it this time. I might have made a strategic retreat at the time, but I'm here now, aren't I, telling you all I know?"

Niall inclined his head. "Good to know. I'll call Hughes, and we can start sorting this out. If you truly had nothing to do with Jason's death, you'll be fine."

Sydney scoffed, crossing her arms over her chest. "Yeah, right. I've got priors for demonstrations and rallies, fighting against the establishment. I know what the cops are gonna think of me. So no, I'm not expecting miracles. No one's gonna save this damsel in distress." She looked away and sat back down as if to wait for the inevitable. The stubborn jut of her chin and the light burning in her eyes spoke of a warrior who understood the world fine. Scales had fallen from her eyes long ago, it seemed.

Right then, the doorbell rang.

As Gus hurried to answer the door, Niall addressed Sydney grimly. "Criminal records do make cops nervous and wary, but the same could be said for your journalistic zeal. I'm not a cop, nor have I ever been one, and I have my doubts about you and your involvement in this mess that has left the body count at three. But I don't have the time or the desire to placate your hurt feelings. I'm looking for a murderer and a bomber, and that's got my plate pretty full."

Sydney paled, apparently mulling over Niall's words. Then she nodded, somber. "I'm sorry if I sounded like a bitch. It's just I've had run-ins with the law, and only a handful of cops have treated me with respect or given me the benefit of the doubt. You, on the other hand, have an ex-detective for a father, so I suspect your experience has been vastly different from mine." With narrowed eyes, she stopped and obviously waited for a response—of any kind.

Niall inclined his head slightly. "I get it, Ms. Keen, I do. But I'm a PI, and I am trying to find a killer and uncover the truth behind a bombing. That's all. Beyond that I've got no ulterior motives when it comes to you or any other Wiccans, including Gus."

Sydney actually grinned and chuckled then. "I seriously doubt you suspect Gus."

Niall smiled in return. "Trust me, I don't think he's not involved simply because I'm sleeping with him."

"Damn. There goes my reason for bedding you. If only I'd known that beforehand." Gus smirked as he came back to the kitchen and winked at Niall.

But Niall didn't get a chance for a smartass retort because trailing behind his boyfriend was a gloomy-looking Hughes. The second he laid his eyes on Sydney, he reached for his gun.

Niall put up his hands and stepped into the firing line. "She's here of her own free will. She's not a threat. She's gonna come with you peacefully, I swear."

If Hughes was anything like Owain, which he was, Niall knew he wouldn't appreciate someone telling him how to do his job. Reluctantly, he lowered his gun. He glared at Niall. "Don't ever do that again, Junior." His warning sounded in his tone, in his stance, and in his eyes. Niall nodded obediently, and Hughes let the matter drop. "I came here to bring news to you two knuckleheads, and here I find you harboring a fugitive."

Niall chuckled, knowing a friendly reproach when he heard it. "Yeah, Gus practically runs an underground railroad. What's the news?"

Hughes kept his eye on Sydney and moved to stand so he had a clear line of sight to her, but he still addressed Niall and Gus. "There's good news and bad news. First, Kerry awoke from her coma, and I interviewed her. The doctors warned she might suffer from temporary memory loss, and her memory of the events was indeed awfully hazy. We'll have to try again in a couple of days when she's better and cross the bridge of memory loss when we get there."

Gus let out a relieved sigh, his hand pressed to his heart. "Oh, that *is* wonderful news. I was worried she might never wake up. That can happen in comas, I think." He spoke to Hughes. "I mean I don't know her. Only what Jules told me. But I'm glad she's recovering, even if her memory isn't all that it should be."

"Me too," Sydney said, and shared an amiable, warm smile with Gus.

"Anyway," Hughes commented, a light growl to his tenor. "The other thing I came to tell you is that both Matty's and Pine Seed's places have been trashed. Every drawer turned upside down, every book opened, every paper in disarray. Computers, laptops, and external hard drives are all gone."

Niall straightened up, his wary battle instincts kicking in. "Ransacked? Like Easton's place?" When Hughes nodded, silent, Niall added, "That is suspicious." He turned to Sydney. "Did either Matty or Piney have anything to do with E.T.?"

Sydney frowned, shrugging. "Not that I know of. Their names never came up during my research into the group. I would've remembered that for sure, even though it's been a few years."

"Who's E.T.?" Hughes cut in, his demeanor revealing how much he disliked being out of the know during a case.

Niall brought Hughes up to speed with the Esoteraphim angle, Sydney's research into them, and Jason's signet ring. He kept the Cabal mystery and Autumnsong out of his briefing. There was no need to stir up more shit when Niall had no clue as to what, if anything, the Cabal had to do with this business. Fortunately, Hughes already knew Autumnsong existed from the Talbot case, so at least when they did have the talk about him, they wouldn't have to start from scratch.

When Niall stopped, Hughes rubbed his forehead and grunted in frustration. "So it's not enough that there's a bombing and a murder, now there's a secret society mixed up with this case too? Just swell. I thought you were joking about all that back at the hospital." He shook his head, inhaling and exhaling to calm himself. "Anything else I might be missing, fellas?"

Niall felt his cheeks flush at the comment. Hughes had that in common with Owain as well, the ability to make Niall feel like he'd been scolded by a parent.

Thankfully, Hughes didn't manage to start his rant, as the doorbell rang again.

"I know it's June and the sun's up and all, but this is still freaking early," Gus mumbled on his way to the door.

A fast-talking Juliette burst in, her manner frantic and her voice almost shrill. "Oh my God, Gus. You're not going to believe what happened. You have got to see this right away. I was going to take it to the police, but Owain suggested we speak to you first. Oh Gus, it's just horrible. I had no idea—"

"Jules, slow down," Gus cut in, holding her by the arms. "I can't understand you."

"Let's take this inside, shall we?" Owain, who stood on the stair landing right behind Juliette, gestured both of them inside. When they all came into the kitchen, Owain added dryly, "I see there's already a town meeting going on. Glad we didn't miss it."

Juliette didn't let anyone else talk. She shoved a wrinkled white envelope in Gus's lap, and her expression was grave and sad and fearful, all at once. "It came in the post this morning. Oh, I almost had a heart attack." Her hand came up to her chest as she spoke breathlessly.

"Now, young lady, it'll be okay," Owain said soothingly, resting his hand on the small of Juliette's back. Niall watched the motion, silent and conflicted. His father was… involved with another woman, one not Niall's mother? She'd been dead for many, many years, so it made sense for Owain to date and see new people. He was still as strong and charming as any man. Yet… the little boy inside Niall wasn't sure how to feel exactly, was perhaps a little bit… bereft and uneasy, or was it even jealousy on his mother's behalf? Was his father's dating too big a change?

While Niall was busy pondering, Gus had opened the letter. His gasp caught Niall's attention. "This is from Matty. He must have sent it before…." Gus swallowed hard, blinking.

Niall moved fast to his side and wrapped an arm around Gus's waist, subconsciously mimicking his father. "It's okay, babe. Take your time."

Gus nodded, his throat moving convulsively as he fought for control of his voice and emotions. "Matty says…." Right after reading the first line, Gus grew silent, frowning in confusion. "He says there's a PO Box in a post office, and that Juliette must be the one to open it in the event of… of his death…?"

Everyone in the room gasped in shock, frazzled by the unexpected news.

It seemed Matty had a secret.

Chapter 13

"YOU THINK Matty sent this before the esbat because he knew he was going to die?"

Niall squirmed on the driver's seat while Gus observed his discomfort. Gus had to ask, not for his own peace of mind, but because his heart refused to believe that happy, smart kid could have set off a bomb to kill them all.

"Babe, it'll do you no good getting upset over it now," Niall said, his rational tone irritating to Gus, who was desperate for answers. "We'll find out soon enough." As he spoke, he swerved to a free spot in front of the post office named in the letter.

Juliette sat in the back, stiff as a pole, holding in her hand the key to the PO Box, the one that had come with the enigmatic but unfortunately short letter. Gus touched her arm, like a fairy-tale prince awakening the sleeping princess. Juliette started but nodded in compliance and got out of the car. Hughes, Owain, and Sydney arrived in Hughes's unmarked cop car, parked right behind them, and exited the vehicle.

The six of them stood in a line on the sidewalk, staring at the post office where one part of the answer to the mystery might be found. Gus prayed with all his might that Matty hadn't confessed to the bomb strike. That discovery would send Gus into a spiral of distrust and sorrow he feared he might never get out of.

Hughes moved first, entering the post office. Juliette trailed on his heels, looking like a convict walking toward her death sentence. One by one, the others followed. No one spoke a word. The mood was positively funereal.

A tall middle-aged man with a neat beard, glasses, and wearing a postmaster's uniform stood behind the counter. There were only two other customers before the six of them, so they soon found themselves in front of the postmaster.

"Hello. My name is Frank. How may I help you, ladies and gentlemen?" Frank recited his standard greeting in a weary voice with words in rapid succession. He most likely said those words a thousand times a day.

Juliette glided forward, moving as though without her own volition. She had tears in her eyes, and Gus inched closer, holding her by the shoulders. Juliette leaned into him a bit, but somehow seemed to find some fortitude as well, for which Gus was grateful.

Clearing her throat, Juliette said, "I have a key to a PO Box."

Frank cocked his head, as though he'd heard it all before and wondered why people bothered him about it. "Yes? Something wrong with it?"

Juliette shook her head. "The box isn't mine, but I have the key—"

Frank's bored expression changed to dubious and guarded. "You shouldn't have a key that doesn't belong to you, ma'am. Interfering in other people's mail is a federal offense—"

Hughes shoved his badge to the window and gave the postmaster a hard stare. "Seattle PD. I need the name of the owner now."

Frank adjusted his glasses and leaned in to see the badge better. But he didn't look any less vigilant, even if his tone took on a slightly more reverent edge. "Do you have a warrant, sir?"

"I have the key and the current owner of said key," Hughes growled out.

"What number?" Frank asked, directing his question to Juliette.

Juliette checked the key for digits or letters. "Seventy-four?"

Frank's expression changed for the second time—to surprise. "Ah. Yes. A moment, if you please." He pulled open a drawer, rummaged inside, and picked up a sealed envelope. He tore the lid open and took out a folded piece of paper with a photo taped to it. The postmaster then said, "Upon his last visit two weeks ago to renew his PO Box for the next three months, Mr. Osborne told me that a woman matching this photo"—he showed them a color picture of Juliette laughing during a party, ritual, or festival of some kind, the pretty photo probably taken by Matty himself— "would come with his key, probably accompanied by a police detective, and that it would be okay. His visit here was recent; that's why I remember it so well."

He offered Juliette the piece of paper, which she unfolded. The writing said only "Ms. Cloud," giving them nothing else to work with.

Frank gestured toward one side of the building, where the entire wall was covered in gray PO Boxes of varying sizes. "Please, go right ahead."

As they all moved in unison, Juliette mumbled in bewilderment, "Ms. Cloud…?"

Since no one had an answer, silence reigned.

Number seventy-four was one of the large boxes. With trembling hands, Juliette unlocked the box and then quickly moved aside to let Hughes take the lead. Owain hugged her, and she slumped against him as if exhausted and relieved that the responsibility had lifted.

Hughes carried the gray metal box to a nearby table. Judging from the way he heaved and lugged the thing around, it was heavy, so clearly it wasn't empty. A loud clank heralded the box's landing, and everyone circled around the table to find out what the mystery box contained.

Hughes pulled open the lid.

Inside were an envelope and a silver tablet computer, an iPad Air 2.

For a moment, no one moved, spoke, or even breathed.

"Since you were supposed to open this, take this." Gus addressed Juliette and offered her the plain brown envelope.

With caution, she accepted it and tore open the side. Onto her palm fell a thrice-folded letter and money, both bills and coins. "Oh!" Juliette breathed. Gus counted the amount in his mind as Juliette shuffled through it, and he and Juliette reached the same conclusion simultaneously. "It's the missing money from the coven. All $317.69, present and accounted for."

Juliette's voice cracked at the end, and she looked about as miserable as a person could when the foundations of her faith in people were shaken. Gus hurried to soothe her. "Maybe Matty will explain why he stole the money. He wasn't a bad guy. What does the letter say?"

Nodding, perhaps searching for a worthy, logical excuse why someone she trusted had betrayed her so, Juliette spread the letter open and started to read. "Dear Juliette. I hope that if and when you are reading this, I will stand at your side, proving my loyalty and friendship to you. You have done more for me than you'll ever know. Please, never doubt that." Juliette stopped, her eyes misting, and both Gus and Owain comforted her with small pats.

"I can read the rest if you want," Gus offered gently.

But Juliette shook her head. "No, I can handle this." She visibly gathered herself and continued reading. "Yes, I stole the money from the coven till, but as you can see, I haven't used a dime. I'm sorry about the theft. I never meant to hurt you. But I needed to get your attention so you'd bring in someone, anyone within law enforcement, to look into the coven. I've learned there's something sinister going on among the group. Find the information I've hidden and see for yourself. Yours with perfect love and perfect trust, Matty."

Juliette wasn't the only one sniffling, but Gus at least tried to hide it behind a scratch on the nose. "Well, that's one question answered."

"And new ones keep popping up," Niall commented sarcastically. His gaze was aimed at the silver tablet in the box, and just like that, everyone else zeroed in on the same object.

Finally, Sydney let out a breath. "Are we just gonna stare at it for the rest of the day?"

Hughes coughed in annoyance, grabbed the device out of the box, and turned it around in his palm, clearly unaccustomed to using it.

Sydney snatched it out of his hands impatiently and switched it on nimbly. "What? You weren't getting anywhere with it."

Hughes snagged it right back, growling. "You're in enough trouble, missy. Here." He chucked it at Niall, who fumbled with it before catching his balance.

"Okay. Jesus." Niall rolled his eyes and watched the screen come alive. Surprisingly, there was no password requirement. Unfortunately, there seemed to be nothing in the tablet, either. The hard drive was empty. "Huh. That's weird. Nothing."

"May I?" Gus asked politely, extending his hand. Shrugging, Niall handed the iPad to him, no questions asked. Gus went through the icons available as standard but Niall had been right. None of the folders contained any information. "He's right. If there was something here, it's not here anymore."

"Shit. A dead end." Hughes wiped a hand over his bald head, frustrated.

That's when an epiphany hit Gus right smack in the brain. "Ohmygod!" He pressed the Google Chrome icon and ran a search. And there it was. "Oh, Matty *was* smart." He lifted the tablet so everyone could see the screen. "He didn't have anything on the hard drive. He backed up his files in an online data storage service—*in a cloud*!"

Juliette shouted in glee. "Oh. Ms. Cloud!"

Before Gus could see what Matty had stored in his cloud service, Hughes beckoned to Owain. "Owain, escort Ms. Keen outside. There's a patrol car coming to take her back to the station for questioning."

"*What?*" Sydney protested, surprised and vehement.

Hughes remained unrelenting. "Ms. Keen, need I remind you that you're still a suspect in Jason Upton's murder. Your presence here is unacceptable." He gestured for Owain to get a move on, and Owain gripped her arm, steering her firmly toward the post office door.

"This isn't fair! I brought you vital information, and I deserve to be present to see…." Her indignant voice drifted off as Owain guided her out of the building to the street where a patrol car had just parked.

Hughes locked gazes with Gus. "Open the cloud, Goodwin."

Gus took one last glance at Sydney being escorted into the patrol car. She was still fuming, judging from the look on her disgruntled face. Since he couldn't do anything about her being hauled away in the back of a police cruiser, Gus refocused on the tablet. The cloud Matty had set up was a trusted service. Someone he had confidence in must have shared access.

"I think you can get in here," Gus said to Juliette, handing the tablet over to her.

Her eyes glimmered with sadness and caring. With reverence, she took the iPad and opened Matty's cloud account with her own e-mail password. "I wish I'd known the full extent of Matty's faith in me," Juliette said, giving the tablet back to Gus. She sniffled. Owain, who had returned, handed her a handkerchief. Gus liked how old school Owain was, carrying handkerchiefs for grief-stricken ladies.

"I think you just learned the depth of his feelings for you, Jules," Gus said, smiling in encouragement. Juliette smiled back, grateful, and leaned a bit toward Owain.

Juliette and Owain made a handsome couple, Gus thought, grinning at the sight.

"What's stored in the cloud, then?" Hughes asked impatiently, snapping Gus's attention back on track.

"Oh, right." With Hughes checking his progress over his shoulder, Gus went through the file folders saved in the cloud. "There are folders here with headings like *assignments*, *research*, and *conclusions*. Matty was in college, so this could be just ordinary schoolwork."

"Click on one of them," Niall suggested.

"Okay." Gus clicked on the conclusions folder. Inside were subfolders for a variety of college assignments, book reports, essays, presentations, and so on.

But one of the subfolders was different. The title was only "E.T.," and Gus swallowed hard as he clicked on the folder icon. Within the folder was only a single Word document. His heart in his throat, Gus forced himself to open the file.

A sheet of paper filled the screen, with half of it covered in writing. Gus read straight from the Word document. "I, Matthew Osborne, was hired on May 12th to look into a potential sect by the name of Esoteraphim—"

"Hired by whom?" Niall asked, stepping closer to peer at the screen. Gus appreciated the support even though he suspected Niall had moved solely out of curiosity.

"Disregard the doofus and keep reading," Hughes cut in, his lips pursed as he cast Niall a reproachful glare.

"Right," Gus agreed and read on. "...a potential sect by the name of Esoteraphim, due to my excellent computer and hacking skills. Here are my findings." Gus tried to read what came after but the text composed of computer slang that meant zero to him, so he jumped ahead. "Blah blah. Here we go. I have determined that E.T. poses no threat to national security—"

"National security?" Niall, Hughes, and Owain exclaimed at the exact same time. Had the DHS hired Matty to look into a secret society? That sounded like a wild conspiracy theory. Then again, they weren't exactly short on those.

Gus ignored the sudden surprised shouts and kept reading. "...for the simple reason that there is no Esoteraphim as such. There exists no global network of opulent, influential power figures behind the scenes in regimes throughout the world—"

"I don't get it," Niall interjected, making Gus pause. "According to Autumnsong, there *is* a group with connections all over the world. Jason had a signet ring indicating membership in this faction." He shrugged, appearing utterly confused. "I just don't get it."

"You gonna let me finish?" Gus asked, unperturbed by Niall's frustration at getting his theory shot to pieces. Niall bowed theatrically, grinning, and Gus smiled back, only then returning to his reading. "Where was I? Oh, here... the world at large. What I did find was a small group (no more than twelve or thirteen at most) of relatively wealthy and moderately powerful individuals with a zealous, pseudoreligious interest in tracking down and collecting all volumes and artifacts referring to—" Gus stopped, reading the rest of the line several times to make sure he got it right. "—to methods of communication with angels." At that point he looked up and saw a sea of faces all appearing just as befuddled as he felt. "I swear that's what it says here."

"Well, that explains their interest in John Dee's grimoire," Niall said slowly, crossing his arms over his chest. "From what I heard, John Dee wanted to find a way to speak with angels and the like. It was apparently the basis of his life philosophy, or something."

"So, it's not just a Christian thing?" Hughes asked, frowning in obvious annoyance at not understanding what was going on. Gus assumed most detectives wanted to know and understand the motivations behind the acts of criminals.

"The Apocalypse is a term mostly associated with Christian faiths," Juliette said, being the authority in the field. "It appears in the Book of Revelation. But a myth of the end of time is an eschatological concept known in many religions and spiritualities throughout the world, no matter how the end presents itself. In Christian denominations, the faithful will be saved while those who aren't perish. In Eastern religions, the world ends to begin anew, a cycle of rebirth and redemption, and humans can be reborn in different forms, with no memory of their past lives. The idea of the end has fascinated the human spirit since the dawn of time, so to speak."

"That's nice," Hughes said politely, though it was clear he'd only absorbed some of what he'd heard, mostly by choice, eliminating useless data. "So, this John Dee guy wanted to chat with a bunch of angels. Why?"

"I googled him," Gus cut in. "Dee wanted to commune with angels in order to learn a universal language of creation. His aim was to show humanity the way to a much-needed unity before the end—as in the apocalypse."

"So that's why this group, which may or may not exist, wants the grimoire," Niall said, snapping his fingers. "They think this missing grimoire will give them the ability to communicate with angels."

"To do what?" Hughes asked, shaking his head. "To end the world?"

"Oh, who cares?" Gus said, frustrated. "I mean, they already have the grimoire in their possession, don't they? They ransacked Rodney's house and stole it, didn't they? So that means if they've figured out how to translate and read the book, they pretty much know how to both talk with angels *and* to end the world, doesn't it?"

Suddenly it was quiet. Sure, the low hum of people doing business in the post office was still audible. But of the five of them, no one said a thing. Gus could have screamed, chagrined at being in the dark like this, with sparse crumbs of information appearing on their path. It seemed their murderous adversaries were several steps ahead in the game.

"Why are we assuming the Esoteraphim are responsible for the grimoire getting lost when Matty tells us in his last confession that the group doesn't exist or is too small to matter in any way?" Owain asked. "If they didn't, it stands to reason someone *else* stole the book. After all, Matty's cloud had a trustee in Juliette, so would he have lied to her?"

"What else is there about the E.T. in the cloud?" Niall asked, obviously having faith in his father's expert opinion. Gus admitted he had overlooked the likelihood Matty wasn't lying, which meant E.T. didn't exist or was composed only of a handful of weirdos seeking to chat with angels.

Gus returned to the main directory. Under the *research* folder were several subfolders. Most dealt with college assignments, but one of them had the heading "E.T. members." He clicked on the icon fast, dying of curiosity. "There are twelve notepads here, all describing one of the supposed members of the E.T."

"Any names in there?" Hughes asked, his bloodhound act intensifying.

Gus checked, then sighed and shook his head. "No. Anonymous. Candidate one, two, three, and so on. Twelve in total."

"This presumed worldwide organization is in reality comprised of just twelve people, probably in the Seattle area?" Niall sounded incredulous, and Gus could relate. "What kind of notes are there? Any hint of who they might be?"

"There are no names, just numbers." Gus scrutinized the memos carefully, not wanting to miss anything important. "However… each file contains a profession, general appearance, and what looks like a psychological and economic profile."

The information wasn't encoded, and no unbreakable cipher had been used. Could it be as easy as this, Gus puzzled, compiling data blocks and matching them with the usual suspects, in this case everyone belonging to the coven? Though he loathed the notion that one of the people he knew, cared for, and trusted could be responsible for the death of three people, he was beginning to accept that possibility.

"So the real person can be deduced from the notes?" Niall concluded, hopeful.

Gus shrugged. "Maybe." As teeming with curiosity as he was, Gus handed the tablet to Hughes. "That's your department, I think. I hope they're worth something—and lead us to whoever put a bomb on Jason's estate and killed... our friends." He gulped, unable to say the names of those now-deceased friends. The words refused to emerge, and his heart hurt.

Hughes took the tablet, a respectful and approving look on his face. "Thanks. We'll do your friends justice, Goodwin. We couldn't have gotten this far without you."

As much as Gus appreciated the praise, considering how hard it was to come by from a man like Detective Hughes, he didn't feel happy, grateful, or proud of his accomplishments. What he wished for was the magical ability to turn back time.

"I'll go over the notes with you, Hughes, if that's okay?" Niall asked. Hughes nodded.

"If the answer is here, we'll leave no stone unturned to find them," Hughes declared.

Gus knew he couldn't change what had already happened.

Did he want to stay on the sidelines and watch others investigate, or did he wish to be in the thick of things, learning the truth on his own? In his heart, he felt the answer as clear as day. Then he had his second epiphany of the day. A devious way to circumvent the mundane paperwork process and break through people's barriers to get at the truth. A card up his sleeve that came from a person they'd neglected to include in the game.

Just like that he knew what to do. "I have an idea."

"YOU LOOK tense. Want a blowjob to relax you? I can do it while you drive. I'll be ever so careful." Gus insinuated his hand toward Niall's crotch as he sat in the driver's seat. Gus's offer was met with a serious glare, and Niall promptly dislodged Gus's hand from his thigh.

"This is by far the stupidest thing you've ever done," Niall commented, frowning, his voice reverberating with fury.

Gus snorted. "What about the time when I jumped on Florian Talbot's back while he was trying to kill you?"

That gave Niall pause, and then he gritted his teeth. "Fine. The second dumbest thing you've ever done."

"What about that time when I went on my own to catch Domville in the woods up the mountain?" Now Gus was just goading his lover, grinning.

Niall growled. "Fine, dammit. The *third* dumbest thing you've ever done."

"If you've got a better idea, I'm wide open and listening." Gus waited for Niall to state his master plan. When nothing came, he sighed and took Niall's hand from the steering wheel and intertwined their fingers. "After everything Hughes's lab boys discovered in Matty's cloud, we've got the element of surprise. Plus, we have an ace in the hole, a wild card. Yeah, we've got this in the bag. In a manner of speaking. Besides, there'll be a gazillion cops on the premises. You'll be in the room with us. Hughes has eyes and ears in the entire house. Nothing bad's going to happen."

Niall sat like a stone statue. Gus squeezed his hand. Finally some of Niall's hard lines softened, and he swallowed, nervousness radiating from him. "If something happens, I'm gonna go all fairy tale on you, and lock you up in the highest room in the tallest tower."

Gus laughed. "If you're there, plus a king-size bed and lube to last a hundred years, I'm game." Niall obviously didn't want to join the merriment, but the corners of his lips twitched like he couldn't help it. "And after this evening's over, I'm gonna ride you all night, stud." Gus winked at Niall, who stared at him wide-eyed, like he suspected Gus had gone insane.

Finally he let out a brief, breathy chortle. "Yes, you damn well will. Even after I make you come, screaming."

Thrilled at his lover's show of domination, Gus chuckled to himself in anticipation. He couldn't wait for Niall to carry out his sexy threat and put Gus in his place—in bed, anyway, where he didn't mind being Niall's boy toy. "Whatever you say. Tigger."

Niall rolled his eyes but said nothing. Still, he grinned wide.

"WHAT ARE we doing back here?" Aeryn asked, her voice loud enough to ascend above the murmur of the others. She'd gotten rid of the crutches but walked with a slight limp.

The crowd agreed with her since their monotonous hum rose to get Gus's attention. He faced their confused expressions for a moment, giving them the time to adjust, and then waved them all to a seat. Grumbling, they obeyed, waiting for an explanation.

Gus had chosen the perfect venue for tonight's proceedings, even if he did feel a bit apprehensive about being so damn close to the spot where he'd thought he might die. A cold shiver went through him, but he shook off his fears.

Jason Upton's mansion had two dining rooms. Gus had gathered everyone involved in the case—at least all those who were still alive—into the more informal of the two. An intricately carved wood table seating twelve was situated in a solarium/atrium that opened to the back patio and lawn, and wooden deck paths led down to the waterfront. The red-and-yellow rays of the setting sun filtering through the huge skylight and the floor-to-ceiling windows gave the white walls an orange glow.

After inspecting Jason's mansion, Gus had chosen this room as the most ideal. Windows provided clear lines of sights in all directions for the police officers in hiding outside, and the chandeliers and candelabras would illuminate the space brightly. Whatever might transpire, there would be dozens of eyewitnesses—who also happened to be law enforcement.

Gus was the only one standing in front of the french doors that opened on the patio, while Hughes and Niall had assumed positions near the doorway to the rest of the mansion, and Owain stood behind Juliette at the other end of the table. The three men were armed, along with the army outside in the shadows, so Gus felt relatively secure in his role of agitator.

Silently, he looked over the sea of faces: family, friends, colleagues, all those Gus would have a month ago deemed trustworthy and ethically inclined. Now he tried to come to terms with the moral ambivalence he seemed to sense from all of them.

Anxiousness making a reappearance, Gus cleared his throat to get everyone's attention, which he already had. "I asked you here with the support of the Seattle Police Department." With a courteous smile, as though he was hiding nothing, he gestured at Hughes, who inclined his head a bit. "We're here to… to do a Tarot reading for each and every one of us."

The low droning resumed, but Gus stepped aside from the head of the table and bid the man outside to enter. Dressed in the old-fashioned garb of a *fin de siècle* gentleman dandy, Guilbert van Es sauntered in and bowed so deep he all but bent in half.

"*Bonsoir, Mesdames et Messieurs*," he said with a smooth smile and in a silken voice that was nevertheless clearly audible.

The other occupants of the room were struck silent.

Chapter 14

"*WHAT?*" MORE than one person asked at once.

Gus nodded emphatically. "You all are part of a coven. One I belong to as well. We all enter the ritual circle with perfect love and perfect trust. Tonight… we will learn how far that trust extends, as I ask you to trust me and participate in this Tarot reading with me."

"Does that mean you're gonna take part in this… this mockery too?" Aeryn asked, her eyes ablaze with righteous indignation. She clearly believed she'd done nothing wrong or morally questionable, and her posture, arms crossed over her chest, emphasized the point.

Gritting his teeth at the suspicion his friends showed, Gus nodded firmly. "Of course."

Gil van Es stepped forward, a charming air to him, a charisma he must have cultivated his whole life. "Ladies and gentlemen, I will speak English during this reading. At least, I will do my best." He gave a self-deprecating laugh, and on a couple of the faces around the table, grins flickered. Gil van Es sure knew how to take a room and mold it into an auditorium of adoring fans. His soft French accent added to his enthralling show. "Please, who would like to begin, eh?"

"I'll go first," Gus offered, not only for playing along, but in the spirit of cooperation. If he wanted others to join in, without coercion, he would have to set an example.

He sat on the right side of Gil van Es, who immediately after took a seat at the head of the table, his movements elegant and yet deliberately slow, as if to display to all he had no sinister intentions. Niall and Hughes both stepped forward and placed nine Tarot decks on the table, but so far from Mr. van Es that he would have to reach for them, in plain sight of all present. Another feat to ensure no cheating was to take place.

Mr. van Es took the topmost deck from the closest stack, flipped open the lid, and then without removing the cards, he politely gestured for Gus to take the deck. "Please, *monsieur*, would you, how you say, shuffle the cards?"

Gus did exactly as instructed, ensuring the cards were in no particular, predetermined order by scrambling them thoroughly in the same way he'd do with any card deck.

Mr. van Es smiled enigmatically. "A Tarot deck has seventy-eight cards.

"The Major Arcana, the Greater Secrets, has twenty-two cards. They depict one's journey through life, or more applicably, the fool's sojourn from childlike innocence to becoming one with the universe. Like regular playing cards, the Minor Arcana or the Lesser Secrets, has fifty-six cards and four suits—Wands (also known as Staffs or Scepters), Swords, Cups, and Coins (also known as Disks or Pentacles)—that describe the people and events a person encounters on his journey through life, shaping his future. The four suits are associated with an element, a cardinal point, a season, and so forth. Wands symbolize fire, power, intuition, action, and conflict; Swords air, thoughts, ideas, communication, and enlightenment; Cups water, emotions, sensations, love, and spirit; and Coins earth, physicality, accomplishment, manifestation, and body. Certain Tarot decks and readers switch the elements of Swords and Wands. *Pourquoi*? *Je ne sais pas*. Also, the seasonal correspondences vary according to whether a pagan or an esoteric deck is used."

Gus listened with only one ear, knowing enough about the Tarot to not need to hear every detail of the account. He focused his mind on the question at hand—would they find out who was responsible for the bomb strike and the deaths involved?

Mr. van Es continued, his voice mesmerizing. "There are many spreads to Tarot, many combinations and decks. This is Aleister Crowley's Tarot deck, or as it is better known, the Thoth deck. A copy only, *malheureusement*. For you, monsieur, the simple five card cross spread." He splayed the deck before Gus into a fan configuration with a swift, agile move. "Choose five cards. In your mind you must have a question. Keep your question at the forefront of your mind and then place the first card in the center, the second to its left, the third to its right, the fourth below, and the fifth above the center card. For now keep them all face down. *Comprenez-vous*?"

Gus nodded and again followed Mr. van Es's lead. By the time he was done, his hands were sweaty, his temples throbbed, and anxiety tightened his stomach into painful knots.

Mr. van Es nodded once Gus was done. "Now. The center card represents the present or the general theme of this evening's reading." He flipped the card sideways until it was face up. "*Et voilà*."

With his heart in his throat, Gus examined the card intently, as though the mysteries of the universe were written on it.

The card was the Knight of Wands, upright. A green knight sat on a rampant horse, a torch in hand and his helmet adorned with the horn of a unicorn.

"Ah, the idealistic, passionate youth," Mr. van Es declared, smiling cryptically. "How befitting." He locked gazes with Gus. "This is who you are today, in the here and now. You are an intelligent, intuitive, and energetic young warrior, only beginning his travels toward progress and strength, with a powerful inner drive to keep moving to reach your goals. You must respond to what is happening around you in order to learn what you're destined to know. You should feel elated. A reversed card would have shown a young man insecure to be who he is at heart and represented a personal or spiritual crisis. *Êtes-vous bien? Bon.*"

Gus wasn't sure how to take the news, so he simply nodded, remaining quiet.

"Now. The card on the left brings forth the influences of the past that still affect your future." Gil van Es flipped the card face up.

It was Justice upright. A blue-green female figure with a mask covering her face held onto a magic sword and the scales of justice, standing tiptoe on the precarious edge of the sword.

Gil nodded, pleased. "You are an ethical, virtuous person. You seek the right thing to do, and that has motivated your actions from a young age, your belief in divine justice and balance. You are able to hold your justified stance not only to maintain justice, but to ensure righteousness, fairness, and karmic balance are reached."

Gus was surprised how accurate the reading already seemed. But then again, he had an ace in the hole. That gave him inner strength and confidence that things would work out. He had to believe that, or he would have risked the lives of his loved ones for nothing.

"The third card," Gil van Es said, his hand hovering above the five-card spread. "This symbolizes the future." He flipped it face up.

It was an upright Tower where the broken spire fell in a fiery upheaval.

The Tarot reader grimaced, and so did Gus. "Uh-oh. An ill omen of what is to come. Troubled times lay ahead, and radical changes will shake your life and uproot what you thought was secure, but these events must take place in order for the wheel of destiny to regain equilibrium. But disasters and catastrophes will eventually lead to revelation because to gain perfection the past must be annihilated into nothingness."

Gus swallowed hard. He feared the implications of what the Tower card signified, and he couldn't understand how liberation could be had from destruction. Chaos waited for him behind every corner, disillusion trailing right after. How transformative this event would be scared him to the core.

"Now, the fourth card." Gil van Es's voice dropped to a husky range, an ominous air creeping into the room. "This will reveal the reason behind your question." With a reverent touch, he turned the card.

It was the Six of Coins. In the card a light blue lotus blossom was surrounded by six orbs in harmony, with rays of light in between shooting outward.

Gil van Es harrumphed. "Hmm. A card of reaping the rewards of all your hard toil, of a successful journey fulfilled, and reaching a milestone. The card also signifies a movement forward, coming to a crossroads or considering a change of direction, and a need for assessment of your levels of commitment. You must decide if you are on the right path as there exists a subconscious impulse that is holding you back from achieving a desired goal. Together with Justice, the Six of Coins means a decision point is imminent."

Gus frowned. For a positive card, it sure held dual meanings. Did it suggest tonight's events would lead to a successful outcome, or that he was destined for a crossroads where he would have to decide between a rock and a hard place? But he knew enough about Tarot to know all cards had different meanings depending on their position—upright or upside down, alone, and in concert with their surrounding cards.

Silently, he waited for the revelation of the final card.

"The fifth and final card," Gil van Es declared, a ring of finality in his tone, giving Gus goose bumps. "It will tell you the potential outcome of this current situation, offering a possible end result for an action taken." He turned the last card with slow deliberation, building the anxiety levels, which were already high, in the room. Gus had to admit Gil van Es was a showman to the last.

The last card was the Hanged Man, who hung upside down from an ankh and a serpent by his left leg, set against a green background, while his right leg was crossed at the knee to form a triangle.

Mr. van Es's face remained impassive, annoyingly blank. Then he quirked an eyebrow, an act of contemplation, as if he had no intention of explaining the card's meaning. But then he said in a lazy voice, "The mysterious figure suspended from a tau cross. The martyr's sacrifice. The paradox of contradictory truths. To control is to let go, to win is to surrender, to master is to yield, to move forward is to stand still. The Hanged Man teaches that the obvious solution may not always be the correct one. When you most wish to act and exert your control over others is the precise moment when you should give up control and accept the will of the divine. Remain passive and be patient, contemplate and wait, and the world will move toward your desired goal—regardless of you."

Gus had never put much stock in Tarot. He understood people finding solace through readings, but he'd never felt the need to relinquish control over his own life to higher powers. He also felt he hadn't really gotten an answer to his question. The vagueness of interpretation was the main reason why he didn't trust predictions. But perhaps tonight, when death was in the air, he had to accept that things might spin out of his control and still lead to a positive outcome.

So he sent a quick prayer to the Goddess for justice—and forgiveness. If the killer was indeed among them, Gus knew he'd have a hard time accepting the truth. He felt vulnerable in his openness, as though the cards had exposed his inner secrets to all. To the inscrutable Gil van Es, all he said was, "Thanks."

Gil van Es flashed a charming smile at the other people in the room. "Who's next?"

"I'M NEXT."

Juliette stood up. She appeared nervous and fidgety, her voice quivering as she spoke, but bravely she soldiered on to take a seat opposite Gus, on Mr. van Es's left side. Gil van Es gave her what was undoubtedly his most efficacious sultry look, and Juliette blushed deeply. Her gaze flicked over to Owain, who had silently positioned himself close to her.

"*S'il vous plaît, Madame.*" He gestured for one of the unopened card deck packages. Juliette chose one and proceeded to pull the cards out and then shuffle them with determination and speed. Then she picked five cards from the deck and repeated the spread Gus had used. "*Bon. Et maintenant, une question.*"

Juliette nodded, and briefly her eyes glazed over as she contemplated her question.

"The first card. The present." Gil turned the card over.

It was the Queen of Coins. A dark female figure clad in reptilian scales and with long curved horns on her head sat on a lush, green oasis while staring back into an arid desert.

Gil chuckled, content. "*Ah, parfait.* The Mother Earth. You are a sensual, down-to-earth woman, fertile and beautiful. You are femininity personified, practical and sensible, domestic and nurturing, big-hearted and loving to a fault, resourceful and trustworthy, loyal and steadfast. Your greatest pleasure is to care for others, and your home is a welcoming place for men, women, children, pets, and plants alike."

Gus chuckled, more relaxed now that the spotlight was no longer aimed at him. "That sure sounds like you, Jules."

Juliette smiled, and it was like sunshine radiated from her. "Hush, you."

"I must add modest to the list, Madame," Mr. van Es quipped, causing Juliette to blush again. "Now, the second card, which represents the past and how it affects the present."

He flipped the second card, left of the Queen of Coins. It was the Hermit, an obscure male figure, dressed in red and carrying a lantern that was the sun, casting pink rays everywhere.

"The Hermit," Gil van Es said solemnly. "In your past you discovered your inner light, your truth, your home within. You have done your soul-searching and introspection, quieted your voice and looked inward. You have sought greater understanding of yourself—but at the expense of the outer world. Due to your inner balance, you felt confident and comfortable enough to become a mentor, a high priestess. But your wisdom is born of solitude, and now this card represents a shadow cast over you. Threatened by what is happening around you, your first instinct is to withdraw to your inner solace. You have turned away from the world, and now it is holding you back."

Juliette gulped, frowning. "It is true there are many things going on right now that try to push me to withdraw." Her melancholy, repentant gaze flicked toward Gus before it was blocked by her descending eyelids.

"You're still listening to us, and you always care for us," Gus said, reaching out across the table to hold her hand. He felt it tremble, and her eyes were moist. "Your truth is our truth too. That is why you're our mentor and our high priestess." Around the table came agreeing sounds and mutterings, and Juliette smiled a little.

"The third card, the future," Gil van Es stated firmly and turned the card.

It was the Lovers. Two figures, one light and the other dark, held hands with a cupid with his bow above them. They were both dressed in regal cloaks and crowns, one bright red and the other glowing yellow.

Gil quirked an eyebrow, curious and surprised. "*Étrange*. The Lovers are an opposing card to the Hermit. There is a huge schism between your past and your future." His twinkling eyes landed on Juliette, who flushed red and steadfastly kept her gaze locked on the Lovers card instead of shifting around the room. "*Très bien*. This card speaks of love, sensuality, romance, a bond being formed, a relationship coming to full bloom. Matters of the heart and passionate love are awakening. It is a message from the universe for you to heed. You must accept that love is an integral part of your future."

Juliette nodded, even though her expression remained incredulous. Like Gus, she said nothing in response to the love letter through time.

"The fourth card, the reason behind your question." Gil spun the card around.

It was the Ace of Cups, depicting the Holy Grail upon a dark sea and lotus blossoms, with a moon at the base to give a shape to nature.

Gil chuckled, seeming pleased with the result. "This card symbolizes giving love, the possibility for deepening emotions and intimacy. Your awareness of a potential object of desire, compassion, and adoring love motivates you, as attraction inside you grows steadily. Love is at the heart of your situation and your question. You are attuned toward an expression of amorous feelings and getting in touch with your deepest desires for a lover and a companion. Your time is coming."

If Juliette had reddened before, now she resembled a boiling lobster. She opened and closed her mouth, but no sounds emerged.

Behind her Owain shifted his weight from one foot to the other while his gaze never left the back of her head. Gus sure wasn't imagining the pinking of his cheeks as well and suppressed a gleeful smile.

"The fifth and final card, the potential of the situation arising from your question and the answers the card have given you, Madame." Gil smirked and flipped over the last card.

It was the Ten of Cups. Ten tilted goblets formed the shape of the tree of life, the cups overflowing with the water of life from the sacred great lotus blossom.

Gil nodded, delighted. "*Ah, precisement*. Fulfillment, joy, happiness, peace, bliss, and love, a contentment of the heart and a perfect companionship of an established pairing. You radiate love, and your cup overflows with joy and good fortune. Your emotions rise far beyond what you thought you would ever be capable of feeling. A newfound serenity grants you harmony and inner peace. Your blessings are abundant. This is the time for deeper connections and greater closeness with your loved ones. Your love transcends earthly delights to the sphere of the divine."

Juliette's eyes widened and her mouth opened into a perfect *oh* of surprise. "Oh."

Smiling, Gil bowed his head like a gentleman dandy. *"Vous êtes une femme heureuse, Madame. Je suis heureux pour vous.* I congratulate you for such a fortuitous reading." With a grin, he looked over to everyone at the other end of the table. *"Qui est le prochain?* Who is next?"

Aeryn jumped up, her eyes fiery, her demeanor defensive and offensive at once. "What the hell, right? I am."

BY THEN the routine was no surprise. But after taking Juliette's seat and while shuffling her deck of cards, Aeryn still managed to deliver a blow of her own. "Just three cards for me, thank you. Past, present, and future. The rest is redundant."

Gil laughed. *"Non, non, non, Belle Mademoiselle. Les règles sont les mêmes pour tout le monde.* One rule for all." He stirred the card deck into a fan and gestured Aeryn to make her five-card selection. Grumbling under her breath, Aeryn grudgingly obeyed. "The first card, the present." Gil turned the card face up.

The center card was the Queen of Wands, who sat on a throne of fire with golden hair and a radiant crown of thorns, her eyes closed to look inward, and beside her sat a lion, her hand on its mane.

Gil chuckled, giving Aeryn a knowing look. "How apropos. The fiery woman. The one who doesn't hold anything back. You are attractive and self-confident, popular and sexy, warm and outgoing. You give every task your undivided attention and total dedication. You are bursting with energy, vigor, and strength, and you lead an active, busy life filled with challenges and admirers. An enviable fire burns within you, and your enthusiasm is contagious."

Aeryn rolled her eyes, crossed her arms over her chest, and scoffed. "Whoopee. How insightful."

As seemed to be his gift, Gil merely smiled in response. "*Merci beaucoup.* Now, the second card." He turned it over.

For the first time the card—the High Priest or Hierophant—was upside down. A man dressed in an orange robe with a pentagram on his chest was surrounded by masks of a lion, a bull, an eagle, and a man.

Gil let out a bereft sigh as he grew serious. "Your past, *ma belle mademoiselle*, is not a happy one. You never conform as you doubt everything. You are always rigid and suspicious since you reject traditions and conformity. You feel overwhelmed by the expectations of people around you and as though you can never give or do enough. You judge a book by its cover and you do not open your heart to others easily or at all. You feel as though you cannot identify with anyone or any group of people, forever the outsider, never one to trust freely or to care for another without a grain of doubt. Your past is filled with anarchy, rebellion, and rejection of those that came before you or tried to teach you with their wise counsel."

When Gil fell silent, one could have heard a pin drop. Gus stared at Aeryn, biting his lower lip, fearful of what might come next. His gaze flicked over to Niall, who stood behind Aeryn, his stance wary and ready for anything. His quick, self-assured nod to Gus told Gus that Niall was on top of things.

Aeryn's eyes narrowed and her lips thinned. Her anger came off her in waves, as her hands fisted on the table. But when she spoke, her words were in stark contrast to her expression and demeanor. "My parents demanded the best from me. I had to excel to earn their love, as though I had no worth beyond top grades, awards, and ribbons, and the highest rung in the career ladder."

Confusion spread around the room like a heavy vapor, only to be replaced by an air of sympathy. Juliette, who sat next to her, took her hand and squeezed it gently. Aeryn nodded rigidly but her eyes glimmered slightly and her jaw quivered as her fists unwound. Gus realized he didn't quite know her as well as he wished and should.

"That was your past, mademoiselle. Your future may be altogether different." Gil said wisely. "The third card shows you a *possible* future." His emphasis didn't go unnoticed as he turned the rightmost card face up.

It was the Two of Swords. They crossed one another, impaling the blue-white flower in the center, a rose.

Gil cocked his head, studying the card silently for a time. Finally he said slowly, "Two swords, crossed. A barrier before you, between you and the world, as you fend off any approaches from the outside. You are coming to a decision, a crossroads of sorts, a path of discernment before you. A mixture of positive and negative. Anticipation and doubt, upcoming truce and impending conflict, a tense balance and a potential stalemate. You are blocking your emotions to avoid a truth about yourself. Are you afraid of getting hurt if you open your heart? Are you refusing to accept a dark aspect of your personality? You must make a choice. That is the only way out of this standstill that is locking you in place."

Aeryn frowned, but Gus sensed it was aimed inward, not outward at Gil. Her low tone depicted the same awareness. "I see." She nodded, mostly to herself, her eyes glassy.

Gil regarded her quietly, his expression impossible to interpret. But something close to admiration shone in his eyes. "The fourth card. The reason behind your question." He flipped the card over.

The card was… Death. A black skeleton dominated the card, holding his scythe and wearing an Egyptian headdress. The twisted form whispered of change, as did the sacred blossoms drowning in mud, the dancing scorpion, the curled serpent, and the phoenix spreading its wings.

Several hushed gasps echoed in the dining room.

"This marks the end of an era and the dawn of a new world," Gil said reverently. "You are closing one door and opening another, putting your past behind you and shedding old attitudes." He smiled as he spoke. "You are going through a profound change, a transition. You are focusing on essentials and disregarding what is not necessary for your transformation. You are about to face your darkest fear and the wide unknown. As the Tarot declares, we die each moment to be reborn in the future." He nodded at Aeryn, seemingly satisfied. "A good omen of things to come."

Aeryn let out a breath, and her features softened. "That's good, I guess."

"*Precisement.*" Gil bowed theatrically. "And now, the final card." He turned the fifth, topmost card while saying, "The possible outcome."

It was the Star. A blue female figure, a water bearer, with long, long flowing hair, held two cups, a golden one above her head and a silver cup beneath her, both pouring ethereal water. A bright star shone above in the sky, with a purple planet giving her a background.

"*Ah, bon.*" Gil practically jumped up and down on his seat, smiling happily. "The sign of hope and inspiration, the light at the end of the tunnel. You are uplifted, ascending beyond fears and doubts to reach for serenity, to see clearly ahead, to regain your motivation and inner strength. You receive your answer as surely as the stars shine in the heavens. Remember, though, that hope is only the beginning, which is followed by positive actions. Promising indeed, Mademoiselle."

At first Aeryn blinked hard. Suddenly she burst into a hearty laugh. When she finally got an intelligible word out, it made the others laugh as well. "I swear, this is by far the best reading I've ever had. I got an answer to my question: What is the point of this exercise?"

The room filled with giggles and chuckles. Aeryn's reading sure seemed to have hit a bull's eye, five by five.

"Should you have told us what your question was?" Gus asked while still giggling. Aeryn might not have confessed to murder but she had spilled the beans about her upbringing. Gus was simply pleased that the plan was working, and a little humor helped to alleviate the dark mood.

Gil shook his finger at him. "*Absolument*! This is not a wish made while blowing out candles on a birthday cake! Of course one may confess the question that plagued one's mind."

"Well, in that case…," Juliette said, smiling wide enough to show her dimples. Gus was thrilled to see her spirits lifted once again. "My question was about my, um… the future of my love life."

Gil winked at her, grinning. "Everyone has questions about their love life. Even if that is not the one people profess to be thinking about." Then, in a flash, he grew deadly serious, even quite ominous. "You will be pleased to hear, Mademoiselle Newton, that your character lends itself to the achievement of perfection. While poison might be a woman's choice for murder, a bomb strike is crude and barbaric, with far too many chaotic variables to successfully control to one's satisfaction. Therefore, it's unlikely, and uncharacteristic, for you to be the guilty party for heinous crimes that have led to the deaths of three people." His relentless gaze swept the dining room and stopped at everyone present. "So, who is next?"

As the warm ambience in the room chilled, Gus had a sneaky suspicion their night of turmoil was just beginning.

Chapter 15

"I WILL go next." Tom stood up, rigid and wary, but bravely he stepped forward to take Gus's seat as Gus shifted to another chair. With steady hands, he opened a pack of cards, took them out and shuffled them, and then chose five cards, which he placed in the cross spread as had the others before him. "I'm ready." His steadfast gaze aimed at Gil, unwavering. As an ex-soldier, he had an inner power no man could undo. Gus was immensely proud of his friend.

Without a word and with an unreadable expression, Gil turned the first card.

It was the King of Cups, where a blue-green male figure sat in a shell-shaped chariot drawn by an eagle.

"The honorable man," Gil said, sounding impressed. Gus wondered how much of that was show and how much true fascination, or if it was another method of seducing a wary audience member. "No matter the tragedy, trauma, or crisis, you are calm and composed, a diplomatic skill to defuse even the most volatile of situations. You are selfless and honest, wise and strong, caring and tolerant. You have a deep grasp of human nature, and you have a gift of seeing into the heart of both things and people. Your quieting, serene sphere of influence extends from friends to strangers, from loved ones to enemies alike. I suspect any and all actions you take are made to help those in need. You possess a gentle touch and a quiet word, as you radiate peaceful energy."

Tom said and did nothing. Like a statue he sat, ramrod straight and indecipherable. No blinking, no tics in his jaw, no nervous fidgeting, not a drop of sweat on his brow. Gus grimaced inwardly. Gil would have a tough time trying to analyze Tom.

"Your past." Gil flipped the card around almost carelessly. Bewildered, Gus puzzled if Gil was losing his cool due to Tom's, well, coolness.

The Ten of Swords appeared in all its gruesomeness. Nine swords aimed at the tenth sword with the symbols of sun and the heart on it, utterly destroying it, drops of blood falling, the background red and brutal.

Gil frowned, but this time Gus believed it was born of sympathy. "The last rays of the sun, of the joy of life, are annihilated. The final remnants of love for yourself and others are ruined. Your foundation is built on terrible misfortunes, extreme disillusionments, and utter desolation of the soul. You hit rock bottom, a devastation laying waste to all light and goodness in your life. War, battle, and strife have scarred your spirit, beaten you down and broken your will, filling you with depression, sorrow, and defeat. You were crushed to ashes."

The silence that fell hung over them all like a death shroud.

Tom stared at the card. "The war…. Yes, it did that to me. All that you said."

"Oh, Tom." Alec hurried to sit next to Tom and rest his hand on his arm.

Tom's features softened immediately. A light returned to his hurting eyes and a flicker of a smile twitched up one corner of his mouth. "Thanks, Alec." He gently patted the hand lying on his arm, a curious fatherly gesture that made Gus frown. The honorable man Tom was sure kept his heart tucked far away from hurt.

"The future." Gil turned another card.

It was the Five of Cups, where golden cups of promise had turned to glass, empty and breakable. Harsh winds of disappointment had torn the lotus blossoms off their roots and withered them.

Gil sighed. "Your future is ruled by disappointment, regret, and loss. Hope is lost, the time for love over, defeat is imminent. You are deprived of love but long to be united with the love of your life. But grief will be your sole constant companion. You may wish to turn back the clock or wish for what might have been, but you have made the wrong choices, so solitude and heartache are ahead of you. Either you will reject your chance for happiness or love will reject you—"

"Stop it! Stop it this instant!" Alec shouted, standing up, his face a mask of fury. Gus had never seen Alec so upset. He turned to Tom, who stared at him, wide-eyed and surprised. "It's not true, Tom. That won't be your fate. He's lying, or he's wrong, or…." He struggled to finish, his voice cracking and fading.

Tom slowly pulled him back down and smiled at him reassuringly. "Don't worry. I'm not easily spooked by dark, decimating predictions. Everything's okay. Calm down."

It took a while, but Alec cooled off, nodding and leaning lightly toward Tom. Gus had to look away, as he felt a tug of sorrow in his own heart. The prospect of losing love stung if you had ever experienced it. His worried gaze met with Niall's. As usual, one confident smirk and wink from Niall, and Gus was right as rain, his troubles lifted.

"Now. The reason for your question." Merciless, Gil turned the fourth card.

The card was the Knight of Cups, who had huge light blue wings on his back and who sat astride a big, leaping white stallion, holding a cup with a crab in it.

Gil actually chuckled, and right after, he tossed his head back and really let it rip. His mirth only confused Gus and the others, if any of their dumbfounded expressions were a clue.

"A new lover, a new passion. An offer of love." Gil gave Tom a smug, satisfied look, and Tom pinked slightly. "This kind and sensitive soul, one believing in true love, is the reason for your question." The suggestive remark made Tom redden more, and this time he did squirm slightly in discomfort. "A romantic worshipper of love's deepest ideal and—"

"Okay. I think we got it." Tom glared at Gil in a way that would have sent lesser men shrieking into the shadows.

Gil merely grinned and shrugged. "The final card. The possible outcome."

It was the Lovers card.

Before Gil could utter a single syllable, Tom beat him to it. "That's been covered. Skip it. Thanks a bunch." He got up, obviously in an attempt to make a memorable exit. He stopped mid-motion, though, and glared at Gil. "So…. Am I the murderer, or what?"

Gil didn't look away, not intimidated in the least. "You have already killed, I see it in your eyes. But… those deaths haunt you, weigh you down with guilt and sorrow, never allowing you the luxury of forgetting. So…. No, I don't think you would invite more anguish and death to hang upon you."

For a second, Tom appeared ready for murder, shaking with pent-up fury, his hands fisted at his sides. Without another word, he moved hurriedly a few chairs away from Gil and his insidious cards, apparently all-seeing third eye, and flamboyant parlance.

Alec, however, quickly yanked him back up. Then he sat down where Tom had sat, and pushed Tom down in his chair with determination.

Apparently Alec wanted a friendly supporter for his reading. "I'm next." His chin lifted up defiantly as he opened a new pack, mixed the cards well, and then spread five in a cross configuration.

Gil smiled, seductive and charming. He turned the first card.

Gus almost swallowed his tongue when the Knight of Cups reappeared.

Both Alec and Tom blushed intensely as they both stared at the card wide-eyed. Then Tom slumped slightly, his eyes lost their focus, and his appearance resembled that of defeat and deep longing. Alec, on the other hand, cocked his head to the side, as if puzzled, like he was seeing something old and familiar for the first time, with new eyes.

"You idealize love, Monsieur Hope," Gil said, his focus on the card alone, his smirk gone. "You always emphasize emotions, express sentimentality, and are aware of the feelings and moods of others. You understand and relate to the pains of others, seeking to relieve it, to ease pain and discomfort. You are creative and artistic, appreciating beauty and pleasure—"

"I understand," Alec cut in stiffly, his lips pursed in annoyance. "Move on, please."

"*Bien sûr*. The past." Gil inclined his head, and flipped over the second card.

It was the Fool, dressed in verdant green armor, with a crocodile beneath his feet, a tiger biting his left thigh, a butterfly and a dove flying above him, and a long umbilical cord, in four circles, attaching him to the cosmic unity. The image was rich with symbols of all kinds, giving room for a multitude of interpretations.

"A true innocent," Gil said, his tone tinted with awe, as though innocence was a state to aspire to. Perhaps he was right, Gus mused laconically. "For you, life is a journey, an adventure, an experience. Once you started on your own path, you felt capable of unlimited potential and you found spontaneity and inspiration in everything new you encountered. Your view of life is a show of optimism and true faith, as you trust that life is worth living and people are ultimately good." Gil gave him a soft, shy smile that Gus was sure wasn't all that real. "I must confess, monsieur, that you are one to admire. Your outlook on things is highly enviable. I tip my hat to you, sir."

Alec obviously didn't know how to accept the compliment, especially from Gil, so he offered a half-assed, unsure smile in return. "Thanks. I think."

Gus could relate. Even back at the esbat ritual, he couldn't understand why Alec stayed with Jason, a man whose love was aimed first and foremost at himself, not his companion. But love, as they said, was a wondrous thing, a miracle capable of deep, profound changes and adaptations, so Gus put the matter out of his mind.

Gil chuckled. "*Je vous en prie.*" He bowed, making a spectacle of the simple act. "*Et maintenant*, your future, monsieur." He turned the third card face up.

It was the Two of Coins reversed. A serpent formed a figure eight that depicted the symbol of infinity, and within the two circles were two coins with the yin and yang symbols. Purple dominated the color scheme.

"*Ah, quelle dommage.*" Gil seemed displeased to see the card, grunting and frowning. "You fear the disharmony, lack of safety and security, that come with change. This should be the time to take a breath and wait for the change to come, to try and see the positive side of change. Your mind is preoccupied with a past event, so much so that it has thrown you off balance. You must resolve this issue in order to regain your balance and reap the many rewards that await you just beyond the horizon. Give yourself time to come to terms and accept the past that haunts you. But… resolve it you must."

Alec swallowed hard as he went pale as a sheet. Like the others, Gus knew Alec was still striving to understand the loss he'd experienced. It was distressing to witness how hard it was for a friend to move on. Alec was stuck, unable to grieve while the question of what was happening remained unanswered. Was Jason a victim or the culprit?

Gus suppressed a sigh, looking away, but feeling every ounce of the pain Alec must have felt. There were times when empathy was a gift and times when it was a curse.

"Don't worry, sweetheart," Tom said at Alec's side, holding his hand and squeezing it briefly. "Take all the time you need to feel sad. You don't have to hide it from me… um, us."

Alec smiled, seemingly relieved and reassured. Sunshine emerged from beyond the dark clouds in his case, and Gus wasn't the only who let out a breath then.

"*Ah, mon ami, c'est pas grave,*" Gil said amiably, awfully close to baby talk. "Time is always in motion, fluid and subject to change. The tiniest flap of a butterfly's wings causes it to swell and stir." He raised a hand in a swish to get Alec's attention, and succeeded as Alec stared at him as if he were the ringmaster of a circus and something magical was in the air. "Now, the fourth card. The reason behind your question."

The revealed card turned out to be the Five of Coins. Against a sinister black and ugly red background, a five-pointed star had turned upside down, standing on one tip, all of which were in the shapes of a coin.

"How dismal." Gil grunted, again appearing dismayed. "The answer to your question is that you are stuck, indecisive, and afraid to take another step on your path forward. Your thoughts are running around in a useless circle, and you see no way out, which breeds hopelessness. And yet, your inner wisdom encourages you to do something, anything, to resolve this standstill. Hence the question that keeps dragging you down back to immobility and indecisiveness."

A flash of despair showed how despondent Alec was, but he hid it quickly. But he kept his gaze lowered, hiding the mirrors into his soul. "I see. Please, finish the reading." His voice was a mere whisper. Like Matty, Alec had been a wonderfully buoyant personality during the ritual, a bright light in the surrounding dim. Now he was but a shadow of his former self, and Gus hated how they had all changed because of all this tragedy and outright ruin.

"*Bien sûr*. The outcome is at hand." Gil turned the final card.

A new wave of gasps followed as the King of Cups was exposed.

Gil explained nothing. His serene gaze moved between Alec and Tom. There was no smirk, no jest, no suggestive remark. Perhaps there was nothing left to say, Gus mused, his eyes also observing Alec and Tom for their reactions.

Tom seemed shaken, and he pulled his hand back from Alec's as though he was trying to appear smaller and unnoticeable. Alec turned to look at him, disappointment and sorrow buried in his glimmering eyes, and then he looked down at his hands too.

But then something amazing happened.

Tom straightened his back, seemingly taking hold of his insecurities, doubts, and fears, and turned to Alec. Decisively he retook Alec's hand in his own, closing his palms around his hand. When their eyes met—one pair steadfast, the other surprised but hopeful—it was as if there were no others in the room but the two of them.

Unable to help himself, Gus stole a glance at Niall, who did the same in the exact same moment. *He loves me. He does. He really loves me.* Gus felt a goofy, happy smile rise on his lips, and Niall smiled back. For an instance, Niall was all Gus saw, the man he had always dreamed of and wished for, and there he was, standing on the other side of the room, giving Gus strength and love without asking for anything in return. *I'm the luckiest guy in the world.*

That was when Gil spoke. "Monsieur Hope, had you killed Jason Upton, or the other two victims, the past would not haunt you so. In your mind you would already have severed your ties to Monsieur Upton if you had decided to kill him. But your emotions of loss, confusion, and pain linger. They tell me you are not the one responsible for these monstrous deeds."

A new voice emerged over the low murmur. "So that's what all this is about? Finding the murderer and bomber with card tricks? You must be joking." Sydney Keen stood up so fast the legs of her chair screeched sharply. Her red hair waved about her as her gestures became wilder and more aggressive. "I refuse to participate in his charade."

"Fine." Hughes grunted, shifting forward like an unsuspecting predator. "Then we'll escort you to the police station for further questioning. Your choice."

Sydney was so enraged she actually shook from the intensity of it, her face reddening with each breath she took. "You have no right to detain me. I have done nothing wrong. You arrest me, and I will not only call my lawyer, but I will take this to the media. How's this for headlines? Police harass investigative journalist. Violations of free speech and civil liberties. Stumped cops—"

Hughes looked like was about to have a stroke. Niall fidgeted in place, about to step in, and Gus rushed to intervene.

But it was the mysterious Gil van Es who got there first, cutting Sydney's rant mid-speech, his booming voice rising above hers as he clapped his hands loudly to startle everyone in their seats. "*D'accord!* Let us move to the *pièce de résistance* of tonight's program. We can finish the readings afterwards." He gave Gus a questioning look. "With your permission, *naturellement*, Monsieur Goodwin."

Frantic on the inside as the time of revelation had come, Gus tried not to squirm and show outwardly how frayed his nerves were and how jittery he really was. After all, this had been the point of the evening all along. So he spoke no words and merely nodded, attempting to appear dramatic and dominating.

Gil grinned in a flash. "Tonight, *Mesdames et Messieurs*, I will perform a séance with Tarot cards. Our goal *du nuit*? To communicate with our deceased friends—Matty, Pine Seed, and Jason—to discover the identity of the vile murderer in our midst."

The shock reverberated around the dining room among those who'd had no clue.

Predictably, Niall, Hughes, and Gus weren't among them.

Chapter 16

"ARE YOU freaking serious?" Aeryn had stood up along with Sydney, only she looked way madder. "We're gonna try to talk to the dead to get answers? This is by far the stupidest thing I've ever heard!"

"No, the stupidest thing would be for us to agree to participate in this farce," Sydney said, shaking her head, her arms crossed over her chest.

But despite the two very angry women and other struck-silent folk in the room, Gil only laughed. "So, are you leaving because you doubt my ability to succeed or because you are afraid I will succeed?" The goading was shameless. Gus had to hand it to him to get the ball rolling. Gil locked gazes with Aeryn. "Why should you have a problem with this, Mademoiselle Newton? The cards have already spoken when it comes to you, *n'est-ce pas*? You are innocent. What more do you have to worry about than wasting a few less than precious hours to catch a fiend who killed your friends?" He tutted in a disappointed manner.

Aeryn worried her lower lip, seemingly conflicted. She faced Sydney, a dead-serious question in her eyes. "If you go, I'll go too." Was that a sisterly act of loyalty or something else? Gus had no idea, even though a month ago he would have professed a deep knowledge of both of them.

Sydney hesitated as well. Her stance remained defensive, her expression a glower, and she appeared more than ready to continue the argument or maybe even start a whole new volley of attacks. Finally she met Juliette's despondent eyes, and the fight left her in a whoosh. "I guess we'll stay." Then she glared a challenge at Gil. "But before we engage in any travesties, I want a reading of my own. Because I. Am. Not. guilty."

She came forward in a hurry, snatched a card deck from the table, yanked the cards out, and shuffled them in a flurry of insane speed and lack of finesse. Then she practically tried to slam the five-card spread through the table, so forceful was her dealing. "Well?" Sydney needled Gil to tell her something she didn't know.

Like a gentleman, Gil acquiesced, as if he were the bigger man. Another irksome gesture on his part. Gus was duly impressed with the man's ability to use physicality as a means of getting an emotional rise out of people. He did his job exceedingly well, managing to exacerbate an already inflamed situation.

"First card. The present." Gil flipped the card.

It was the Knight of Swords. A male figure wore golden-green armor and had four translucent wings attached to his helmet, rode a white war horse at full gallop, and held in his hands a long sword and a short sword. He moved with purpose and fervor.

Gil chuckled, quite pleased with the card. "A strong, masculine personality. An alpha male. Of a sort." It seemed to be some kind of inside joke since he giggled at his own jest. "You, Mademoiselle Keen, have a uniquely sharp mind. You have your goals in sight, and nothing stands in your way, or you will cut through it with your strength of wit and sharpness of tongue. Each one of your many irons in the fire is fueled by an emotional bond, and they stoke the fires of passion. Nothing quenches the thirst in you like knowing more, learning more, being more. You use every skill at your disposal, be it feminine wiles or masculine command. You are ambitious and opinionated, even rude and tactless at times. Your personality is a mix of opposites. You are both direct and crude, authoritative and overbearing, and incisive and cutting. What makes you strong also gives you a corresponding weakness."

Sydney's eyes flashed angrily. "I guess that's why my coven name is Flame and my journalist nickname Newshound. I'm a hunter, and I'm proud of it."

"Ah, accept no prisoners and show no mercy, eh?" Gil grinned. "*Très bien*. The second card, the past."

The card was the Chariot, reversed. The driver, wearing golden armor with ten crystals embedded in it, sat still in an unmoving red chariot with a blue roof. He held the Holy Grail, which symbolized the Wheel of Fortune. Four green sphinxes—bull, lion, eagle, and man—stood before the chariot, ready to start the imminent journey.

Gil nodded to himself. "Ah, now your ambition and drive make sense, Mademoiselle Keen. You were forced to a standstill, into making a compromise against your will, which held you back from what you were destined to be. Envy and avarice mark your past, as the sparks that have led you to your current path. You had no control over your own situation, and as a result you felt less than what you believed you were meant to be."

Sydney stared at the card, her expression less angry, and more… pensive. "Yes, I…. My parents…. I was a competitive child. My father thought a girl should not be ambitious. He held me back, pushing me toward a more, shall we say, traditionally feminine sphere of life. A house mouse with a working husband and a litter of kids running at my feet as I slaved over by the stove." Her eyes sparkled like diamonds, hard and relentless. "Naturally, the second I was old enough to decide for myself, I chose a different path. And not once have I regretted my choice."

All that was news to Gus, who began to realize he'd only thought he knew his coven friends. He had no idea Sydney's childhood had been so… oppressed. Gil was right: knowing these details about a person's life did shed light on who they were today.

Gus was ashamed he was so poorly versed in the lives of the people he called friends, and he vowed to change that. Well, after the current conundrum was over and done with, and the killer rotting behind bars.

"Your future," Gil said and turned the third card.

It was the Sun, reversed. In the center of the twelve signs of the zodiac shone the sun in all its brightness, with a rose in the middle and two dancing children with butterfly wings below.

Gil muttered something under his breath. "*Oh, je déteste cette carte! Quel malheur.*" He shook his head as though angry at the card for making an appearance. "Your light and warmth, your vitality and splendor, are all negated, buried under the massive, oppressive weight of your inflated ego. Your ego, born from oppression, has grown into something you may no longer recognize. You are blind to it, a character flaw. Whatever it is your mind is focused on right now is victorious behind a barrier of your ego, preventing you from dispelling the harmful impact. You withdraw from all that is rational and meaningful in order to pursue St. Elmo's fire that will lead you… nowhere of any true consequence."

At first Sydney appeared truly upset. Gus had a sneaky suspicion Gil was referring to Sydney's quest into secrets like the Esoteraphim and the Cabal. Sydney could bang her head against the wall of secrecy all she liked, but all she'd get out of it was a headache and a nasty bruise. Still he sympathized because Gus believed the world would have been a much, much darker place without free press.

Then Sydney let out such a deep breath she almost seemed to shrink. "I see. I do." She inhaled and nodded, regrouping. "I have strayed quite far from my typical journalistic zeal, from all matters relating to the environment. Pure journalism and verifiable facts, not shadows in the bushes. Thank you, Mr. van Es, for giving me something to think about."

As a gentleman, Gil bowed his head. "*Le motif de votre question.*" He turned the fourth card with a solemn gesture.

It was the Two of Wands, where two fire-red staffs with symbols of thunderbolts were crossed. The heads were in the shapes of horse heads and the tips adorned with serpents.

Gil nodded firmly. "Whatever your question, Mademoiselle Keen, this explains why. A fiery drive burns within you, demanding dominion and power over all knowledge, all deeds, all situations. Pure will, a voracious hunger for learning, controls your actions. Strength of character is your foundation, while your ambition and lust to see, hear, know, and experience all are the means. You are daring and courageous, and you take risks to get what you want. Personal power will lead you to greatness. Your hunger… will never be satisfied."

Sydney paled. Gus assumed her question had something to do with how to get more information, how to learn and know more, probably about secret societies like E.T. If that was so, it explained her reaction as she confronted her own choices in life, the ones that had made her into the career- and truth-oriented journalist she was today.

"I…." She hesitated, her voice vibrating slightly from nerves. "My question… it was about knowing more, about how I might get it, how I'd reach my objective." She looked away, part infuriated, part embarrassed.

"*C'est pas grave, Mademoiselle,*" Gil reassured her. "Your questions are not between you and me, but between you and the divine, you and the universe, you and your soul." To alleviate the tense atmosphere, he moved on, turning the last card. "The result."

It was the Empress.

Pastel hues of white, red, green, and blue gave the picture sensitivity and a dreamlike quality. The calm female figure was surrounded by a heavenly arch, blue flames, globes of earth and moon, a pelican, and a coat of arms depicting a two-headed eagle. In her hand, she held an open lotus blossom. She faced east, to the future.

Gil smiled. "Mademoiselle, if you play your cards right—pun intended—you will find harmony and radiance, beauty and wholeness. All aspects of femininity will be combined within as you grow as a woman and as a person, and reach your full, yet unlimited potential."

"So, is that my get-out-of-jail-free card?" Sydney asked, a half smile on her lips, with a touch of self-deprecating humor in her voice.

Gil burst into a full, deep belly laugh. The sound stopped suddenly, like it was cut in half with a knife. "Your personality lends itself to making your opinion and judgment known. So yes, as your emotions take control over your sensibilities, you are more than capable of setting off a bomb to prove your point or to exact revenge."

Sydney jumped up to her feet, her eyes ablaze. "I didn't do it! I'm innocent!"

Gil smiled enigmatically. "Therefore you are innocent."

That halted Sydney's rant before it began. "Say what?"

"Had you truly bombed your coven and killed two in the process," Gil said rationally, "you would have admitted it when prompted. You would have done so for the simple reason that you believe you would have been in the right and others in the wrong."

It sounded like such a simple statement, like an already known fact. Yet judging from people's mystified expression, they didn't get the gist of it any more than Gus. How could Sydney's personality be a possible match for the bomber and at the same time be proof against her guilt? That made no sense, as Aeryn would say.

ONLY THREE people remained huddled in their seats at the other end of the table. All of their expressions showed fear. But undoubtedly for different reasons, Gus assumed.

Rodney's dread was palpable. He sweated bullets, squirmed in his seat, and looked pale and about to collapse. If Rodney wasn't guilty, Gus contemplated, his worries were the result of his situation in life. Rodney's feverish stare at the cards could have been from fear of the cards telling him that the breakdown he'd suffered had been his own fault—not born of stressful circumstances, but of his own weak character. And, what if the cards predicted he'd never recover, and that his state of unemployment and poverty would last the rest of his life? Those kinds of concerns could make even the strongest man cower and wither.

Kerry's expression was slightly different. She frowned as if she couldn't understand why they were involved in this charade. Her gaze flicked from the cards to Gil, from Rodney and Joy to Niall and Hughes, from the table to Gus, and so forth, in a repeating cycle. She came from an ultrareligious background. Her fears could have stemmed from learning through the cards that she wouldn't find peace through spirituality, let alone from her new life, free from the oppression and tyranny of family. At least, that's what Gus theorized.

Joy looked about, eyes wide, her full lips apart in an *oh* of mystification, and her gaze never stopped anywhere either. There was an ounce of trepidation in her, but it was mostly clouded by perplexity. Her head was cocked and she frowned slightly, as though she was trying to make sense of things but didn't quite have the faculties. She wasn't stupid, Gus knew, but she was kind of an innocent, a bit naïve and easily misled, which had led her to troubles in the past. From her point of view, the cards probably appeared as divine portents that would tell her she would never be more than she was now, no matter how spiritual. That her wisdom would not grow, and she would continue to be blind to the dangers in the world.

Of course, Gus's reflections were predicated on his knowledge of the three remaining coven members. As recent events had shown, he couldn't exactly boast of his superb judgment of character. Was he just a fair-weather friend? How could he have bared his soul to these people at rituals since he was obviously so lacking in intimate knowledge of their lives? How could he have been so... blind and deaf, and purposely too? It wasn't like he'd exerted himself trying to learn the small details of what made these people tick. Had it really felt like such a... a burden?

Frowning and angry at himself, Gus vowed for the second time to change his approach and conduct, take the time to get to know these folks, who had prayed to the same goddesses during rituals. Yes, that was definitely on the agenda.

"Who would like to step up to the plate next?" Gil asked. Gus glanced at him, puzzling how a foreigner was so well acquainted with American idiom. How curious. "*S'il vous plaît.* Don't be shy. I won't bite." He winked playfully, grinning.

But Rodney, Kerry, and Joy didn't seem to be on board the this-is-just-a-game train.

By now, Rodney looked positively ill, almost going green. Gus had to wonder if he was about to throw up, and a spell of sympathetic nausea hit his throat. Joy seemed out of it, not having a clue as to what was going on and why she had to be a part of it. Kerry had the same doubtful and wary expression that Aeryn and Sydney had had, and her reluctance to participate was easy to spot.

"Be brave and come forth to—" Gil's voice cut off abruptly as he gasped, his eyes aimed skyward, glazing over. "Oh. Oh. *Oui, oui. Mon Dieu.* I sense... a presence." His arms spread, and his eyes widened to saucers as he stared up, as though seeing something besides the glass roof of the solarium. Then, in a flash, an exalted, rapturous expression replaced the shock. "*Ah, oui.* Our noble guests have arrived."

Gus's skin broke out in goose bumps. By the gods, the man had a flare for melodrama, a true showman. Even though Gus had anticipated this scene, he was ill prepared.

Without looking, Gil grabbed a deck of cards and spread them in a fan configuration on the table. Yet he never looked at them, his gaze still turned upward. "Speak to me, oh visitors from the great beyond. Tell me what you wish us to know. Show us your truths. We will listen and we shall obey."

"What the hell...?" Aeryn muttered, appearing bewildered and in shock. No general murmur followed, as everyone focused solely on Gil and his theatrics.

"Who comes?" Gil asked, his tone low and ominous. He swiped a card from the table in front of him and flipped it over.

It was the Moon, but reversed. Dominated by the colors blue, green, and black, symbolizing midnight and fear, in the card hung a waning moon above a narrow path between barren mountains, guarded by two ominous-looking, jackal-headed figures, representing Anubis, the Egyptian God of Death and Afterlife. Yet, below was the sacred beetle carrying a sun disk, a promise of a better tomorrow.

"The time of fear is upon us," Gil said without even seeing what the card was. "A warning comes from the other side. Lies and deceit fill this room, emanating from... from...." Gil let out an odd wailing sound, like a desperate death cry into the night. "Inner demons gnawing at the good within. Chasing after fantasies, the impossible. A nameless dread walking upon the cold, dark waters. No...."

Gus felt a chill in his soul as he, like the others, was mesmerized by the sight, unable to look away. Like moths to a deadly flame, they were all drawn toward the majesty of Gil.

Gil closed his eyes, a reverent, ecstatic look on his face, a small smile flicking up the corners of his mouth. "Yes, I hear you. I feel you. Come closer, I beg of you." He swayed a little, as if lost in a trance or a world of his own. "A young man. Laughs a lot. Wears silly shirts.

Genuinely likeable. What a wonderful strategic, yet playful, mind. Yes, I see." His fingerprints hovered over the fan of cards. Another card was flipped over, almost carelessly, and it landed on top of the Moon card.

The Knight of Coins appeared.

Wearing a red-brown cloak, a weary knight sat on an exhausted horse, staring at an unrelenting harvest sun, and the horse lowered its head toward the ripe wheat field. He held a flail to work the fields, to slave hard to reap the rewards of abundance.

"Yes, I hear you still," Gil spoke slowly and slurred a bit, as though his mouth wouldn't work normally anymore. "Your name.... Matty...?"

This time the dining room filled with loud, shaken gasps and the creaking of chairs as people leaned forward to hear and see better.

"Tell me more," Gil prompted the ghost only he could apparently see, his tone half-pleading, half-commanding. "You are, what... a prince of clouds now." Gus damn near swallowed his tongue. Was Gil referring to Matty's cloud storage? Damn, he was good at this subterfuge by means of the performance arts! "You wish to speak of... seedlings...?"

Juliette let out a helpless yelp. "Oh Goddess, Seedling was Pine Seed's coven name!"

Gil acted like he hadn't heard the interruption, continuing to behave as if he were enraptured—or intoxicated. "Seedling was... an agent of order...? No, that's wrong. Ah, yes. She was an agent for... for the government."

"What?" Juliette, Aeryn, and Sydney yelled out at once.

"*Ah, oui, je comprends.*" Gil swayed in place, his eyes closed, the smile ever-present. "Seedling asked you to—no, told you to... research... angels?" Gus was sure his eyes would pop out of their sockets any moment, what with all the astonished ogling he was doing. "No, that was wrong. Look into... worshippers of angels? Ah, yes, that is correct."

"Angels?" Aeryn asked loudly, confusion marring her beautiful features.

Beside her, though, Sydney fiercely shushed her and listened intently.

Gil frowned, as though he heard something he didn't agree with. "I will tell them but I—Of course I will. *Oui, bien sûr, mon ami.* He wishes you to know that... a vengeful spirit has latched on to him, a possessive personality. A... a killer." Gil gasped along with others but he didn't snap out of his trance. "He says someone in this room harbors an embarrassing secret, one that could tip the scales of justice. He urges, yes, he begs of you to speak out before it is too late."

He turned another card, seemingly at random. It was the High Priest again.

Gil groaned like he was in agony. "*S'il vous plaît, mes chéris*, speak the truth now, before it is too late. For the sake of our coven, for the sake of our religion, for the sake of honesty and integrity. Cast aside your fears and doubts, your self-recriminations and humiliation." He drew in a sharp breath and paled. Though his eyes were shut, his horror was plain to see. He was even starting to sound like Matty, if it weren't for the French words. "*Mon Dieu*. The shadow, it nears…. In life, I was afraid, forever watched and spied upon, never alone. Always the shade following, wanting, craving me…. Ahh…. Jealousy, anger, unrequited lov—"

Gil's voice was cut off when, shaking like a tiny leaf in a storm, Rodney stood up abruptly, trembling though he was stiff as a board. "I… I must tell you…. I must confess…." He pushed his chair back and was about to begin his trek toward Gil and the Tarot cards.

But all of a sudden, he rubbed his forehead, mumbled something incoherent—and fell down on the floor in a wobbly heap of limbs, passing out cold.

"Shit." Hughes hurried to his side and checked for Rodney's pulse. He sighed in relief. "He's fine. Just… unconscious." He looked up at Niall sarcastically, "Guess the stress got to him."

"I'll take him to a couch and place a cold, wet towel on his forehead. That should ease his sick feeling and revive him," Niall offered. He snaked his strong arms around Rodney's midsection and under his arms and lifted him up like a rag doll.

Grunting, he heaved the lump of lifeless flesh toward the door to the large, spacious living room, which spanned two floors and boasted not less than three suede couches, along with floor-to-ceiling windows and a view to the nighttime Lake Washington guaranteed to soothe even the most anxious of souls.

Everyone in the dining room exhaled a sigh of relief, and started to resume their places.

All but one.

"Hey, Pryor's gone! Where'd she go?" Hughes called out loudly.

Like the others, Gus turned toward the place Kerry had occupied a moment ago, but her seat was empty and she was nowhere to be seen. "I don't know," Gus said, a second later feeling rather silly for stating the obvious.

"Maybe she went to the bathroom," Joy suggested. "Perhaps she felt ill, like Rodney."

Bless her heart, the saint among us petty mortals. Gus had serious doubts about Kerry and her innocence. "I don't think so." While still confused about a possible motive for Kerry, Gus looked at Hughes. "You should probably radio in her sudden and suspicious departure."

Gil straightened the lapels of his fancy coat and said coolly, like a totally disinterested party, like the séance had never happened, "She did not run past me to get outside, Messieurs, but deeper into the house, I believe."

"Nobody leaves," Hughes barked to everyone waiting shocked and silent in the dining room, and Gus nodded his agreement. As he hurried toward the living room and adjoining open kitchen, Hughes shouted orders to the camouflaged police officers on stakeout on the estate grounds. The buzz, hiss, and rattle of the radio faded as he moved farther away until silence reigned in the house and the only sound was the trills and songs of the nocturnal birds coming from the garden.

"Was this the goal of this mockery?" Aeryn asked, having calmed down before anyone else. "A fake séance to provoke the murderer to run?" She no longer sounded furious or even bewildered but tired and sad.

Gus nodded slowly, slightly ashamed. "Yeah, kind of."

"*Je proteste!*" Gil van Es said, indignant, as though mortally wounded. "I do not fake anything. There was a true presence here in our midst, one close to all of—"

"So, none of these readings were on the level?" Juliette asked, cutting off Gil's upset rant.

"Mr. van Es had character profiles of all of you, which accounted for the accuracy of his predictions," Gus explained.

Gil growled then, an angry sound for the first time. "*Faux! Vous avez tort!* I may have learned a few minor details about you, but my predictions, Mesdames et Messieurs, were not wrong or lies or fabrications. They were true. *Ils étaient vraies.*" He seemed terribly hurt about doubts of his abilities, so Gus decided to placate him, but he didn't get the chance.

"Are you claiming that Pine Seed was really a government agent?" Sydney interjected, the pitch of her voice rising to an alarming level. "That was true?"

Gus nodded firmly. "After his death, Matty confided to Juliette via a tablet computer that he'd been hired to investigate a secret society called the Esoteraphim. According to conspiracy theories and wild online rumors, E.T. was the alleged powerbase behind most regimes in the world. But during his examination into the sect, Matty learned E.T. is nothing more than a small group of moderately influential people in the greater Seattle area." Fraught with empathy, Gus looked at Alec, who had a right to know. "I'm sorry, Alec, but I have to tell you that… that it looked like Jason was a member of E.T., and that was probably what got him killed."

Taken aback, Alec just blinked, apparently unable to absorb the information. "No. No. I don't believe that." He kept shaking his head, as though the motion alone could keep the truth at bay. "It's impossible. He would've told me if…. He wouldn't have…." He swiveled around in haste, his shoulders shimmying like he was crying, but no sounds could be heard.

Hesitantly, Tom stepped closer, putting his hand on Alec's shoulder. Alec started, and for a second it seemed he wanted no part of what Tom offered. Nodding glumly, Tom moved back to give Alec some space. But in a heartbeat Tom had his arms full of Alec, who clung to him with gusto. Tom let out a deep, shaky breath, and embraced Alec back.

It was clear the two of them were headed toward some sort of relationship. Gus smiled at the happy, loving sight in the midst of all this emotional and spiritual turmoil.

"Gus? Hello?" Sydney waved a frustrated hand to get Gus's attention. "Pine Seed?"

Worrying his bottom lip, Gus decided to come clean. It seemed like a safe bet since Kerry was in the wind, potentially the culprit. They wouldn't really know until they caught her and got the story straight from the horse's mouth. "Yes, Piney was a government agent. Really and truly. Well, an agent of sorts. Apparently, she'd been recruited in college, her first year, due to her interest in neopaganism. At the time, the DHS had also heard rumors about E.T. and believed it was based on religious fanaticism. These days, those words ring with a menacing echo. Because she was into Wicca, Pine Seed was chosen. To hide her involvement, she hired Matty, as a computer expert, to look into E.T. on the down low."

Most everyone was still standing following Rodney's passing out, but now, one by one, they sat down heavily, as if the weight of the world were upon them. Sydney appeared stunned in disbelief, and Aeryn part angry, part hurt. Juliette sat at Owain's side, dazed and silent, like she was processing the news but hadn't made it to the finish line of normality yet. Sympathetically, Joy had come to sit on Juliette's other side, and she held Juliette's other hand.

"I can't believe this is happening," Juliette whispered, her gaze glassy, her voice low and frail. "I just can't...." She frowned, irritated at her own ignorance. "Now that we're confessing things.... Matty was the thief who stole from the coven till."

"What? Why?" Aeryn demanded to know, her aggravation only growing.

Juliette sniffed, her head downcast, her brown tresses covering most of her face. "To get my attention and that of law enforcement to investigate the odd goings-on in the coven."

But Aeryn wasn't buying it, apparently. "That makes no sense. If Jason was a member of this, what was it, Esoteraphim, and Kerry, who's now on the lam, is a possible member too, then why would Kerry murder Jason? If they're allies, I mean, there'd be no motive for her to kill him."

Gus had to admit that was a damn good question. He sure had no answers to offer. But he did know he was tired of sitting in the dining room. "Let's all go to the living room and find out if Rodney's regained consciousness. The cops will likely come there too to let us in on the hunt for Kerry."

His suggestion was met with quiet nods and everyone rose from the chairs to head for the living room. Gus had a sinking feeling the night was far from over, and that didn't help his mood one damn bit.

Only one thing did: Niall. Gus put all his faith, trust, and love in Niall. If anyone could solve this dilemma, it'd be Niall. That thought did give Gus's step some optimistic bounce.

Chapter 17

"HEY THERE," Niall said in a quiet, soothing voice as he wiped Rodney's forehead with a damp, cool cloth. Rodney started coming around, blinking wearily. "How ya feeling?"

Rodney groaned in pain, trying to reach up and touch his head, but Niall gently pushed his hand back down. "W-what happened…?"

"You passed out. You were about to confess something." Niall was well aware he was being fucking obvious, heading straight for the cause of Rodney's anxiety, but a killer was on the loose, and Niall was running out of time and patience.

Rodney first paled, then flushed scarlet. "Oh, y-yes, I remember now." He gulped like he was fighting some pretty substantial inner demons. "The cards…. They were right. I felt so ashamed when I realized how foolish I'd been." His pleading eyes met with Niall's. "Did Matty…? Was he really there…?"

Niall decided to ignore that bit for a lot of reasons. "What did you wanna tell us?"

Three uniformed officers walked into the room from different locations, settling close to the entryways to keep clear lines of sight in all directions. Niall, for one, was glad they were there. The living room, or lounge to be precise, was massive. Fifty people or more would've easily fit in there. Wood-paneled walls, a stone fireplace, and plump, cozy furniture gave it an unusual warmth for an opulent estate. The only signs of affluence came in the form of art—antique vases and paintings by well-known artists—an expensive rug, and crystal glasses and a silver decanter by the bar area, which also housed an assortment of expensive bottles of wine and liquor.

"Rodney?" Niall prompted cautiously. "Whatever it is you know, now's the time to come clean. You gotta tell us." Niall left out the part about Kerry having done a runner since that would be dealt with, sooner or later, without them.

Rodney nodded frantically, though it was obvious the situation was hard on him. "Yes. Of course. I'll tell you everything."

Before he could get another word out, however, Gus, Juliette, Owain, Aeryn, Sydney, Tom, Alec, and Gil van Es entered from the dining room, all appearing distraught—barely holding it together, but managing somehow. All except Gil, that is, who wore a professional mask of cool detachment. Niall nodded to Gus, who offered a weak smile and a haunted gaze in return. Niall worried about him, and decided then and there to take him on a holiday soon. As soon as this mess was dealt with and the killer apprehended—or shot down by the police.

Niall turned back to Rodney, who had shifted to a sitting position, though he still looked ill and a bit green. "Rodney?"

With an appearance of a whipped dog, Rodney mumbled miserably, "I didn't know, you see. I thought he was on the level. I thought he was a fine, upstanding citizen. How could I have known he was a bad man? I have no experience with such... duplicitous, dangerous people. He had a stellar reputation, you see, so naturally when Jason entrusted me with the grimoire for study and safekeeping, I—"

"Rodney, you're rambling," Gus said quietly from across the room.

Rodney was clearly about to burst into tears. "I know, I know. It's just this is so awful and terrible, and I was so foolish and gullible—"

This time Niall interrupted him, his tone soothing. "Rodney. Take a deep breath and speak slowly and calmly, okay? Good man."

Rodney closed his eyes, did a hysterical male version of Lamaze breathing, and relaxed a bit, enough to speak. "I met him the day after Jason gave me the grimoire for research. He led me to believe he was a serious connoisseur of sixteenth- and seventeenth-century literature, especially of grimoires. I'd heard of him, of course, during my time as a professor, but I'd never actually met the man." He shuddered, blood draining from his face again, and sweat beaded his forehead. "Until the day after I met Jason. He came to my home, you see, and I... I...." Shaking his head vehemently, he harrumphed loudly, angry at himself. "He mentioned Jason's name. That, plus the name recognition, and I believed him, let him in, and allowed him to see the grimoire. I valued his insight and was eager for his expert opinion, you see, because he's reputed to be a descendant of John Dee himself! That's why I saw no reason to deny him access to the grimoire, since it was a part of his family's legacy and heritage."

Before Rodney could draw breath and keep going, Niall intervened. "Who, Rodney? Who is he?"

Rodney slumped, defeated and humiliated. "I didn't recognize him at first. He was shining that flashlight right at us when he came through the gate the night of the esbat, and I only saw a glimpse of his face when he started to leave." He took a shuddery breath and spoke in a watery voice. "Ignatius Ashe. But of course he wasn't the *real* Dee scholar by that name. And I sincerely doubt he's Dee's descendant, either. The true name he was born with is John Abrams."

Niall was speechless for a second or two, dumbstruck. "Abrams? Jason's next door *neighbor* Abrams? The same Abrams who interrupted your esbat ritual by starting a shouting match? That Abrams?"

Rodney nodded, a miserable sight indeed. "Yes. His bodyguard, a tall blond beefcake who accompanies him, trashed my house and stole the grimoire."

"Oh, Rodney." Gus sighed, sat down next to Rodney, and took his hands into his own. "Why didn't you tell the police, or us, or anyone?"

Sniffling, Rodney said, "I was embarrassed, humiliated, ashamed, and… I couldn't admit even to myself I'd let him in and welcomed him to my house. Until now."

A shot suddenly pierced the air, a loud bang in the silence of the night.

Everyone started, and the officers by the doorways ran toward the sound. Niall stood, took his gun out from his belt, and clicked off the safety. He stared in the direction the police had exited but remained in place, fixated on ensuring the safety of his loved ones and their friends. No one was going to get past him if he had any say in the matter.

The rest huddled closer to each other for safety, their gazes also aimed at the door.

Time ticked away so slowly Niall suspected it might have actually stopped, suspended in a moment of gruesome death, great danger, and ensuing panic. His palms were sweaty and his stare so intense his vision began to blur. He had to blink several times to clear it. The urge to do battle was strong within him, the instinct that had grown into a monster inside him during the war. He hated being in this situation again, pitted against a murderous foe on the edge of a knife.

A bulky shadow loomed in the doorway, and everyone gasped, holding their breaths, grasping at one another. Niall aimed the barrel of his gun at the shape that was forming.

"Don't shoot. It's just me."

Hughes entered the room. The collective sigh of relief was loud, followed closely by a spate of nervous laughter as stress relief.

"What happened?" Niall demanded to know, his own stress level remaining high.

"Pryor was shot," Hughes grunted. "In the chest. But there was a pulse. The paramedics took her a second ago. Good thing we had them on standby."

Niall clicked the safety back and holstered his weapon, then finally allowed himself to relax, sitting back down on the chair. They were out of danger, the situation defused, the case over. "Fuck. That was tense. I almost...." *Flashed back to the war zone.* Niall suppressed the admission.

"What? Almost shot me?" Hughes chuckled. "Good thing I know your aim sucks."

"Fuck off, man. This has been a shitty day." Niall turned back to the others, relieved to see them recovering from the crisis, sitting and standing close together, their unity restored. But then he saw something was amiss. "Hey, where's van Es?"

Surprised, everyone looked around, but the mysterious Gil van Es was nowhere to be seen, as elusive as the shadows themselves.

"Maybe he went back to the dining room," Gus suggested. "He could have gone to the kitchen to get a drink or something. I'll go check." After a quick nod from Niall, or in spite of it, Gus left the room.

Niall faced Hughes again, feeling the urge to needle a comrade-in-arms, to bring some humor into the recent dire situation. "Good thing you had your gun ready, Virg. Funny, but I figured you'd be the one to suck at shooting."

Hughes rolled his eyes and shook his head. "I happen to be a crack shot, Junior. But in any case, your congratulations are misdirected. I didn't shoot Pryor."

Niall stared at him confused. "Then who did?"

Hughes shrugged. "Abrams. The guy from next door. Apparently, Pryor had gone there for some reason, maybe to hide, or to steal some money or a means of transportation, or whatever. Anyway, Abrams had heard the commotion going on over here, so when Pryor came in, he was already armed and shot on instinct. It'll most likely be ruled a justifiable shooting, considering the circumstances. Case closed."

Scratch that. Case still very much open. Gritting his teeth, Niall was ready to leap into action. No way was it a coincidence that Kerry Pryor had gone to hide at Abrams's place. If Abrams shot Kerry when Kerry had an opportunity to disappear, in Niall's mind that could only mean one thing: Kerry had sought safety and sanctuary from an ally or a boss, which suggested they were on the same side—part of the Esoteraphim.

That was when Gus returned from the dining room. His face radiated confusion as he came in, carrying a round wine glass with a Tarot card in it. "He's not here anymore. Gil van Es, I mean. He's disappeared." He raised the glass. "This was all I could find."

"What is it?" Niall asked, just as puzzled, as he pointed at the items Gus held.

Gus shrugged. "There was a single red rose in it, but I took it out. Gil had it stuck in his lapel. I saw it before." He picked up the card and turned it around so everyone could see it.

It was the Universe, the final card in the Major Arcana.

An individual's unity with the cosmos was represented by a naked dancing female. She held a sickle, a serpent around her, the Eye of Horus aimed at her, and the webs of mortality and physicality tore around her, lifting her beyond them to a form of pure spirit. Four cherubs blew winds of new beginnings at her from the four cardinal corners.

"I admit I'm a novice when it comes to Tarot," Gus said slowly. "But I'm pretty sure this marks the moment of release from all constraints and the past. Ultimate freedom and oneness with the universe is achieved. A final purpose has been reached, and all masks and cloaks are cast aside as useless." He sighed as he stopped. "Masks…." He frowned, but then again so did others in the room, Niall included. Then he flipped the card around to look at the back. "Oh my God…," he gasped aloud, shock clearly evident on his face. "Look!" He made sure the back of the card was visible. Over the gray uniform back was a big letter C. "C for cyanide," Gus said, his voice caught in a tremor of bared emotions. "C for…."

Niall snapped his fingers as the important dots connected in his brain, firing him up. "C for the Cabal." He jumped to his feet, angry at himself for missing the obvious. "Van Es is with the Cabal." Then he cursed out loud. "And Abrams is with the Esoteraphim! Fuck, we gotta get over there. *Now*!"

NIALL WAS already running, with Hughes following him, and so was Gus, who was bubbling over with questions. But Niall didn't have the time to answer anything at the moment. He had a bad feeling. Van Es had heard Rodney speak of Abrams, who not only had stolen the grimoire but had claimed to be a descendant of John Dee as well. If van Es really was with this Cabal, then they were rivals.

Through the lawn, under the hedge archway, and over the tiled patio, Niall rushed onto the Abrams estate. Abrams's mansion was a modern architectural masterpiece, with only metal, glass, and black leather as interior design, giving it a cold feel.

There, at the foot of the safety glass stairs, stood a uniformed officer, writing in a note pad. On the floor lay a dark pool of blood, undoubtedly Kerry Pryor's. Niall tried not to shout at the police officer so as not to spook Abrams. "Where's Abrams?" he insisted in a voice as low as he could muster, all the while urgency beat inside him, demanding him to stop yapping and take action.

The officer frowned, abashed, but as soon as he recognized Hughes, he replied, "Mr. Abrams was a bit shaken and wanted to wash his hands and face. He went to the upstairs master bathroom, sir." He pointed at the stairs.

Niall jumped over the pool of blood and dashed up the stairs, with Gus and Hughes hot on his heels. From the top of the stairs, several hallways opened, but only one room was lit, so Niall assumed it was Abrams's bedroom.

The master bedroom was huge. Two chandeliers illuminated it from above and bedside lamps from below, while floor-to-ceiling windows would provide daylight when it was available. One corner was occupied by a round, towerlike space containing an armchair and a small coffee table. Next to it stood a whitewashed fireplace, an urn filled with fresh flowers, and the door to the master bathroom. On its right sat a king-size bed, now unmade, its sheets and pillows rumpled. On the other side of the room, there were no windows, and a bookshelf and a study desk dominated the area.

Above the desk a painting of stormy shores hung outward on a set of hinges, revealing a safe embedded into the wall behind it, its metal door now wide open. Inside were several boxes, stacks of papers and documents—and a small book stand covered by a dark-red velvet cloth, now empty.

"The grimoire," Gus panted, breathless from the run over. "It's gone."

"Two guesses who snatched it," Niall growled and hurried to the master bathroom.

The faux-wood-paneled door was ajar. No sounds came from the other side.

Niall and Hughes both snatched out their guns, and Niall waved Gus back. He was glad this time Gus obeyed without protest.

Hughes kicked the door open, and it slammed against a cabinet.

Another spacious room, Niall observed, with white-and-blue tiles, marble counters, stone sinks, and a wide oval bathtub with jets on the sides—and a man's body in it. The dead man had on gray sweats, a T-shirt, and an oddly carved wooden mask that vaguely resembled a human being but was decorated with strange symbols.

Chapter 18

GUS GASPED from behind Niall, who couldn't reproach him. "W-who is it…?"

Hughes approached and yanked the mask off.

The dead man was Abrams.

He hadn't been shot or stabbed, Niall noted, but his lips and partly out-lolling tongue were peppered with red blisters.

Hughes bent down to take a pulse from the jugular artery, waited a few seconds, and then shook his head, glum and furious. "He's gone." Suddenly he sniffed the air, dipping down a bit. "Bitter almonds."

"Cyanide," Niall concluded. "The same weapon that killed Jason."

"If Gil van Es murdered Abrams with cyanide, does that mean… he also killed Jason?" Gus asked, going pale in shock. "Oh God, Niall…. If I hadn't come up with my stupid plan to use Gil, the con man and cold-reader, to expose a murderer, none of this would have happened! He was there the whole time, right under our noses. Under mine."

Niall closed the gap between them, gripped Gus by the arms, and gently drew him as close as he could without making a scene. "No, babe, that's not true. I think Kerry was disposable. Abrams didn't need her anymore."

"Abrams…? You think Kerry, too, was a member of the Esoteraphim?" Gus asked, his eyes blinking as the idea dawned on him and took a foothold.

"Yeah, I do. She could've run. But instead she came here, I'm assuming to get help from an ally." Niall nodded, firm in his belief because he trusted his instincts, no matter where they led. "I also think van Es was going to kill Abrams once he found out he was with E.T., same as Jason. The only thing van Es didn't know was the identity of the person behind Kerry and who'd stolen the grimoire."

Gus hugged Niall, decorum be damned. "We don't know any of that for sure."

"The police will search into Kerry's life until they find out what she ate for lunch in kindergarten, so don't worry. It'll all come out in the end."

Niall kept rubbed soothing circles on Gus's back, letting Gus lean on him for support. "Besides, if my theory's right, Kerry could have exposed Abrams, which gave him a solid reason to shoot her. And Rodney, who also knew part of the truth, would've been next. Without your plan, we wouldn't have known about the threat against Rodney, and Abrams would have disposed of him too, sooner or later. You saved his life, Gus. That's worth a hell of a lot."

Gus was quiet for a moment. "I guess you're right." He took a deep breath and seemed to calm down, the tension and anxiety flowing out of him. "Why does the Cabal want John Dee's grimoire?" Gus asked, sounding sleepy now. "Are they fans of angels too?"

That was another damn good question, and it was also one Niall didn't have an answer for, not even a made-up one.

Several pairs of heavy footsteps came from the stairs. Gus quickly pulled away from Niall, straightening up and putting on a brave face. Niall understood. No man wanted to be seen as weak or frail in public.

The Crime Scene Unit team of four technicians, wearing white coveralls and carrying metal cases with their gear, entered the bedroom.

"I want pictures of everything, and gather every damn piece of evidence you can find. Hair, fibers, blood—everything and anything," Hughes told them in his authoritative voice. "Start by taking photos of the open safe and dust it for fingerprints." He pointed a finger at Gus and Niall. "Once they're done, I want you to go through what's in there. If there's any proof of Abrams being a member of this E.T., you two will likely recognize it before anyone else." He then pointed at one of the uniformed officers who stood by the doorway. "Martinez, stay with them at all times. I don't want any more bodies."

Another officer hollered from the hall. "Sir? I think you better see this."

"What now?" Hughes grunted and followed the young man downstairs, disappearing from sight.

Gus bit his nails while waiting, his nervous gaze aimed at the safe. Niall could relate since he, too, itched to see what was there. The grimoire was gone, of course, but there had to be at least something to connect the dots in this case and prove that Abrams was involved in this mess. The theft of the book from Rodney's place, at least, was something they could prove.

Martinez spoke softly to another officer who came to the doorway. Then he addressed Niall. "Sir? Detective Hughes has ordered you to be kept informed of every aspect of this case. You might like to know that we've detained Mr. Abrams's bodyguard, and he's on his way to the precinct for questioning. Also, Ms. Pryor has made it to the hospital and she's been taken into surgery."

Niall nodded. "What are her chances?"

"I'm sorry, but I don't have that information, sir."

"Any news on van Es, the psychic?"

"I'm afraid not, sir. There have been no sightings as of yet." Martinez returned to stand guard at the threshold, his game face firmly plastered on his roughly handsome features.

"Niall, take a look at his." Gus waved him over to the safe, where he already had a pile of papers in hand. The CSU team must have finished while Niall talked with Martinez. Niall joined Gus, who leafed through the stack in a rush, clearly excited. "There's everything we need here, Niall."

"Files or notes about the other members of E.T.?" Niall asked, enthusiastic as well.

"Yes, all that plus a contact book with their names, numbers, and addresses. Abrams has also kept a kind of journal of his dealings with E.T." Gus gave Niall a few papers and a black notebook. "Look at the last dozen entries."

Niall flipped to the right page and read, "Jason Upton successfully recruited and set up next door. Advised him to purchase a specific book at the black auction in order to avert unwanted attention falling on the group."

Niall looked up at Gus. "That's gotta be the grimoire. Jason said at the hospital the book was recommended to him. Now we know by whom."

"That's what it looks like," Gus agreed. "Read on."

"Damn that Upton. He refused to give the grimoire to the group. Now we have to find the infernal thing and then deal with Upton permanently."

Niall shuddered. "That means E.T. killed one of their own."

"One who rebelled," Gus noted. "Guess that's why Jason gave the grimoire to Rodney. Not just to do research on it or find a rich buyer, but for safekeeping. He must have suspected the group would try to get the book back."

Niall nodded, finding the explanation rational. They would still have to find a way to prove their theory. "Grimoire not at Upton's place. Abe searched the mansion top to bottom, with no results. Damn Upton must have stashed it somewhere else. Must find out where he's been during the last couple of days."

"Abe must be the blond bodyguard," Gus commented.

"Guess so." Niall shrugged, since he didn't know for sure. "Found out who's got the book. Rodney Easton. Sent Abe to toss his place upside down. I want that book."

Niall harrumphed. "This guy reads like a poor excuse for a mobster. Pathetic."

"Niall," Gus said with obvious reproach in his tone. "The man is dead. You shouldn't speak ill of the dead."

"Not even the bad guys?" Niall knew he sounded skeptical, but when Gus pursed his lips like he did when he was disappointed, Niall acquiesced. "Sorry." Gus smiled, and Niall's world was better once again.

He continued reading. "We have the grimoire. Easton's a scared little mouse. He won't talk after the mess we made of his house. No need to get rid of him."

Gus puffed out an angry breath. "What a bastard."

Niall quirked an eyebrow, trying not to grin. "Hey, what happened to your policy of not talking trash about the dead?"

Gus's cheeks pinked, and he looked a little sheepish. "An exception to the rule. The situation called for it."

Niall chuckled. "Uh-huh." Then he resumed his inspection of Abrams' journal.

"Found out about Kerry's one-sided crush on that geeky Osborne kid. Told her nothing would come of it. She didn't believe me. She's ruled by her emotions, not her common sense. I knew it was a bad idea to recruit her in the first place. But Cummins outvoted me, the rat bastard. He's got a soft spot for young, innocent skirts. A hard spot, if we get technical. I still think she's unfit for the group, and I'll make this known to the others at our next meeting. We gotta get rid of her."

"Cummins," Gus repeated, pensive. "I think I saw that name in one of the files. Wait a sec." He skimmed through the stacks of papers until he pulled one out. It was a character profile of one of the twelve members of E.T. "Clarence Cummins, United States Court of Appeals for the Ninth Circuit." Gus looked up, horrified. "He's a judge!"

Niall nodded that he understood the magnitude of the discovery. He continued reading. "Found out Kerry has planted a bomb on Upton's lawn. From what I've been able to gather, the target of the strike seems to be that Tash tart who's been seen with Osborne on several occasions. Guess Kerry's jealousy finally got the better of her, if she plans to dispose of her romantic rival with such drastic means. She's off her rocker for sure. This is just the sort of information I can use to get to the group to accept the fact we must do away with her."

Niall had to stop there, too appalled to speak further.

Gus didn't have the same problem, but he spoke with tears in his eyes. "Kerry thought Matty and Piney were having an affair because they were seen together. When in truth Piney just ordered Matty to research E.T. There was nothing romantic between them. Matty disliked Piney, and since she was a government agent, that kind of makes sense. But Kerry… she didn't know any of that. And that's why she… why she…."

Gus couldn't finish, just kept swallowing and blinking. Niall gripped his lover's arm and pulled him in, embracing him tighter and rubbing more soothing circles on his back. "Love can make us do great and horrible things. Considering how sheltered Kerry was before learning of the ways of the world, I suppose she didn't know how to handle the jealousy born from unrequited love."

Nodding a bit, Gus unwound, and Niall inwardly sighed in relief. Comforting wasn't his strong suit.

"I'll keep reading, okay?" He pulled back and met Gus's green eyes, now misted. Gus frowned and looked away. He didn't like to act overly emotional, Niall knew, at least not in front of him.

Without further comment, Niall returned his attentions to the journal. "The group managed to convince Kerry that the bomb idea was a bad one. But… I found out that the Tash woman isn't just a plain old witch; she's an undercover operative of the government, investigating me and the group, and with Osborne's help in computers. So… I decided the bomb strike wasn't too radical for my agenda after all. When Upton wasn't home, instead of removing the bomb entirely, I simply moved it to another spot. Now it will destroy four nuisances in one shot: Kerry, Tash, Upton, and Osborne. I, of course, will serve my humble citizen's duty as an eyewitness. And the blame will fall on Kerry and her insane jealousy. No fuss, no muss. Best plan I've ever had."

"Oh. My. God." Gone was mournful Gus; in its place was vengeful, furious Gus, whom Niall not-so-secretly found hotter than hell and sexier than sin. But now was not the time for sex-laden thoughts. "If Abrams wasn't dead, I'd kill him myself."

"Gus…," Niall tried to reach his boyfriend, the truest part of him that never believed violence was the answer.

But as quickly as fuming Gus had appeared, he vanished again, replaced by sad Gus. "Now I get it. How Kerry was that night before the esbat. There was so much sorrow and longing in her eyes. She believed Abrams had removed the bomb, and she had let go of her hopeless dream of being with Matty." A small, hollow chuckle escaped his lips. "I wasn't wrong about her after all. She saw the error of her ways and tried to change. But… it was too late. No good came of it at all. All because of Abrams's duplicity and betrayal."

"He's paid for it," Niall said, attempting to be rational. He expected having to argue his point to a mourning Gus.

Gus exhaled, sagged, and nodded, all in one fluid move. "No, he didn't pay for it. He should've gone to prison for the rest of his life. Now that he's dead… I'd say he got away with it."

"I disagree." Niall locked gazes with a puzzled Gus. "After all, he was murdered in his own home and his prized possession is gone. He lost the game, or whatever this weirdness is between E.T. and the Cabal."

Gus pursed his lips in concentration. "I hadn't thought about that. Guess you're right."

Niall grinned. "I could stand to hear that more often."

Gus rolled his eyes. "Keep reading, egomaniac."

Niall winked before resuming. "Bomb went off as planned. Walked into the scene as the upset neighbor, screaming my head off, and hit the remote. I had a one-minute window. I was brilliant. The acting world lost a talent with me."

Gus grimaced. "Is that douchebag serious?"

"Ego boosts." Niall shrugged and went on. "Plan failed. In part. Kerry's alive but in a coma. Let's hope she doesn't wake up. Upton's alive, too, but in his second surgery, so he might not recover either. Tash and Osborne are dead." Niall skimmed a few lines with information that wasn't relevant to the case before continuing. "Something's happened. Upton was poisoned in the hospital. He's dead. It wasn't me or anyone in the group. There's someone else out there. Gotta keep my eyes open for anything suspicious."

"E.T. didn't kill Jason after all," Gus said, gasping. "That means…."

"Then it must've been the Cabal," Niall concluded Gus's thought. Suddenly he snapped his fingers as a memory clicked in his head. "Wasn't there a male nurse back at the hospital that kept refilling the jug?"

Gus frowned, obviously recollecting. "That unkempt-looking dude? Yeah, I remember him. He didn't refill the jug but replaced it with a new one. Heck, that jug must've been laced with cyanide. How could we have missed that?"

Niall scolded him, "Gus, unlike gods and goddesses, we humans aren't all-seeing or infallible. How could we have paid attention to something we didn't know about? Besides, we kind of had other priorities that day."

"That's true." Gus nodded toward the journal. "What else?"

Niall read onward. "Abe ransacked Tash and Osborne's apartments for incriminating evidence against the group. None found. Nothing suggests Tash had contacted or reported back to her superiors. Might be safe after all. All we found at Osborne's place were piles of games and lots of half-assembled computers, school books, and empty pizza boxes. It seems he didn't have anything on us either. Looks good."

"That part we already knew," Gus commented, trying to get sneak peeks at the journal even though Niall would have happily given it to him had he simply asked.

"Easton's been talking to the police and some PI. Looks like we have to deal with him after all. Abe will try to make it look like an accident. Also, one of the group members informed me of a reporter who's been sniffing into our affairs, has for quite some time. Why I was kept out of the loop, I don't know, but I will, and when I do heads will roll. In any case, this reporter—by the name of Keen—I will handle myself. I'll make an example of her. Should prove titillating."

"Syd...," Gus whispered, his features contorting in shock, fear, and pain.

Niall touched his arm gently. "He's dead, Gus. And the rest of E.T. will soon be behind bars for good." He nudged Gus to look up at him. "See? Your plan saved another life that we'd never have known about or connected to this."

"Yeah. Yes." Gus visibly shook himself from his saddened state, even managing a tiny smile.

"This is the final entry," Niall said and kept reading. "The police have set up some kind of sting at Upton's place next door. Kerry's awake, but she hasn't breathed a word about the group. According to the medical report, she might have amnesia. Whether that's true or not, I gotta get rid of her. She knows the names of over half the group. I'll keep vigil if whatever they arranged proves successful. Best to keep a gun at the ready too. If not to tie up loose ends, then to try and make an escape."

"Abrams didn't know if Kerry was faking it," Gus commented, appearing perplexed.

"Neither did we," Niall observed. "But considering she escaped to Abrams's house, I'd wager she either recovered her memory tonight or she faked it entirely."

Gus frowned. "I met her the night of the esbat. She was nice. I find it hard to believe she was that a good an actress." Then he let out a long, pained sigh. "Then again, over the past couple of weeks I've learned a lot of things about people I thought I already knew, inside and out."

"Your trusting nature isn't a handicap, babe," Niall said forcefully. "It's a strength, and one of your defining characteristics. Made me fall for you."

Gus blushed cutely, and Niall didn't have a shadow of a doubt he was a lucky man.

Hughes returned to the bedroom, clearly fuming, his hands shoved deep in his pants pockets, grumbling. "Well, we figured out how Pryor got here without anyone seeing her outside." He thumbed over his shoulder. "There's a connecting underground passage between Abrams's and Upton's mansions."

Gus harrumphed. "That explains that bit in the journal where Abrams mentioned how he'd arranged for Jason to take up residence next door. He must have known about the passageway and decided to put it to good use. Wonder if Jason knew about it?"

Niall shook his head, doubtful. "Abrams didn't strike me as the kind of man who had a habit of sharing information, even with his allies. And let's not forget, Jason betrayed Abrams by not handing over the grimoire once he'd acquired it. Surely Jason would've made sure the passageway was either blocked or locked up tight if he planned on deceiving his so-called buddy."

Hughes listened to them quietly and then took stock of their progress. "Find anything useful?"

Gus smiled. "We hit the mother lode. Do not let any of this stuff leave your sight even for a second. There's everything here. Names, dates, accounts, journals—you name it, it's here." He took the journal from Niall, and placed it over another stack of papers and notebooks. "Thankfully, Abrams was a crook who kept detailed records."

Hughes chuckled. "Okay, kids. Time for you to head on home. We'll take over here. Let you get some sleep. God knows you deserve it. The others have already given their statements, but you can fill in the rest tomorrow." His gaze swept over the workload on Abrams's desk below the safe. "I have a feeling I won't be getting any shuteye. Lucky bastards…."

Niall and Gus shared a secret smile between each other before passing their friend and heading out of the disaster area.

The drive back to Gus's home was quiet, both of them lost in thought, their emotions in disarray, their memories too vivid for comfort, and their bodies and spirits exhausted. Neither had the inclination to hash things out again tonight.

They parked the car on the street and made their way to the stairs at the side of the building that housed both Gus's shop and home, only to find a yellow sticker on the door.

Gus snatched it up and read it slowly. "Left a gift for you out back. Do with it what you will. Autumnsong."

Gus stared at Niall in surprise but at least without trepidation.

Apprehension tightening like a knot in Niall's belly, he gripped his gun and hurried to the small back garden—surrounded by a wooden fence and tall hedges—making sure he got there first. He wasn't taking any chances with Gus's life, even though technically the property belonged to Gus. Niall figured that since they were moving in together, he had every right to act protectively.

As he cautiously rounded the corner, wary of the shifting shadows of the back garden and the small greenhouse for Gus's tomatoes, Niall crouched, ready to take on an army.

In front of the shop's back door, on the cold stone slabs, was a black lump.

Niall crept closer, sensing Gus tight on his heels.

But he needn't have concerned himself. As soon as he saw what the "gift" was, he let his gun hand drop and his guard relax.

On the ground lay an unconscious, bound, and gagged Gil van Es.

"Huh. Guess the Cabal didn't want him either," Niall commented, shrugging.

"I think we should leave the unwrapping of this gift to the cops," Gus said dryly from behind Niall.

Finding that the funniest thing he'd heard in a while and unable to help himself, Niall started laughing hysterically. Gus's sarcastic eye roll and the amused twitching of the corners of his lips just made Niall cackle more, like a hyena on a roll at a comedy club.

Shit, what a fucking day this has been.

Chapter 19

"I STILL can't believe that fake psychic was simply delivered at your doorstep," Juliette said with a smile as she held up a glass of mango juice and sipped it.

"Yes. I wish more criminal organizations would be so obliging," Owain commented, his half grin belying his dry tone.

Gus chuckled, pouring a shot of bourbon for Owain. "Autumnsong is quite an unknown factor in any murderous equation. Whatever we think might be his motive, we could very well be wrong."

"Maybe he's got a crush on you, babe, and wanted to get your attention." Niall pressed closer to Gus from behind and kissed his nape.

Gus blushed. "Shush, you." He playfully slapped Niall's arm.

Niall grinned. "Well, whatever his motive, the organization Autumnsong belongs to is something we all definitely need to keep our eyes open for."

"Good thinking, son." Owain's praise had Niall beaming almost to the point of preening.

"Yet Autumnsong didn't leave the grimoire to us," Gus noted smartly. "That suggests he had a need for it too. We just don't have a clue what it is."

It was the morning of the summer solstice, and they had gathered together to celebrate the upcoming festival. Only the four of them were at Gus's place, while the others—Joy, Tom, Alec, Rodney, Sydney, Aeryn, and Hollister—would meet Juliette at her place later. The Litha festival would be held at noon, when the summer sun hit its zenith.

"How on earth did you get van Es to help you out?" Owain asked, curiosity etching his handsome features.

Niall nodded at Gus. "Ask the poindexter over here."

Gus elbowed Niall gently. "It was easy. We didn't give him a chance to refuse after we figured out his showman facade. Or should I say fake identity?" At the baffled looks he got, Gus explained. "Like in the Talbot murder case, it was Autumnsong again who pointed us in the right direction. He laughed at van Es's name. When Niall told me about that, I wondered what it meant."

"And?" Juliette asked, leaning lightly forward, intrigue sparking in her eyes.

Gus winked. "It took me a while to figure it out. Gil van Es is an anagram of Svengali, a fictional literary character who manipulates people." Juliette and Owain shared an astonished look between them. "Svengali led me to the Svengali deck, which is one of several trick card decks. And that finally led me to conclude that van Es was a con man using card tricks."

"That's amazing," Juliette said in awe, shaking her head slightly.

"Yeah. Gus did really good." Niall wrapped one arm around Gus's midsection, again planting a soft smooch on his neck. "Turns out van Es is a wanted felon, according to the FBI and Interpol at least. We don't know where's he from originally or what his tie to the Cabal really is, but he's got a criminal record in France and the Netherlands and outstanding warrants in other aliases in St. Croix, Tortuga, and New Orleans. He's a new breed of cosmopolitan con men," he added in jest.

"Of course, we didn't know about those things when we elicited his help to catch the murderer," Gus interjected, solemn. "I only suggested I might be inclined to inform the police about a con man using Tarot and séances to trick his marks. I should have realized something was up when he so readily agreed to my plan in exchange for my silence. Especially since I had no proof of his wrongdoings."

"That's not your fault, Gus," Niall cut in, miffed. "Someone like van Es would have found out about Abrams's involvement with or without you and taken him out somehow because we have no idea what's really going on between the Cabal and E.T."

"What have the police done about the Esoteraphim?" Juliette asked, shivering and hugging her arms. "How terrible it is to know that groups like that can exist in this fair world."

"With all the evidence collected from Abrams's safe, the twelve members of E.T. were quickly identified and charged with criminal conspiracy to commit murder, and the chief prosecutor might throw in some domestic terrorism charges because of the bomb strike." Niall frowned, unsure if anything tangible would come of those trials, other than a bit of bad press. "There were low-level judges, minor bankers, small-time businessmen and the like among the twelve members of E.T."

"No one high profile, then?" Owain commented.

"Minor celebrities in their chosen fields. Not anyone who people would recognize on the street. At least not until now." Niall grinned. If bad press was the only consequence these people would have to endure for their part in the conspiracy, that would at least ensure their names were out there, tucked away in some dark corner of cyberspace, safe and ready to be whipped out if necessary. "Plus they all had those weird wooden masks. Apparently, they used them in their secret meetings, to create an aura of mystery. Even though they all knew who the others were. And, the best part of all: Kerry survived the shot, and she'll testify against the rest. For what it's worth."

"Rodney will add his testimony as well, even though it'll likely make him a laughingstock among his peers," Gus cut in softly. "He's brave for stepping up to the plate and admitting Abrams pulled the wool over his eyes, deceiving him with a fake scholar persona. The real Dr. Ignatius Ashe has been told of the smirches on his name and reputation, but thankfully he took the news in stride. Oh, and as a curious side note: we have no idea whether Abrams was in fact related to John Dee. Now that he's dead, we may never find out. Perhaps that was just part of the ruse he used to get Rodney to show him the grimoire," Gus said, shrugging.

Juliette snickered. "I'd be really surprised if he truly were Dee's descendant. I mean, really. How would he even have learned such an amazing thing?"

"A genealogy search, maybe?" Owain suggested with a shrug. "People are interested in their predecessors even today, probably because it's easier these days to employ a professional to track down lineages than it was before."

Juliette arched a brow, looking skeptical of the merits of his notion. "Yes, perhaps."

A moment of silence followed as they all got lost in their thoughts.

"How's everyone else dealing with what happened?" Gus's voice went small, his brow marred with worry lines and a kind of sad longing pulling his mouth down.

Juliette made a sympathetic sound in her throat and embraced Gus heartily. "They all understand what you did for them. Rodney and Syd are most eager to thank you properly for saving their lives. But I asked them to give you some space to deal with things first. I hope I did the right thing?"

Gus smiled again, though it wasn't his usual full-on, sunshiny smile. "Yeah. I needed a little time to... to accept that I did help my friends—even though my actions caused people to die." His voice cracking, he ducked his head so his blond, curly bangs fell to hide his face. "It's... it hasn't been easy. I know rationally I did more good than bad but... it's just been hard, is all."

Niall sighed inwardly. Over the past couple of weeks since Gil van Es was delivered to their back door like a lump of coal, Gus had been more glum than usual, quiet and pensive, with a haunted look on his face. Niall had tried to tell Gus many times that he'd done nothing wrong and his actions had helped save people. Gus seemed to know this, but he clearly had trouble accepting the truth of it. The mind accepted it; the spirit remained unwilling. Niall was aware of the ethical and moral standards Gus aspired to, and the wave of deaths that had come with this case had seriously undermined Gus's faith in his essential goodness. Nothing and no one seemed able to get through to him.

Nonetheless, Niall tightened his grip of Gus, who exhaled slowly and deeply, leaning into him for support. "It's like you always say, babe. Time heals all wounds."

"Niall's right," Juliette said with deep strength of conviction. "Joy's opinion of you, for example, is unchanged. You're still her hero, Gus. You saved her from being buried alive. How dare you think less of yourself after you've done something so precious and miraculous?" Gus opened his mouth, but Juliette's frown and pursed lips stopped him cold. "That van Es might have been a charlatan, but his card tricks showed Tom and Alec a possible future. And did you know that they're planning a vacation together this coming fall? Yes, they're dating. Tom wanted to wait, but Alec.... He'd been miserable with Jason for a long time, and now he's got someone who adores him. That couldn't have happened without you. So how can you diminish their love with your loss of faith in yourself?"

"Jules, I—" Gus tried again.

"You already know what you did for Rodney and Syd." Juliette went on like a steam engine, unstoppable. "And Aeryn... well, you know her. She's a master of holding grudges. But if even she can see the worth in what you did, then you—"

"Jules, please stop. I get it, okay? I get it." Gus let out a long breath after succeeding in halting Juliette's rant before it turned into an endless harangue. "Geez, guilt-tripping me much?"

Juliette's eyes flashed intently. "We think the world of you. You should do the same."

Gus rolled his eyes, a sure sign he felt better. "All the way to the other end of the ego spectrum? Arrogant worship of my heroism?"

"Oh, you." Juliette smacked his arm, looking stern and scolding. But she calmed down quickly. "So, will the police recognize publicly your service and all the help you gave solving this case?" she asked, her eyes wide with anticipation.

Niall might have burst into laughter had he not known intimately how fierce she could be, the warrior princess of witches. Carefully dodging that bullet with a cough, he said, "The police department is not in a habit of recognizing civilian help in high-profile cases with lots of media attention. Besides, I think it's better Gus's name is kept out of this, for the sake of his friends if nothing else."

"What about your contribution?" Juliette insisted, frowning. "You're a PI and need the publicity to attract new clients, don't you?"

"Nah. Small price to pay for my Gus."

Gus practically melted in Niall's arms, turning his head and kissing him tenderly on the lips. "Thanks, Niall."

Juliette preened, all but jumping up and down in glee. "Oh, you two are just the most adorable—" She stopped immediately when both Gus and Niall cringed at that word, and then she started giggling. "Men." She fussed with her hair briefly. "Well, that's our cue to skedaddle. After all, I still have some baking to do before the noon ceremony. I was thinking… vegan crab cakes."

"Ooh, yum." Gus licked his lips in a way that caused Niall's cock to harden.

Juliette winked. "I'll be sure to save some for you." Her gaze flicked between the two men. "Are you going to celebrate Litha together?"

Gus chuckled mischievously. "I might ask you the same thing, missy." He looked at Owain knowingly.

Juliette blushed crimson and Owain rubbed the back of his neck, clearing his throat.

"Gus," Niall warned playfully.

"Oh, okay. Killjoy." Gus flashed his tongue at Niall, causing Niall's erection to grow. God, but he needed that ass sooner rather than later. But Gus had returned his attention to Juliette. "Will everyone be there for Litha? There'll only be eight of you."

"Nine." Juliette batted her eyelashes as she glanced sideways at Owain.

"Ah." Gus smiled, and this time the gesture was his genuine, upbeat, positive smile again. Niall couldn't have been happier to see him in a better state of mind.

"Have a nice day, you two," Gus said.

Niall moved off his boyfriend the second he got his wayward dick under control and went to hug his father. Gus did the same with Juliette, and then they switched. Waving good-bye, Juliette and Owain left, hand in hand the moment the door closed behind them.

WATCHING THROUGH the window in the door, Niall smiled to himself. He had to admit Owain and Juliette made a handsome couple, and they seemed well suited for each other.

Warm hands slid up from the small of his back to his shoulders, and Gus whispered in his ear, "Are they gone?"

"Just getting into the car," Niall replied, letting some of his weight rest against Gus behind him. "Why? You got something planned, Grasshopper?" He grinned over his shoulder at Gus's gasp of surprise. "Did you think I didn't know about your nickname? Jules mentioned an incident about jumping over a bonfire naked as the day you were—"

"Yes, yes, a funny anecdote—for another day," Gus talked loudly over Niall, and Niall laughed. It was wonderful to see Gus so lively again, smiling like the sun emerging from behind a dark cloud.

"Will you celebrate Litha with me?" Gus asked.

Niall snorted. "When have I ever said no to you?" Gus nuzzled Niall's neck, planting soft kisses there, giving Niall goose bumps. "Didn't you want to spend Litha with the coven?"

Gus froze briefly. "No." Then he resumed his amorous attentions.

"Why not?" Niall pressed. He felt strongly that Gus needed to deal with his issues about the coven.

Gus harrumphed in exasperation, as though he was annoyed Niall was still pursuing the subject. "I want to give them time. To give me time. Us time, you know, to sort stuff out." Suddenly he burst out loudly, "I'm not hiding."

Funny, but that had been Niall's first thought, which was why he'd insisted on knowing the answer. But he wasn't about to say that. Gus would speak and act when he felt comfortable doing so. Any further pushing would only backfire. "Okay."

"Okay?" Gus seemed surprised and perplexed by the reply. Then he sighed, and Niall sensed him unwinding. "Okay." He kissed Niall's neck, the deed hesitant and barely perceptible. "So... you still want to celebrate the summer solstice with me?"

"Now?" Niall asked, though it was a rhetorical question. He leaned back into Gus again.

Gus bit Niall on the fleshy junction of his neck and shoulder, then licked across the same spot, smoothing the sting. "No, not quite yet. Litha is celebrated at noon, when the sun is at its highest point in the sky, at its most radiant. We still have a few hours."

"Is that right?" Niall swayed a little, as if they were slow dancing together. "What's on your mind?"

Gus chuckled. "Dirty thoughts, naughty deeds, wicked ways."

"Ah. My wicked witch of the Northwest, I'm all yours." Niall meant every word.

"Good." Gus began to drag Niall backward by the back of his dress shirt. "'Cause I'm in the mood for some lovin'."

Niall murmured his approval, following Gus blindly as he was led toward the bedroom.

"Did you know that Litha is all about honoring love at its fullest?" Gus asked.

Niall grinned, and though Gus couldn't see it, he must have sensed it. "I did not know that. Will there be another love chase? 'Cause I caught you last time too... wabbit." Gus laughed at the Bugs Bunny reference, as Niall knew he would.

"Sun is shining at its peak of the day and year," Gus educated Niall while tugging him into the bedroom. "Litha is known for flowers, leaves, and lush vegetation."

Niall chuckled. "Ah, so that's why you decorated both the backyard and the doors and windows with floral garlands and birch wreaths, and brought some into the house too." Niall liked that their house smelled of aromatic flowers, fresh birch leaves, and grass, even soil and hay.

"Yes." Gus spun Niall around and in quick order popped open the buttons of his shirt, revealing his muscular, hairy chest. "This is the festival of fertility, abundance, and fires burning through the sunny day and the night of the midnight sun." He shoved Niall's shirt past his broad shoulders and down his thick biceps, letting it pool in a heap on the floor. Then Gus devoted himself to opening and divesting Niall of his pants too, his fingers swift and dexterous. "This is the day and night of amorous magic and love spells."

"Oh, is that right?" Niall grinned as he watched the man he treasured undressing him.

Gus nodded, smiling seductively. "Uh-huh. Like running naked through the fields and bathing in moonlit dew, gathering seven different flowers and sleeping with them under our pillows so that we may dream of our perfect mate in life."

Niall quirked an eyebrow. "Did you dream of me last midsummer?"

Gus smiled enigmatically, hiding his eyes behind a veil of golden lashes. "Not telling." Then he looked up at Niall, love shining in his gaze. "You're here with me tonight, so I don't need to dream of you. But... I will try."

Niall planted a tender kiss on Gus's lips, tasting pears and apples on his breath, which was normal for him. "Me too, babe."

Gus pressed up against Niall, wrapped his arms around Niall's neck, and kissed him again, more intently this time, with ardent purpose.

Only when they pulled apart, both breathless and hungry for more, did Niall notice all the lit candles spread around the bedroom. "So this is where you disappeared to just before our guests left."

Gus licked Niall's jawline, nipping it every inch or so. "Traditionally, bonfires were lit throughout the night. We can't have outdoor fires, so I thought candles would do the trick." With an impish grin, he added, "After all, Litha is all about worshipping the heights of light, nature—and lovemaking. Beltane had love chases; now the chase is done and it's time to enjoy the spoils."

Niall chuckled, pulling the playful Gus closer, and rubbed their hard cocks against each other. "I like that."

"I knew you would." Gus shoved his hand through the flaps of Niall's boxer briefs to grip his heated dick. Niall groaned as Gus manhandled him roughly, greedily. "More than any of the other sabbats, this is the time for rejoicing, for mirth and affection, music and dance."

"Didn't you dance for me during Beltane?" Niall whispered, tilting Gus's head back so he could nuzzle the column of his neck, feeling his lover's pulse quicken with his sensitized lips. "I recall a sexy little twirl around a pole. Well, two poles, actually."

Gus giggled breathlessly. "A dance of life is given in honor of the Mother Earth."

Niall moved aside the simple necklace Gus wore, with a yellow crystal dangling from it, to kiss Gus's neck where he wished. God, but Gus tasted like paradise. "Uh-huh?" Niall was close to forgetting what they were talking about, as arousal and pure unadulterated need grew within him.

Gus fumbled to touch the crystal. "This… this is a sun crystal… a symbol…. I've worn it since dawn to… to charge it with the sun's… the sun's energy and light and strength…." He was out of breath, clearly also succumbing to the pleasures of being touched.

Suddenly Gus pushed Niall off him, startling Niall with the rejecting act. "What…?"

Gus panted heavily, backing off toward the bed. He removed his T-shirt and threw it to the corner. He unbuttoned his jeans, his bulge pushing past the open flaps, and he slid backward onto the bed to lie atop the gold and green sheets, covers, and pillows.

Niall watched, rapt at the sensual sight. He gripped his own cock and rubbed along the length, titillated and anxiously awaiting whatever Gus was about to surprise him with next.

"For the past two sabbats," Gus said slowly, solemnly. "You have joined me at my side, celebrating with me. Litha is a day and night of fires burning, dancing around them, jumping over them, treasuring their life-affirming light and warmth."

Niall smiled crookedly. "One day you're gonna tell me all about that sabbat when you jumped naked over a fire and earned that nickname of yours, babe."

Gus blushed, but he quickly dodged and deflected the statement. "I decided to… have fun during this Litha. I'm going to… seduce you."

Niall's cock leaked precome. He couldn't believe how lucky he was. "I promise to be an easy catch."

Gus laughed. "Really? Darn it. I'd prepared to woo you with sweet scents." He pointed up at the ceiling where he'd hung herbs to dry, especially red heathers, and scents mixing the sugary with the bitter wafted down on them. "And with flowers." Gus hovered his hands over the covers where gold blooming flowers appeared on green fields. "And with… these." Gus flushed bright red as he reached under his pillow and fished out yellow and green specialty condoms and lube. "Gold for the sun, green for nature."

Niall snatched one for inspection. The latex glittered. "Colors *and* glitter?"

Gus smirked. "They even glow in the dark."

Niall laughed so hard his stomach hurt. "Now I've heard it all."

"Not yet." Gus pushed up onto his elbows, spreading his legs in blatant invitation. "You'll have to choose. Gold or green?" Niall frowned, baffled, but thankfully Gus explained. "At the hour of the solstice, both the Sun God and the Oak King are at their strongest. Are you a golden hero of the hour? Or the horned god of the season?"

"The horned god?" Niall lifted the green condom, raising an eyebrow. "I do feel pretty horny."

Gus chuckled, his hips shimmying slightly. "That's why we're gonna celebrate Litha… in bed." Niall stepped closer to the bed, getting more voracious by the minute. "You see, during the ritual, I'd use a… phallic staff and plunge it deep into a cauldron ringed with flowers." Again he slipped his hand under the pillow—he'd certainly made preparations, Niall mused—and carefully took out a garland of flowers, placing the crown over his blond curls. "A lance into the cauldron, a knife into the cup, spirit into flesh, man into… man, the sun into the earth," Gus spoke reverently, clearly a passage from the rite. His eyes burned as he stared at Niall. "Then you sink your sword into my… cauldron. And you give me the five-fold kiss—plus any others you wish." He sighed contentedly. "I'm yours."

Gus lay on the bed, spread-eagle, his lean body ready and waiting to be plundered. Who was Niall to argue with that? If Gus wanted to celebrate the summer solstice with a fuckfest, Niall was able and willing to oblige.

"The rising sun will climax our love," Gus said solemnly. If he was attempting reverence, he ultimately failed because his lips curled up and he laughed.

Niall cocked his head, a recollection inching forth. "Isn't that the rising moon will climax our love? You know, from *Heavy Metal*?" Gus's jaw dropped. Clearly he had assumed Niall hadn't seen the movie. "Gotcha, babe." Niall grinned, and Gus blushed. "So…." Niall shoved his boxer briefs down and kicked them off, standing at the foot of the bed stark naked. "You're the sacrifice for this day?"

Gus grinned. "You've been reading again."

Resting one knee on the bed for leverage, Niall leaned in leisurely, took a firm grip of Gus's jeans, and drew them off. Gus whimpered, and his legs spread farther apart in a wanton gesture, his erect cock and tight balls on sexy display.

"Sometimes your witchy rituals read like smut, babe," Niall commented as he inched forward, skulking like a big cat, until he was above Gus. Then he lowered himself onto Gus, and they both inhaled sharply as their hot, hard cocks kissed wetly.

"How dare you. Wiccan rituals are *not* smut." Gus's protests came in weak whispers as arousal built and ruined his intellectual resolve.

Niall dipped down and conquered Gus's mouth, silencing any further outcries. With a deep-seated need burning through every fiber, Niall entangled his tongue with Gus's, demanding his utter submission. Gus moaned and went limp against Niall, succumbing to him, and Niall purred in satisfaction.

As he slowly pulled back, he bit Gus's lower lip, keeping his hold tight but without drawing blood. When he finally let go, he swiped his tongue over the swollen place, soothing the sting and ache.

"Gonna make you mine," Niall murmured, his voice low and forceful. "Gonna make you scream till your lungs hurt. Gonna make sure you'll be mine forever." He barely heard his own words, only feeling their power and how deeply he meant every one.

Entwining his limbs around Niall's body, Gus whimpered, "Yes, please."

Shifting to sit on his haunches and reaching for the condoms and the lube, Niall peered down at Gus, the rosy-hued, debauched witch beneath him. Even as he slid the condom down over his burgeoning cock and gave the hot, rigid pole a good lathering with the lube, Niall sensed this moment was a watershed event.

Something bigger than love grew in his chest, burning to cinders all doubts and fears, filling the emptiness with something warm and sparkly. Niall felt alive, more than he had in a long time or with any previous sexual partners. He and Gus had moved in together, they had spoken words of love, had declared their feelings and begun a true relationship.

But something was still missing.

Niall held his dick up, aimed at Gus's pretty hole, and looked straight into Gus's eyes.

"Gus? Will you be exclusive with me?" That sure as shit didn't come out right, Niall knew, frowning at himself.

Gus met his gaze with heavy-lidded eyes, half smiling in bewilderment. "We moved in together, Niall. And I'm not sleeping with anyone else, so isn't it a given that we—"

"Wait. No." Niall placed a hand over Gus's mouth gently. "What I meant was…." His nerves almost got the better of him, and he physically forced the words past his lips, praying that he wouldn't hear a rejection. "Will you marry me?"

Wide eyes, a dropping jaw, and a sharp gasp welcomed Niall's query.

Gus blinked. Then he stared. Then he blinked some more.

Niall worried. "Gus? Babe…?" He felt his dick start to deflate. "Look, if you don't—"

"Yes." The word burst out of Gus's mouth. "Yes," he repeated, nodding. "Yes." This time there was firm finality in his voice, a steadfast resolve.

Niall released a breath he wasn't aware he'd been holding. "Yeah?" Gus nodded again, silent but grinning ear to ear. "You sure?" Gus nodded for the third time. "I mean, we just moved in together, so if you don't wanna rush—"

"I'm positive." With a whoosh, Gus pulled Niall down on top of him and proceeded to kiss the breath out of him. In fact, Gus did things with his lips, teeth, and tongue that made Niall's head spin and his dick harden to steel. "In me, Niall. Now." Gus's order was growly, a sexy sound Niall rarely heard, but sure as shit loved.

Niall pushed his sheathed cock inside Gus's ass in one slippery slide. "Gonna be quick, babe."

Seeming to understand, Gus moaned back in response and wound around Niall like a vine around a tree trunk. Niall began to rock within Gus's hot, tight channel, the pressure exquisite and the friction to die for.

They both groaned as one. Mad with desire and crazy in love, Niall increased his pace and fucked Gus long, hard, deep, and fast. Briefly he worried his special brand of lovemaking was too rough on Gus, but his blond beauty only called out for more, so that's what Niall gave him.

Ramming into Gus's sweet behind with wild abandon was something Niall couldn't remember ever having done before. They'd fucked before, lots of times, but this time there was a furious element of recklessness, a pure animalistic drive that forced them to copulate in a frenzy of torrid passion. It was like the solstice sun burned away their humanity, leaving behind solely the basest of desires and a feral, untamed passion that ensured they would be forever changed by the act.

"Gus, I love you," Niall growled against Gus's skin, sucking up marks of claiming.

"Niall, I love you too," Gus whispered, his voice nothing but a breathy moan.

Practically simultaneously they found each other's mouths and kissed like their lives depended on it. Niall held onto Gus's thigh and his shoulder, and thrust into Gus like a savage. He couldn't help himself. The blaze within him was too intense.

"Niall, oh, oh… I can't… I need…." Gus shifted to suckle on Niall's neck and then bit down harshly, undoubtedly leaving teeth marks. "Gonna come!"

Niall growled something unintelligible back and somehow managed to fuck Gus even more resolutely, gaining an inch or two, driving in ferociously until his own orgasm exploded inside him, blowing him to smithereens. Fireworks danced before his closed eyes as he pumped his seed within Gus's convulsing channel.

Hot, sticky rain landed between their writhing, sweaty, smoldering bodies as Gus, too, came, crying out like a banshee, his twitching dick pumping out all the contents of his balls. With a shaky hand, Niall swiped a few droplets and licked them off his fingers.

"You always taste like apples and the sun," Niall muttered, collapsing on top of Gus, his hunger only temporarily sated.

Gus chuckled, partly panting. "Thank you kindly… my horny Tigger."

Together they laughed, their dicks still half-hard, snuggling cozily and smothering one another with more kisses—and gathered their potency for a second circuit around the solstice sun.

Author's Note

The text refers to Aleister Crowley's Tarot card deck, also known as the Thoth Tarot deck. The order, names, and meanings, however, are a blend of the Thoth, the Classical, and the Rider-Waite Tarot decks, depending on the application of the cards to the plot events and to the characters in the story.

Glossary

athame: A ceremonial dagger, double-edged, with a black handle.

besom: A broom.

Book of Shadows: A hand-written book containing spiritual texts, instructions for magical rituals, and spell-work. First known copy written by Gerald Gardner and Doreen Valiente. Covens can have one BoS for all, and each individual can have their own.

cabalism: A group of people coming together to promote a common interest, thus forming a cabal. Note: not to be confused with Cabala, which is an esoteric method of spirituality connected to Judaism.

Charge of the Goddess: An inspirational text/speech spoken by a High Priestess after the ritual of Drawing Down the Moon, where she embodies the invoked goddess. Several versions exist, most notably those written by Gerald Gardner and Doreen Valiente.

cold-reading: A set of techniques used by mentalists, psychics, fortune-tellers, mediums, and illusionists to determine details about a person by analyzing the person's body language, manner of speech, etc.

coven: A group of neopagan witches. Covens are autonomous and nonhierarchical even though they are usually led by a High Priestess and/or a High Priest, the title mostly apt only in ritual settings. Ideal number of coven members is thirteen but not mandatory. A Wiccan need not belong to a coven.

deosil: Clockwise.

esbat: In broad terms, an esbat is any coven meeting that doesn't fall on a sabbat festival. In stricter terms, an esbat is a ritual observance of the lunar cycle, typically celebrated on the night of a full moon.

grimoire: A textbook of ceremonial magic, describing how to create spells and incantations, talismans and amulets, and how to summon supernatural beings. Term used mostly of historical books on magic, but can also be used to describe any type of book on magic.

Hermetic philosophy: A philosophical and esoteric tradition based on the works of Hermes Trismegistus that claims the existence of a single true theology present in all religions.

Illuminati, the: A name attributed to a multitude of so-called secret societies and groups, both real and fictional, historical and modern. The term means enlightened.

Litha: Summer solstice festival, midsummer, height of the sun's power, a festival of love and nature's bloom.

Major Arcana: A suit of twenty-two cards in a Tarot deck describing the person's journey through life in symbolic and spiritual representations, starting from the Fool and ending in the World.

Minor Arcana: Fifty-six suit cards comprising four suits (wands, cups, swords, and coins/pentacles). These match modern playing card decks with spades, hearts, diamonds, and clubs. Each suit is numbered from one/ace to ten, followed by court cards (princess/page, prince/knight, queen, and king).

Ouroboros: An ancient symbol depicting a snake, drake, or dragon biting its own tail to form a circle.

Rede: The only rule that all Wiccans follow—*An it harm none, do what ye will.* ("An" is an archaic form of "if.")

sabbat: The Wiccan Wheel of the Year consists of eight seasonal festivals called sabbats. Four of these are the two solstices and the two equinoxes, also known as quarter days; the remaining four are called cross-quarter days and represent the beginning of the four seasons (spring, summer, autumn, winter).

sunwise: Same as deosil, east to west following the sun.

Tarot: A pack of playing cards used in divination, mysticism, and the occult, originating in fifteenth-century Europe. Several Tarot decks exist, for example the Thoth deck and the Rider-Waite-Smith deck.

tau cross: An older form of the Christian cross symbol, named after the Greek letter tau, resembling the letter *T*.

Wicca: A modern pagan witchcraft religion first introduced by Gerald Gardner in the 1950s. Wicca is both pantheistic (belief that nature and the universe are the divine) and duotheistic (worship of a mother goddess and a horned god), and magic is a focus in most rituals. Wicca is at heart a nature religion that defies strict descriptions. It has no central authority figures, no controlling priesthoods, no one-type-fits-all ritual patterns, and no holy scripture per se (See: Rede).

Wiccan ritual: Consists typically of several phases wherein the invocation is the most significant. A circle is purified and cast, an invocation of the Guardians of the four cardinal points and an invocation of the Goddess and the God is spoken, a seasonal ritual is performed if it's a sabbat, magic is worked (called a cone of power), and cakes and wine are shared among the participants and deities. Media has needlessly sensationalized the ritual practices of skyclad (in the nude) and the Great Rite (a symbolic joining of the masculine and the feminine, typically done with the use of an athame and a chalice, not actual sexual intercourse).

widdershins: Counterclockwise.

Don't miss how the story began!

Sparks & Drops

The Wheel Mysteries: Book One

By Susan Laine

Magic is in the air when Gus Goodwin, a pagan shopkeeper and owner of the Four Corners' occult shop, meets a Niall Valentine, a mysterious PI investigating the disappearance of a local witch named Joy. What starts out as harmless flirting and information gathering soon turns into a partnership, with both men determined to solve the case.

Then bodies begin to pile up. Someone is using fire and water to kill witches associated with Joy, and it is up to Niall and Gus to find out what's going on. But when their friendship blossoms into something else, the unknown dangers looming ahead become even more frightening. If they can't solve the murders soon, they're going to get themselves killed.

http://www.dreamspinnerpress.com

Devil's Own

The Wheel Mysteries: Book Two

By Susan Laine

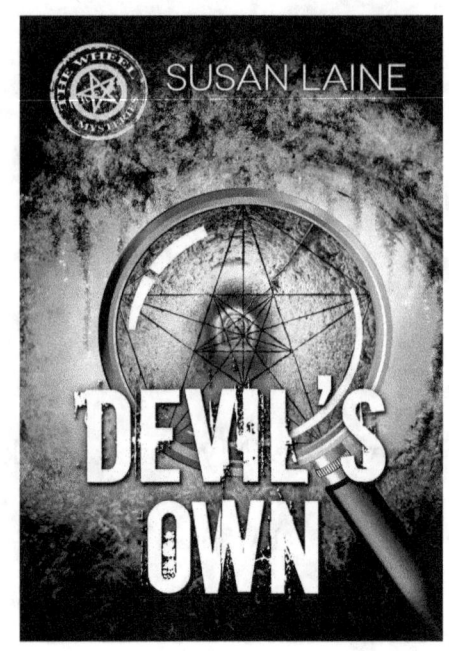

A month and a half into their relationship, PI Niall Valentine and his occult shopkeeper boyfriend, Gus Goodwin, are hoping for a little time alone, but they're thrown into another murder mystery.

Niall's client, Angelina Talbot, is certain her new husband attempted to kill her, ambushing her in their bedroom, half-naked and covered in blood. Scared out of her mind, Angelina hit him with a lamp and ran away. Florian Talbot lies dead in the bedroom, his head smashed in with a lamp—but the door is locked from the inside. Is Angelina truly an unwitting murderer, or are more sinister forces at play?

With a family of eccentrics, borderline criminals, and Satanists, the real killer could be any number of people wandering the mansion that night under the cover of darkness. The entire Talbot clan thrives in secrecy. Still unfulfilled and utterly perplexed, Niall and Gus are tasked with shedding some much-needed light on the shadowy case.

http://www.dreamspinnerpress.com

SUSAN LAINE, an award-winning, multi-published author of LGBTQ erotic romance and a Finnish native, was raised by the best mother in the world, who told her daughter time and again that she could be whatever she wanted to be. The spark for serious writing and publishing kindled when Susan discovered the gay erotic romance genre. One of her books, *Monsters Under the Bed*, won the 2014 Rainbow Award for Best Gay Paranormal Romance.

Anthropology is Susan's formal education, but she has set her long-term sights on becoming a full-time writer. Susan enjoys hanging out with her sister, two nieces, and friends in movie theaters, bookstores, and parks. Her favorite pastimes include pop music, action flicks, chocolate, and doing the dishes, while a few of her dislikes are sweating hot summer days, tobacco smoke, and purposeful prejudice.

Webiste: http://www.susan-laine-author.fi/
E-mail: susan.laine@hotmail.com

Falling for Rain

By Susan Laine

Matt Wetherton is just an average-looking tax attorney until he breaks up a gay bashing and unwittingly becomes a hero. He isn't looking for a date, but when he meets the man he rescued, he finds himself longing for one anyway. Rain Deveraux is a beautiful, effeminate lounge singer—and utterly unwilling to be Matt's damsel in distress, even if he does wear women's clothing for his performances. When common courtesy prompts Rain to pay Matt a thank-you call, it's the beginning of the romance of their lives.

Before long, Matt and Rain fall for each other hard and fast, but both men are stubborn: Rain clings to his right to express himself even though Matt worries for his safety. Despite their occasional clashes, the passion between them is undeniable.

When an accident compromises Rain's independence as well as his singing voice, it tests the strength of their newfound relationship. It is up to Matt to help Rain find his music again before depression sullies the brightness in Rain's soul.

http://www.dreamspinnerpress.com

Haunted Heart

By Susan Laine

Duncan Kerr is the art director of Enamored Press, an erotic romance publisher based in Seattle. An open submissions call for new artists yields an imaginative book cover with rich details and bold colors that catches his interest. After a few more samples of work and some e-mails, Duncan is determined to hire the talented young artist on a permanent basis.

But Ruben Winterbottom isn't an average freelance artist. His agoraphobia leaves him terrified to set foot outside his secluded house in the woods by the Olympic National Park. Living alone, fear is Ruben's sole companion.

When the two men meet, Ruben has a panic attack and hides away. Although confused, Duncan sees past Ruben's anxiety to his artistic gifts and beautiful soul. So he sets out to coax the young man out of his shy shell.

Falling in love with a broken boy, however, might be the first draft of heartbreak.

http://www.dreamspinnerpress.com

Sauna Lover

By Susan Laine

SAUNA LOVER
Susan Laine

When Shawn Wells learns a planned development project threatens the quaint gay neighborhood of Trickstown, he jumps into action. This is his home turf. Plus, his favorite hangout, bathhouse Hot Haven, is the heart of the community--along with its owner, Toby Macintyre, who has been a sort-of friend to Shawn for years.

Surprisingly, Toby seems opposed to Shawn's community-wide campaign to save the uniqueness and unity of the area. Even so, an unexpected attraction sparks between them, further fanning the flames of change.

Shawn has to fight for the future of his community, his beloved bathhouse, and for Toby. The sauna lover quickly finds himself in some real hot water.

http://www.dreamspinnerpress.com

The Sensualist &
the Untouched

By Susan Laine

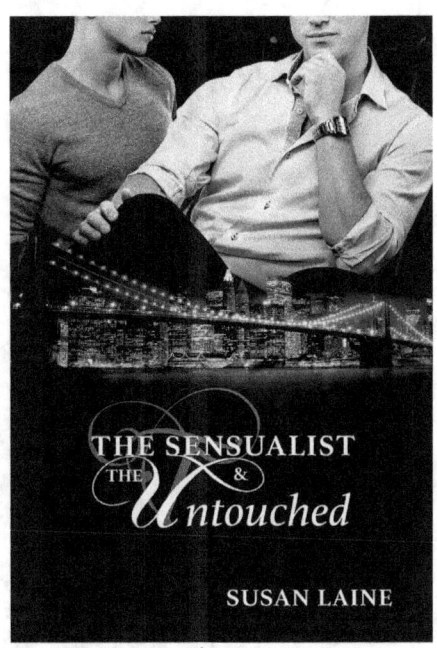

Being over thirty is not an issue for Corey Paige. Being frigid and a virgin, however, is a huge problem for the only son of a newspaper magnate. No matter the risk, Corey's intent on resolving both problems in one go.

Enter Lucian Allard, a wealthy hedonist with a notorious reputation at club Boudoir—and an unconventional sexual mentoring program for those who suffer from dysfunctions. As the two men begin a sensual journey to awaken Corey's libido, Corey's frigid body isn't all that begins to melt. His untouched feelings also spark to life.

Though a family emergency puts a halt to awakening Corey's senses and desires, Corey and Lucian grow closer as friends. Then an unexpected kiss from Lucian in Corey's most desperate hour changes everything. Now Corey must decide if the program is still an aid or an obstacle to two lonely men trying to maintain a professional detachment but falling hopelessly in love.

Isleshire Chronicles

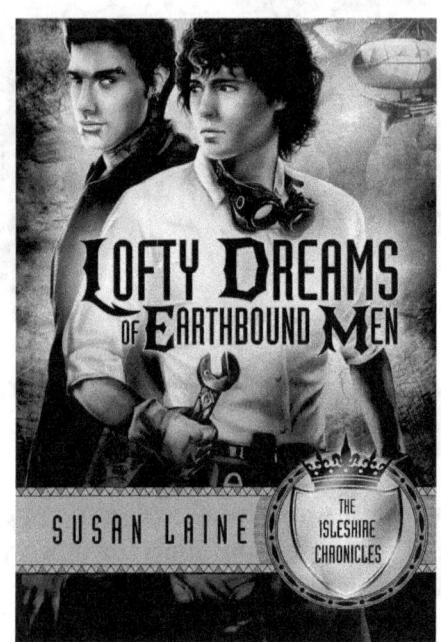
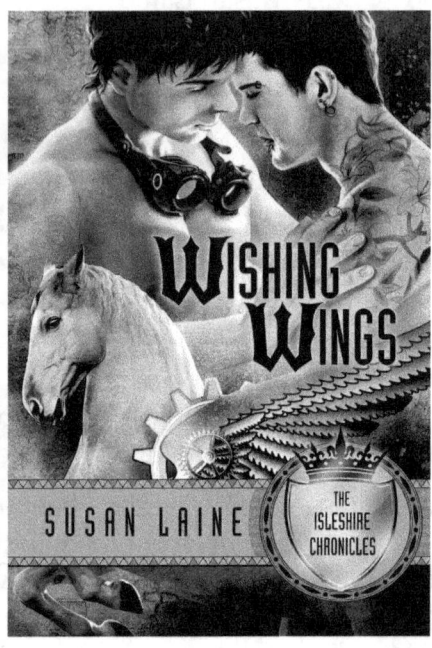

http://www.dreamspinnerpress.com

The Wolfing Way

Lifting the Veil: Book One

By Susan Laine

Kris Ellis thought that the time of arranged marriages was long past—but that was before the Great Unveiling revealed creatures of myth living among humans. Now a routine medical test has determined that Kris has a mate, a werewolf named Rafael King.

Kris is fresh out of college and has plans for his life. None of them include being tied forever to someone he's never met. But then Rafe calls him, and Kris starts to reconsider. After all, what must it be like to wait for your soul mate for two hundred years?

Rafe is patient, strong, and kind, not to mention attractive. True to what Kris has heard about mates, sparks fly the second they meet. But Kris and Rafe are very different, and the werewolf way of life is dangerous. Is the fight for love really worth it?

http://www.dreamspinnerpress.com

Genie's Wish

Lifting the Veil: Book Two

By Susan Laine

Ten years ago, the Great Unveiling revealed the presence of supernatural beings living on Earth. But the residents of the ruined city discovered in Majlis al-Jinn are long dead—or so junior archaeologist Pip Butler thought until he accidentally unleashed a very naked genie named Jinn.

Even though he's been shyly pining for his charismatic supervisor, Val Velde, Pip has a hard time refusing Jinn's flirtatious advances. He barely has time to even consider the fact that he has an all-powerful genie and three glorious wishes at his fingertips when ruthless mercenaries sweep down on the dig to collect the most valuable artifact of all—Jinn's lamp.

So Pip, Val, and Jinn have to work together in a race against the clock to discover the secrets of the ancient city, free their captive colleagues, and keep Jinn from the mercenaries' clutches—all while trying to sort out their romantic tangle.

http://www.dreamspinnerpress.com

Hunter's Moon

Lifting the Veil: Book Three

By Susan Laine

Ten years ago, the Great Unveiling revealed the presence of supernatural beings living on Earth, but not all humans know much about them—or care about them as anything other than a paycheck.

Kieran Knight is a freelance mercenary who hunts mythical beings for money. He abducts a man called Gabriel King, intending to turn him over to his client. But Gabriel isn't any ordinary cowboy. He's a powerful werewolf and the beta of his pack—and as he and Kieran soon discover, he is also Kieran's mate.

Kieran knows next to nothing about how mating works, and he isn't gay—but that doesn't mean he doesn't feel the chemistry heating up between them. To save Gabriel, Kieran orchestrates an escape, but his clients won't give up their werewolf without a fight.

http://www.dreamspinnerpress.com

Monsters Under the Bed

Lifting the Veil: Book Four

By Susan Laine

When PI Sam Garrett is hired by eccentric billionaire toy maker and child genius Mozart "Mo" Chance—*after* his apparent suicide in the hills of San Francisco—Sam takes the case out of sheer curiosity. In a world where the Veil lifted a decade ago and exposed mythical beings living among humans, Sam faces a big challenge as the mystery surrounding the case deepens.

The inheritors of Mo's fortune—the uncle, the butler, the nanny, and the bodyguard—all possess secrets, and some are willing to protect them at any cost. The trouble is that Sam's partner and lover, Rex Ford, is suddenly under suspicion as well.

Clouded by doubt, Sam continues to search for answers as tapestries of crimes begin to unravel and powers beyond his imagination are unleashed. If Mo endured horrific nightmares about monsters under his bed, there's no telling what dangers await a nosy PI. What dangers lurk in this darkness? Sam is about to find out.

http://www.dreamspinnerpress.com

Love of the Wild

Lifting the Veil: Book Five

By Susan Laine

Trying to jumpstart his waning career in travel and nature journalism, Jim Faulkner jumps out of a plane in the middle of the night to get the inside scoop on werewolves in Connor's Crossing, Wyoming. Unfortunately, he lands in a tree and gets stuck. His rescuer is a mysterious and solitary man living in a cabin in the woods. Although Jim feels an odd connection to Dakotah, Dak's silence is all but hostile.

Jim won't give up though—he finds ways to be around Dak, both for the bond and his belief that Dak is a great source for wilderness information. As Dak continues to dismiss him, Jim is suddenly surrounded by progenitors—the most powerful werewolves in existence—who all seem to want Jim as their mate. After one abducts him, Jim has to fight for his freedom and for his one true mate. No matter how reluctant said mate is.

http://www.dreamspinnerpress.com

Accidental Chemistry

A Second Chances Story

By Susan Laine

Zane Roscoe's evil day job at a musical instrument store is supposed to teach him responsibility. What he really wants is the fun, excitement, and artistic challenge of being a musician. Joshua Norton is in college, training to become a pharmaceutical chemist, and he is Zane's complete opposite: introverted, intellectual, and quiet. When the two meet at a gay night club, their relationship begins with a case of mistaken identity and a wounded ego.

They try talking but stumble over one miscommunication after another. So Zane decides they better stick to sex—except a series of bumbling disasters, accidents big and small, and minor mishaps leads to frustration. Afterward, Zane wants to apologize for his behavior. But Joshua ran, and finding him turns into a test of character, as does earning Joshua's forgiveness. Can they find the new beginning they need for a second chance at love?

http://www.dreamspinnerpress.com

Twice by Chance

A Second Chances Story

By Susan Laine

As a teenager, Addy Monroe had a life-changing experience—although technically the "experience" was happening to someone else in the steamed-up backseat of the taxi stuck in traffic next to him. Six years later, at a club in LA, Addy meets rock singer Zak Roscoe—the man who unwittingly taught him who he is—and gets a shot at experiencing Zak for himself.

A private and guarded person, Zak finds Addy's determined advances both annoying and intriguing, and he allows himself to be seduced for a night of pleasure. Unfortunately, some old habits die hard: Zak's postcoital nature leaves something to be desired, and Addy quickly realizes that sometimes fantasy and reality don't have much in common. If wishes were second chances….

http://www.dreamspinnerpress.com

Senses and Sensations

http://www.dreamspinnerpress.com

Senses and Sensations

http://www.dreamspinnerpress.com